THE MALE RESPONSE

Brian Aldiss, OBE, is a fiction and science fiction writer, poet, playwright, critic, memoirist and artist. He was born in Norfolk in 1925. After leaving the army, Aldiss worked as a bookseller, which provided the setting for his first book, *The Brightfount Diaries* (1955). His first published science fiction work was the story 'Criminal Record', which appeared in *Science Fantasy* in 1954. Since then he has written nearly 100 books and over 300 short stories, many of which are being reissued as part of The Brian Aldiss Collection.

Several of Aldiss' books have been adapted for the cinema; his story 'Supertoys Last All Summer Long' was adapted and released as the film *A.I. Artificial Intelligence* in 2001. Besides his own writing, Brian has edited numerous anthologies of science fiction and fantasy stories, as well as the magazine *SF Horizons*.

Aldiss is a vice-president of the international H. G. Wells Society and in 2000 was given the Damon Knight Memorial Grand Master Award by the Science Fiction Writers of America. Aldiss was awarded the OBE for services to literature in 2005.

Also by Brian Aldiss

BRIAN ALDISS

The Male Response

HARPER
Voyager

Harper*Voyager*
An imprint of HarperCollins*Publishers*
1 London Bridge Street
London SE1 9GF

www.harpervoyagerbooks.co.uk

This paperback edition 2015
1

First published in Great Britain by Dennis Dobson 1963

A catalogue record for this book is
available from the British Library

ISBN: 978-0-00-748238-2

Set in Minion by Born Group using Atomik ePublisher from Easypress

Printed and bound in Great Britain by
RR Donnelley

Introduction

'To travel is to discover everyone is wrong'

Aldous Huxley

I should like to thank the editors of the *Encyclopaedia Britannica*, whose invaluable articles on 'Africa', 'Computing Machines' and 'Sex' I consulted before daring to attempt this story. My chapter headings are quotations from the 'Ode to Autumn', by John Keats, to whom I would also have liked to offer thanks.

For advice on the contents of this novel I communicated with celebrated author Aldous Huxley, then living on the western shores of the U.S.A., whose responses proved very helpful.

Brian W. Aldiss
Oxford, 2015

PART ONE

Dark

Chapter One

'… borne aloft or sinking …'

'Of course, if they had had any sense they'd have routed us via Cairo,' the engineer from Birmingham said.

This is the miracle of our age: that one may be borne swiftly and smoothly along in winged luxury, constantly fed and reassured, while underneath one unrolls the great viridian mat of central Africa, that territory to be flown over but never conquered, whose mysteries deepen as the rest of the world grows shallower, whose beasts and peoples breathe a secret, greener air, whose prodigality seems to make of the continent a very planet, subject to its laws and psychologies – this, I say, is the miracle, that one may be borne over all this superbity to the tune of turbo-props and notice nothing of it because of the vacuous gossip of an engineer from Birmingham.

'I mean, Dakar just doesn't compare with Cairo in any way,' he added, 'as regards amenities or anything else.'

Soames Noyes did not remember the chatty man's name. They had been introduced rather hurriedly by Sir Roger at the Southampton airfield. Soames never remembered names upon introduction; although his thirtieth birthday was creeping up on him as surely as a tide, he was still paralysed on all meetings with people. For an instant, he would be back at his kindergarten, Miss Munnings would be conducting the Deportment Class and saying, 'Now, when you are introduced to somebody, you stand with your feet so, left hand resting gently on the hip so, right hand extended so, and you say "How do you do?" Now, Soames, will you come out here and give the other boys and girls a demonstration?'; and little Soames would go sacrificially before them all and stick out his rump and hand in such a way that the class burst at once into derisory laughter. And in the moment it took for this splinter of memory to flush through his brain, Soames would have missed the name of the new face, even when the new face was saying, 'Pleased to meet you, Mr Noyes. Of course, managing the Midland branch of Unilateral, I've never come in contact with you, but we've all heard of you, even up in the wilds of Birmingham.'

'How are they all in Birmingham?' Soames asked facetiously, mainly because he guessed that this plump, grey-faced engineer would be what in the lower echelons of the firm was called 'a good, solid Unilateral man'.

'Fine, fine. And a lot of them a fair bit envious of your and my little trip to Darkest Africa, Mr Noyes, I don't mind telling you.'

There were four Unilateral men on the 'little trip'. In the seat opposite Soames and the nameless Birmingham man were two more engineers, one a cheerful type called Wally Brewer, one a quiet, wiry man called Ted Timpleton who was now white round the jaws and sat looking steadfastly away from the plane window. Soames was not a technical man; he belonged to what was spoken of as the Unilateral façade. His job was to talk charmingly and not too intelligently to Unilateral clients, to soothe away their little worries over expense-account dinners, to reassure them that Unilateral electronic computers were the best in the world, to ingratiate.

The plane contained a fifth passenger: Deal Jimpo Landor. He looked the typical African, clad in magnificent tribal costume, with one black, almost purple, arm resting nonchalantly over the back of the seat in front of him. In fact, he was an eighteen-year-old ex-public schoolboy with a manner, as Soames had already discovered, more reminiscent of a Teutonic philosopher than of the Uele warrior stock from which he came. The playing fields of Eton had made him frightfully earnest. His deep eyes were abstracted now, as if his thoughts ran ahead to his own country of Goya, which the aircraft was rapidly nearing. His father was head of Goya and would have a suitable welcome awaiting his firstborn.

The most valuable part of the pay-load lay not in the five passengers nor the pilot but in the storage compartments of the plane. There, carefully packed, crated, stencilled and numbered were the component parts of an Apostle Mk II, Unilateral's newest, most svelte electronic computer, bound for the palace at Umbalathorp, Goya.

Six weeks had passed since Unilateral received the order for this machine. Deal Jimpo Landor had come in person to the glossy showrooms in Regent Street. To give his visit an additional touch of unreality, he was dressed in the full official regalia of a Princeling Son of the President of the Republic of Goya. Awed Regent Street assistants ushered him into the manager, Waypole's, office, where Soames, as it happened, had dropped in for a gossip.

Having been primed for the audition by a hurried phone call from below, Waypole and Soames rose from their chairs and executed stiff bows to the gaudy new arrival.

'You are not the owner of this firm?' Deal Jimpo asked, when the introductions were completed and he had accepted a seat.

'I fear not,' Waypole said, nervously flicking a speck of pollen from his carnation. 'I am in charge of this branch of our organisation, however, and can contact our chairman by phone, should that be necessary.'

'I do not want to cause trouble,' Deal Jimpo said. 'Please do not bother the chairman yet. I am wishing to buy just one of your very best computing machines.'

5

'May one ask – is it for yourself, sir?' Waypole said.

'No, it is for my father's republic in Africa,' the young negro replied. 'In Goya, we are most progressive and have everything on Western principles without any bother from reactionaries. Perhaps you read *The Times* yesterday where my republic is referred to as "the black Scandinavia". To become still more progressive we require one computer. I think my people would like best a red one.'

'They actually are all turned out sprayed slate grey,' Waypole said faintly, 'but of course we can make alterations to suit customers' requirements. Please excuse me just one moment.' He turned to Soames, who was fighting a stubborn rearguard action to keep his face straight, and said in a low, agitated voice, 'Soames, my dear man, for heaven's sake go downstairs and check up if this place Goya exists. I always thought it was a painter. Unless I am mistaken, this is a practical joke being played on me by an odious fellow called Betts-Lewcombe who was on my staircase at Balliol.'

Soames returned from this quest a few minutes later and, standing behind the Princeling, made an involved gesture intended to explain to Waypole that a quick phone call to the *Daily Telegraph* Information Bureau had revealed Goya to exist in very fact as a small republic wedged between the Congo, the Sudan and a bit of ex-French Equatorial Africa, with a flourishing cocoa bean industry and a President called M'Grassi Landor; that it looked as if, in this instance at least, the odious Betts-Lewcombe's name was cleared.

Enough of this signal was comprehensible to Waypole for him to gather that its opposite, the bum's rush, had not been mimed. Casting his eye more benevolently upon Deal Jimpo, he said, 'I have here some brochures of our various computer models; perhaps you would care to look at them at your leisure and see which you think would best suit your – er, peculiar circumstances.'

Fishing in a drawer of his desk, he produced a batch of sumptuous folders and handed them across to his visitor.

'Thank you,' Deal Jimpo said, opening the top folder. Inside was a colour photo of a smartly uniformed young lady pointing smilingly at the bulk of an Apostle Mk II.

'I will take this one,' Deal Jimpo said definitely, planting his thumb on the machine.

'Er, *that*,' said Waypole, smiling as if in the throes of gastroenteritis, and nobly giving the stranger a chance to change his mind, 'is the star member of the entire range of our machines and is only just in full production. We have sold it to Edinburgh, Harwell and the Air Ministry, but so far our only clients overseas are the Saga Uns people in Hamburg and the Sûreté. Its basic price is £400,500.'

'It sounds as if it should be very suitable for Umbalathorp, thank you,' Deal Jimpo said gravely. 'I will write you a cheque now but I shall not require the machine until tomorrow.'

The edges of Waypole's carnation curled. He slumped slightly in his chair.

'There may be a slight delay in delivery,' he said, a wave of emotion rippling on his voice.

'Of course – for the red painting,' Deal Jimpo agreed. 'Well, no hurry at all. I do not sail for home yet for two days.'

It was at this moment that Waypole caught sight of Soames frozen in a column of silent laughter behind the Princeling. His air of distraction relaxed, washed away by a peevish grin. Some of the rough edge which had won him the manager's chair began to show.

'You must allow us to make the delivery for you,' he said, carefully choosing his tone so as to show Deal Jimpo only its silk glove and Soames only the iron hand within it. 'We shall be delighted to fly the Apostle out to Umbalathorp (do I have it correctly?), and our liaison man here, Mr Noyes, will go with it, so that any little difficulties or misunderstandings which may arise can be dealt with on the spot.'

And that was how it had all begun.

'Well, I don't know about you, Mr Noyes, but I shall be glad to get out and stretch my legs,' the Birmingham man said.

'Same here,' agreed Soames. It was a phrase he never used.

'I wonder what sort of a place this Umbalathorp is?' the Birmingham man wondered, and then – sagely guessing just how worthwhile any answer of Soames' would be – he turned round and called to Deal Jimpo, 'What sort of a place is this Umbalathorp we're getting to, Prince Landor?'

His voice implied that he might have been requesting information on the nearest brothel from a street tout, but Deal Jimpo replied equably enough.

'Umbalathorp is the capital of Goya. It is a healthy city without much sickness. Everyone is progressive in outlook and content in spirit. It has a railway which may perhaps one day connect it up to other cities. Its population is ten thousand and rising rapidly.'

'All natives, I suppose,' the Birmingham man said flatly.

'All natives of Umbalathorp,' said Deal Jimpo with equal flatness. The remark completely won over Soames, who felt a new eagerness to investigate this curious little jungle republic; he had already begun to like Deal Jimpo.

The Birmingham man was not snubbed. Giving Soames a dirty wink, he remarked, 'I hope the native women aren't tabu, Prince, anyhow.'

Deal Jimpo did not smile.

'You will find our standards equal to Western standards,' he said. 'Which means promiscuity among the females. Morality was higher under the old tribal customs, that must be admitted.'

'After you with the old tribal customs!' exclaimed the Birmingham man, slapping his hands together and making succulent smacking noises in his cheek. He dug Soames in the ribs. 'Ever tried a bit of the old tribal customs?' He lowered his voice confidentially. 'I had an Arab bint once during the last war. Talk about strong! She got her legs wrapped round me and dug her heels in the small of my back like a human nutcracker. Scared me stiff at first, it did – I was only a youngster in those days.'

'Quite,' agreed Soames, feeling enthusiasm was required of him. The Birmingham man was goaded into fresh revelations, so that Wally Brewer and Timpleton leant over to catch what he was saying.

'I knew a good thing when I found it,' the engineer boasted. 'Ah! I was back round there again next evening. "Dig your heels in again, missis," I said. And she did. Strewth! We'll be okay if they're like that in this Umbalathorp, I tell you. She was a nice little bit, that Arab bint. They shave off their pubic hairs before marriage, you know.'

This anthropological detail reminded Brewer of something he had heard.

'A lot of these African women slap goat dung on it to improve the sensation,' he said. 'It's like using curry powder with meat.'

It was Timpleton's turn to chip in.

'You haven't lived till you've had an Italian girl,' he said.

'Japanese,' Brewer contradicted firmly. 'Japanese. Nothing like a little Jap girl – up to all the tricks, they are, taught about it from the nursery. When we set up that computer in Yokohama last year …' He guffawed to show that the sentence could not be completed in words, not even over the wilds of Africa.

'Just let us loose in Umbalathorp, that's all I say,' Timpleton remarked.

Soames said nothing. He could not casually reveal his sexual experiences in this way – not that he had ever felt anything so exotic as an Arabian heel grip in the small of his back. Obviously it was time he asserted himself.

Ignoring the chatter of the other men, he fell into a reverie. Now or never, presumably, was his chance to break the bonds of his confounded reserve, to leap free from the constraints of a cold temperament and climate. On this trip he would prove himself a man or die in the attempt.

Sexual fantasies surged through his mind. Massive thighs opened up before him, pair after pair, like doors down a Versailles corridor. Soames went through them all, unruffled, laughingly denigrating his own prowess. The tenth woman, who could speak a little English, cried aloud for mercy.

'Mercy!' exclaimed fantasy-Soames. 'My good woman, this is only a dress rehearsal.'

'But I cannot exhaust you. You are a Casanova among men.'

'Nonsense, chicken. It's just – well, I'm a branch of a lusty family.'

'Branch, sir? This thing, it is more like a trunk!'

'It happens to be a prominent feature in the Noyes family, that's all.' And as he left, tossing a few dollars negligently to the bowing and awe-struck proprietress, he called over one shoulder. 'Try and find some fresh girls for me tomorrow night, madame – something with a little fire in it.'

The madame was weeping, trying to give him his money back.

'Please do not come here again, sir,' she pleaded. 'You wear out all my best girls.'

But the girls were protesting to her, begging to be allowed to lie with Soames just once more.

'All a beautiful dream,' Soames told himself, sighing heavily.

He glanced out of the window to see if there was any break in the tousled green carpet beneath them. The plane was lurching in rather an un-English manner as if investigating a new way of coping with turbulence. This might have been either because they were flying over a range of mountains or because half of one wing was trying to detach itself from the plane.

This latter phenomenon riveted Soames' attention. He no longer felt capable of joining in the small talk about him, which had now turned to the possibilities of hunting in Goya. Instead, he gazed sickly at the wing. It was making the leisurely flapping movements of an old pterodactyl; a girder inside the leading edge must have snapped even as Soames looked, for the flapping became abruptly more pronounced. The pterodactyl had sighted food.

Soames was petrified – not by fear but by a less wholesome emotion. He was the son of a doggedly timid father and an assertive mother, and the war between his parents had been perpetuated in him. Now the urge to stand up and do something useful was quenched by a conflicting urge which said to him, 'Think what a fool you would look if you walked through into the pilot's cabin, tapped him on the shoulder and announced "one wing's coming off, pilot" – and he turned round and said, "Yes, I know; mind your own business".

The Birmingham man and Wally Brewer were discussing the rival attractions of football and game-hunting with Deal Jimpo. Ted Timpleton stared whitely ahead like an actor whose lines had gone from him for the night – the first night. The sedate flapping of the wing had changed now, changed into an angry shaking, as if the cargo plane were an animal just waking to the hideous injustice of having to carry humans in its digestive tract.

Breaking at last from his trance, Soames stood up. As he did so, the loudspeaker in the cabin broke into life and the pilot's voice said harshly, 'I'm going down for an emergency landing. We've developed a fault. Strap on your safety belts and sit tight, all of you. No need to panic.'

'What the hell's the matter?' the Birmingham man asked. 'Do you think we ought to see if we can give him a hand, Mr Noyes?'

'We're going to crash!' Timpleton said, standing up. 'My wife warned me …'

'Sit down at once, and do as the pilot says,' Deal Jimpo said, loudly and firmly.

Both Timpleton and Noyes, rather to the latter's annoyance, at once obeyed the command.

'Bugger that, I'm going to see if I can help the pilot,' the Birmingham man said, running forward and disappearing through the connecting door into the cabin. They were diving now, the turbulent green lurching up uninvitingly to meet them, the plane bucking as it set its nose down. A small suitcase of the Princeling's shot out of a luggage rack and scuttled down the gangway after the Birmingham man.

'Oh my God,' Timpleton said. 'Now we're for it, Mr Noyes.'

'N-nonsense,' Soames replied with an attempt at a joke, 'the pilot knows the Apostle is too valuable a cargo to damage.'

Long afterwards, he recalled with surprise how loudly Deal Jimpo and Wally Brewer laughed at his remark; and even in the face of what might conceivably be death-in-a-veil, he found himself

11

resolving to try and make more jokes in future. Then Wally caught his eye, winked broadly to indicate that this was for the abject Timpleton's amusement, and began to sing 'Abide With Me'.

The noise in the cabin was so deafening that they could scarcely hear him. The earth which from the serenity of a few thousand feet up had looked as smooth and inviting as an electric blanket, now revealed itself in its true colours: a savage, Jurassic world of broken hill and valley, loaded with rivers and trees. Space in which to land was absolutely nonexistent. Uneasily, queasily, Soames tensed himself for the fatal shock. Just through the window, the wing was a giant fist shaken at him. It sounded like a madman's banging on shutters.

Now they seemed to be clipping the tree tops. Startled giraffes broke through a tiny clearing and galloped beneath them. The suitcase was shuffling its way back up the gangway.

Four passengers with dry, open mouths sat clutching seat-backs. Their flight was so bumpy they might have been leaping from tree top to tree top. Wally Brewer's oil-coated hair flapped up and down on his head.

'We're going too fast,' Soames whispered.

Abruptly the jungle stopped. A sea of grass rushed beneath them. The plane dropped towards it. Now they staggered in for a landing, forest fringing them on either side, more rising up like a wave a mile ahead. It had to be now or never.

Their wheels touched the ground. A mighty hissing, a boiling sea of grass-noise, rose round them. And in that instant the loose wing struck the flowing earth.

With a crescendo of noise, the plane was flung round off its course, pitched back into the air, hurled on to one shoulder.

Timpleton screamed and somersaulted across the gangway. He had not buckled his safety belt properly.

A mighty mvule, outrageous, irresistible, spread out its branches to them. Foliage slashed across their windows. With a last heave, the body of the plane struck something solid. Everything in the universe rattled.

Maniac sound, maniac silence.

Chapter Two

'... *whoever seeks abroad* ...'

The men and dwarfs seemed to be carrying an ocean liner, which was made of rubber and only semi-inflated, so that it flopped about as they dragged it up Everest.

Soames jerked out of his dream and opened one eye.

'Yes, I'm inside the liner,' he thought. 'It's clear to me now. It's not made of rubber; it's made of grey plastic and filled with special grey air ...'

His mind cleared. He squeezed his eyes, opened them both, took a deep breath, roused, remembered.

He was still strapped in his seat. He was lying on his back, for the plane had come to rest with its nose high in the air, standing like a tower among a tangle of branches.

All Soames could do for some while was stare stupidly straight above him at the pilot's door, some feet over his head. He was exceedingly cold. It occurred to him that the grey light was the light of early dawn. They had crashed at about six, or perhaps an hour before sunset; he had been unconscious for some twelve hours. He was too numb to attempt to check this observation by lifting his arm and looking at his wrist watch.

Instead, he turned his attention to the other passengers. Over to his right lay Wally Brewer, in a position much like Soames' own, except that his head was twisted backwards in such a ghastly fashion as to make it obvious even to Soames – a tyro in such matters – that his neck was broken and he was dead. The grey light, filtering through the leaves, pressed against the windows, lingered complacently on Wally's staring eyes.

There was no sign of Ted Timpleton.

Twisting himself round with an effort, Soames looked backwards and down to where Deal Jimpo Landor had sat. There was no sign of him either.

He wondered how the pilot and the Birmingham man had fared, but there seemed no possible way of getting up to them in the forward compartment. As he stared rather dreamily upwards, the communicating door opened slightly and a head was poked into the cabin; it wore the flamboyant bushwacker hat the Birmingham man had deemed appropriate for the journey.

Soames was about to shout out to him when he recalled he did not know the man's name (Duncan? Dobson? Hobson? Hobhouse?); again absurd inhibitions overcame him and silenced him. And now the head turned, allowing Soames a glimpse of gleaming teeth and a hairy shoulder.

Just for a startled second, horror invaded Soames. Was the Birmingham man a werewolf? Had the crash released lycanthropic tendencies in him?

Then a grinning chimpanzee, still wearing the bushwacker hat, launched itself into the cabin, swinging down from seat to seat with all the trained abandon of a Palladium act.

'Shoo!' Soames said with appropriate force.

Startled, the chimpanzee shed its headgear and beat a retreat back into the pilot's compartment.

Thoroughly roused, Soames undid his safety belt and set about climbing out of the wrecked plane.

He swung down the seats in a clumsy imitation of the chimpanzee and reached the door, which had been broken open by the force

14

of the crash. Looking out, he found himself some forty feet above ground level. The plane was standing on its tail against a giant tree whose damaged branches seemed to extend like broken tusks all round the fuselage, piercing it in some places.

Unexpected elation coursed through Soames. He was alive! He was romantically in the mysterious heart of Africa. Life was suddenly something worth a hearty cheer. He took a grateful breath of morning air, and found it smelt much like eggs and bacon.

There was no exit for him this way. He jumped down on to what had been the rear wall of the cabin and lowered himself through the door, now hanging open, into the rear of the plane.

Passing the little galley and toilets, he climbed down through another open door into the cargo hold. Here, all the crates containing the component parts of the Apostle Mk II looked still to be in position and unharmed; thanks to careful packing, they had not budged an inch. Working his way carefully down them, Soames reached the cargo hatch. It gaped open, and a steel ladder extended from it down some fifteen feet to the ground.

Descending the ladder, pushing through twigs and leaves, Soames could see that the crumpled expanse of tail plane acted as a pedestal for the wreck. He reached ground and there, a few feet away, Ted Timpleton, sleeves rolled up, was frying eggs and bacon over a stove.

Directly he saw Soames, he came running up, throwing out his arms and clutching Soames' hands.

'Oh, Soames,' he exclaimed. 'Oh, how good it is to see you! Oh, what a ruddy relief; I quite thought you had had your lot. You've not a clue how terrible it felt here – the only white man …'

With Soames' anger that this little man should have crept out of the plane without, apparently, attempting to help any of his fellows, went a detached interest in the sudden use of his own Christian name, with all the camaraderie in the face of danger it implied; then these sensations were banished by a more urgent one which rose conquering from the pit of the stomach.

'Is breakfast ready?' Soames asked.

In the frying pan, deliciously, joyously, six eggs sparkled and wallowed like suns in the lively fat; close by, waiting to welcome them when they were cooked, stood two plates already loaded with crisp bacon and gleaming rounds of potatoes. A groan escaped Soames' lips.

Even as he wondered if Timpleton had been intending to eat all this glorious food himself, Soames caught sight of Deal Jimpo propped with his back against the bole of a tree a few feet away. The young negro was covered by a rug; his eyes were closed, he breathed heavily.

'I had a dickens of a job getting His Highness out of the plane,' Timpleton said. 'Nearly broke my back. Of course, it was dark when I came to, and that didn't make things any easier. He was already conscious and groaning like a boat. I got to him and brought him down here somehow. Then I fixed his leg up in splints. He's broken it badly. Funny a big chap like that should get his leg smashed up and here's these eggs with their shells not even cracked.'

'You did jolly well, Ted,' Soames said warmly.

'I don't know. I was in the Navy in the war.' The word of praise embarrassed him. He gestured awkwardly at the sleeping man and said, 'We'll wake old Jimpo up now and give him a plate of grub. He'll feel twice the man. I got some coffee out the galley, too.'

He squatted by the stove, slightly smiling, a little wiry Londoner turning grey above the ears, conscious of Soames' eager looks. Producing a third plate he put the eggs, now done to a turn, two on each plate and shovelled bacon and potato beside them until the plates were equally loaded. He produced knives and forks from a box and handed a pair to Soames.

'Eating irons coming up,' he exclaimed. 'Blast! Forgot the salt! We'll have to rough it this time. I can't climb back up there again till I've had my grub.'

'Quite,' agreed Soames, and before Timpleton could get over to the sleeping man he had begun the attack on his plate.

After coffee, all three of them felt much better. Jimpo, as both the white men had instinctively dropped into the habit of calling him, bore the pain in his leg stoically and assumed command of the party, to Soames' secret relief.

For the first time, Soames had an inclination to look round. They were at the bottom of a thickly forested slope, among whose branches monkeys chattered. The open ground before them was churned by the crash landing and littered with small branches. Two hundred yards away, forlorn and innocent now, lay the culprit length of wing.

'One of you must climb to the nose of the aeroplane and see if the two men there are alive,' Jimpo said. 'That is first essential.'

'I will go,' Soames offered, eager to show his readiness to do anything, for he wanted his two companions to realise as quickly as possible that he was a good chap.

It was not an especially hard climb. Soames took it stage by stage up through the aircraft and, with a final jerk that it would have done his old scoutmaster good to behold, hauled himself up into the pilot's cabin.

The chimpanzee had vanished. Silence reigned here now. A mighty bough had crashed through the small compartment, shattering the instrument boards and pinning both the pilot and the Birmingham engineer, who had taken the spare second pilot's seat, beneath it. The Birmingham man's torso had completely caved in; he lay with his profile turned from Soames, glass frosting his hair. His tongue had been forced out of his mouth like a length of tie. When Soames pulled back the leafy branches, so incongruous in this little, man-made shell, it was to find that the pilot's skull had been shattered. His face was indistinguishable; a few large blow-flies were inspecting the damage.

Sickened, Soames let the branches sweep back into position. He could do nothing here. Yet he stood there, silent, the air heavy with petrol fumes and sunlight coming in horizontally through the wound in the hull. He was regretting he had not been more genial with the Birmingham man while a chance for geniality existed.

Looking up through the shattered glass, he perceived a face watching him from a branch outside. It was a thin, eroded face, lined with despair, from which peered two hanging-judge eyes; its beak was like a tarnished blade. Even as Soames and the vulture regarded each other, another great bird in its funeral garb came clattering down to take up its perch beside the first. Then they both stared down at the living man without comment. By the time he had disappeared back into the body of the plane, two more friends had joined them; the leader stepped forward and flubbed heavily down into the cabin.

'This is our best plan,' Jimpo told them, leaning back against the tree. 'We cannot be many leagues from my country. That is a fortunate chance, for my leg will allow me to proceed only slowly. Just now I have observed a herd of topi, and from their movements, I suspect there may be water in *that* direction, through the bushes. We will walk to that water. If it should be a river, it is good for us to make camp there and wait for men to come by in boats. They will take us to my father's republic.'

'What you say goes, of course,' Timpleton said, scratching his neck. 'It's your country. But I thought the usual stunt in these situations, from what I've read, was to walk to safety. Even if we have to take it slowly, it's better than just sitting spinelessly by the river waiting for someone to show up.'

'You have read too many adventure stories, Ted,' Jimpo said. 'These jungles are bad and we become quickly lost. We are not Biggles & Co. Best to wait by the river! I will teach you to trap crocodile.'

'If we set fire to the plane, someone would be bound to see it and come and investigate,' Soames suggested. 'We could get all the food out first.'

Something like bad temper flitted across Jimpo's face.

'You think I get the computer so near to home and then burn it?' he asked. 'That is a silly notion, Soames. Help me to my feet and we will walk to the water.'

They trudged slowly through the waist-high grass. While Soames was in the plane, Timpleton had fashioned a sturdy crutch for Jimpo, with which he was able to proceed without too much discomfort.

The sun was high in the sky and they were sweating profusely by the time they reached the water; by English standards, it was a fair-sized river. The approach to it lay through a thicket of head-high bushes, but on the other bank rose true jungle, dense and unwelcoming. The river itself was deep and flowed so sluggishly it had the appearance of being semi-congealed.

'This is ideal place,' Jimpo said. 'Now I will light fires to scare away the snakes and one of you will go back to the plane to collect the equipment I shall name. It can be dragged back here on the rug with maximum comfort. Which of you likes to go?'

'Toss you, Soames,' Timpleton said promptly, producing a coin and laying it on the back of his fist with his other hand over it.

'I always lose these things,' said Soames hopelessly. 'Heads, I suppose,' and lost. Thus it was he who had the surprise, when he got back, sweating, to the plane wreck, of finding a green bicycle with four-speed, propped against the crumpled tailplane and gleaming in the still sunshine.

'Who's there?' Soames called nervously and then recollecting that this might well be what was French Equatorial Africa, 'Er – qui est là?'

No answer came to him except the superbly contemptuous twittering of an insect in the long grass. He walked quietly about the wreck and saw nobody. The owner of the bicycle must have climbed up the ladder and entered the cargo hatch.

Slightly nonplussed, Soames was staring up this ladder when a black face appeared at the top and a negro wearing khaki shorts and bearing a spear shinned down like lightning to confront him. They faced each other with rather similar silly smiles before the negro began to talk volubly, pointing to the plane.

'Sorry, I don't understand a word,' Soames said, commencing an elaborate pantomime with swooping hands and explosive sounds to depict the whole drama of a plane crash in which all but three passengers, two white and one black, were killed, the other two being by the river about a mile distant, and would you kindly follow there now bringing your bicycle if needs must …

19

All this the negro watched politely before shrugging his shoulders in a gesture of bafflement.

When Soames, after taking a refreshing swig from the water container Timpleton had left under the tree, began to head back for the river, he beckoned industriously to the negro and saw him seize up his bike, swing it over one shoulder by the crossbar, and follow. 'Good boy … that's it … someone who'll be able to make you savvy when we get there … yes, come on … he'll make it worth your while … good,' Soames muttered in a kind of dreary undertone of encouragement as they proceeded.

The negro fell in beside him, cutting off the mumble with a long account of his own which he interspersed with frequent laughter, rather to Soames' irritation.

'What's the good of going on, old boy, when you know I don't understand a word?' he enquired, but the negro was still laughing and talking when they reached the river bank. Pushing his way forward, keeping his bicycle miraculously free from entanglements with bushes, he came to where Deal Jimpo was lying.

The latter uttered a few curt sentences, evidently announcing who he was, for at once the newcomer lay down beside him and clutched his hand; he broke into what sounded like an incoherent address of welcome to Jimpo. While they were talking together, Timpleton reappeared, grimy and hot, having set fire to the grass according to Jimpo's instructions. Soames rapidly explained to him what had happened.

'We have fortune in some things at least,' Jimpo said, rising with the newcomer's aid and leaning on his crutch. 'This good man, Tanuana Motijala, tells us we are less than a day's journey – even with my slow progress – from Umbalathorp itself. He will escort us along the trail and we can leave at once.'

This was indeed good news. Both Soames and Timpleton had had private dreams of spending a week by the surly river, beating off crocodiles, rhinoceros and water snakes with fragments of girder from the plane.

'Thank him very much indeed and ask him where the hell he got his push bike,' Timpleton said.

A brief exchange between the two black men followed and then Jimpo explained, 'He won it in a raffle.'

Once more they did the journey to the plane under the blazing sun. Jimpo assured them that directly he reached the capital of Goya an expedition would be despatched to bring back everything from the wreck, including their luggage, and on this understanding they set off light-handed, Timpleton and Soames bearing haversacks containing water and food.

Tanuana's trail lay some distance beyond the plane. It was a relief to find themselves in the shadow of the jungle, but this benefit was short-lived, for soon the trail was winding uphill fairly steeply. Both white men began to blow hard, and Jimpo's face was grim with effort; Tanuana, noticing nothing, chattered and laughed in the same cheery way he had done when Soames first met him.

'Whatever is he talking about?' Soames enquired irritably at last, when the trail momentarily levelled out.

'Saying he explore wreck of flying plane before you appear,' Jimpo said. 'Saying he kill four vulture birds in nose of flying plane. Saying they eat too much, too fat to get out hole they come in by. Saying he got four good beaks in saddle-bag.'

Thereafter they lapsed into silence. Gloom rose in Soames. He disliked the way Jimpo's English was growing worse; it might be only the pain he was suffering; or it might be that the eighteen-year-old ex-Etonian was reverting to type. Now that Umbalathorp actually lay ahead, it no longer seemed the inviting haven it had a few hours earlier. Obviously the first thing to be done was to get a radio message through to Unilateral, asking for rescue at once. Primitivism cast no spell over Soames; he was a *Guardian* man.

Gradually the distances between the figures grew. Ahead was Tanuana, sometimes uttering a brief snatch of song. A short way behind him came Jimpo, with Soames following close and Timpleton much in the rear. The jungle, moody and fascinating

21

at first, soon became, like an expanse of moody and fascinating contemporary wallpaper, something to pass with averted eyes.

The morning drew on, the trail widened, every step became a burden. After a long time, when there was no sign of Tanuana ahead, nor had been for some while, Jimpo halted, leaning against a tree until Soames caught up with him.

'You look bad, Jimpo,' Soames exclaimed, seeing his haggard look and grey face. Sweat sprayed from both their foreheads.

'Is nothing. We will stop here for rest. Bloody man Tanuana go too fast for me. Wait for Ted to bring us water.'

They both lay down and rested. Ten minutes later, Timpleton appeared, trudging with his head down, his thumbs hooked into his haversack straps.

'Don't they have any ruddy buses on this route?' he asked, sitting down beside them and swinging his haversack off his back. His morale was so good that Soames' also improved.

As they ate canned peaches and cheese biscuits, Jimpo announced that they were near a village; he 'could tell', he explained. He thought that Tanuana might soon return with villagers to help them.

'What, a lift?' Timpleton asked. 'Litters or elephants?'

'Possibly a handcart,' Jimpo said. 'Now we will press on again. We must remain on our legs.'

'If you will stay here with Ted, I will go on and hurry them up,' Soames said. 'I don't think you are in a fit state to walk any further.'

'It will not be fit state for my father's people to find me lying down,' Jimpo said. 'Help me to stand.'

They had been on the move again only another ten minutes when they came into a clearing. From the other side of it, a reception committee was approaching. Ten men, among whom were Tanuana with his green bicycle, several women, and a flock of naked children, jostled round a large barrow loaded with flowers. The three from the plane were rapidly surrounded by people and voices.

With a splendid show of patience, Soames and Timpleton stood for a long while listening to speeches all round.

'What's it all about?' Soames asked.

Jimpo eyed him rather superciliously.

'They made delay to decorate my triumphal cart appropriately,' he said, as willing hands bore him up on to the bed of flowers. The procession then gradually moved off, the two white men following behind the main crowd.

Some hours later, when shadows lengthened over patchily cultivated land, they entered, the capital of Goya, and an old man of benevolent aspect came forward with pineapple ice cream, smearing it ceremoniously over their faces and hands.

Chapter Three

'… And full-grown lambs loud bleat …'

Without putting too philosophical a shine on the matter, we may say that cities are places where men gather. It follows therefore that, as no man is perfect, no city he builds is without fault. Hong Kong has its overcrowding, Peking its interminable walls, London its traffic, New York its pavements, Bombay its hideous buildings, Paris its foreigners, Buenos Aires its residents. Umbalathorp has its biting things. It was a peevish Soames Noyes who climbed from his rush bed next morning and cursed all the nocturnally feeding species who had banquetted upon him.

'We'd have done better to stay in the plane,' Timpleton said, running a thumb-sized bug to earth in his arm pit.

'Jimpo said we'd be moved to the palace today. It should be slightly less inhabited there.'

'Soames … Do you reckon those black women'll come and bath us again like they did last night? That was a queer stunt, if you like.'

Soames emitted a giggle. He had yet to orient his feelings with regard to that ceremony.

'They did you all over,' Timpleton said musing. 'Christ, I ask you, Soames, if they'll wash your crutch what else won't they do?!'

'The same thought occurred to me, Ted,' Soames admitted solemnly and was surprised when Timpleton burst into laughter.

The bathing ceremony had occurred at dusk last night, shortly after the weary travellers had arrived. By then, Jimpo had already left them to be carried to his father, informing them they would be well looked after. That they certainly had been, and the three girls apiece who scrubbed Timpleton and Soames, despite their coy protests, in ceremonial concrete baths, had not lacked ardour. Soames had to admit that the only offensive note in this covertly erotic ceremony had been the emptying of an entire carton of detergent into their water.

While they were still being dried by their handmaids with wads of cotton waste, an English-speaking native appeared. He escorted them, when they were ready, to a brick building where an excellent meal was served. Then he took them through the strange-smelling darkness to this beehive-shaped hut in which they had served as nourishment all night.

'All Umbalathorp men make to you much apologise for this dead-end-kid mansion,' he told Soames and Timpleton. 'Better you to sleep here one night while room for you in President palace not sweep. Tomorrow room in palace be much sweep for you. Be nice for you. Be clean like England hospital tomorrow. Only tonight not sweep.'

'I suppose it never occurred to the blighter that this place wasn't sweep either,' Soames grumbled, when the man had gone, after producing – or so it had seemed – a lighted candle for them from his pocket.

'This must be where they usually keep the palace tigers,' Timpleton said, sniffing suspiciously.

'Subtle effluence of cat,' agreed Soames.

'Subtle? Have you got cotton wool up your nose?'

Now Soames emerged into the open air, nervously rubbing his hands together. He wore, with an uneasy air, the European clothes the handmaids had given him the night before, in exchange for his own sweat-stained garments. The clothes did not fit properly, hence his nervousness; to a casual observer he might have been taken for a repentant amateur clothes thief, or an ex-jailbird without the strength of his previous convictions.

Directly Timpleton joined him, similarly disguised, their guide of the night before appeared and escorted them to breakfast.

'After this foregoing meal you are have a shave in the barber's and next then go to palace,' he told them.

When they left the barber's shop, a large hut with a number of smelly charms for sale on the walls, a rickshaw was waiting to take them to the palace. This ride gave them their first good chance of seeing Umbalathorp. The capital, although small, was dispersed over uneven ground broken by several streams and bounded on the one side by a hill they later knew as Stranger's Hill and on the other by the Uiui River, whose opposite bank rose in places to become almost unscaleable cliff. In the town itself, streets and roads, with few exceptions, were sketchily marked, huts, bungalows and larger buildings facing this way or that according to the whim of their owners. Patches of cultivation or strips of jungle stood even in the heart of the town, giving Umbalathorp a desultory air. The total effect was as if Bideford had suddenly been elected capital of England, whereupon everyone's garden had grown eaves high, and the town council, to celebrate, had planted thousands of giant straw beehives in the streets as far as Northam and Buckland Brewer.

Many people were about, mostly negro, the variety of their features suggesting that several races mingled here; a number of Indians could be seen, carrying umbrellas and looking important. Once Soames thought he saw a European, but the man vanished into a shop. A few American cars were in evidence, outnumbered by pariah dogs by ten to one.

The rickshaw made its way slowly through the market place, its owner adding his voice to the babble of the crowd; they swerved down a wide road and came unexpectedly on the Presidential palace, from which a crimson, scarlet and black flag flew. Guards at the gate waved to the vehicle as it passed them and turned up the drive.

The palace looked like one of those great grey barracks the British used to build with such tedious frequency in Central India, but its gauntness was relieved by a riot of creeper which attempted to swarm up every balustrade and into every window – something never permissible in Central India, for fear the local women took advantage of this unorthodox staircase to accost the troops. From the tessellations which crowned the building floated a great brown banner bearing a word that, in these unexpected surroundings, took on a resonant ambiguity: DUNLOP. On the wide steps below, flecked by the droppings of a thousand brightly coloured birds which flitted ceaselessly in and out of the creeper, ten black soldiers in white uniforms stood with rifles at the slope, open umbrellas attached to the rifles in place of bayonets, lest they should become flecked like the steps on which they stood.

This impressive scene was marred only by a discarded bath full of Coca-Cola bottles and rainwater lying by the drive, from which a dog drank in insolent disregard of the nearby soldiery.

When Soames and Timpleton dismounted from their chariot, their guide paid off the owner and led them quickly up the steps. They proceeded through an archway and down a corridor to a small room, the door of which the guide opened for them.

'Please wait here; someone else come see you soon, gentlemen.'

'This is like a dentist's waiting room only more so,' Timpleton remarked, as the guide left.

On the benches round the room two men were already sitting, as far apart from each other as possible; Soames and Timpleton selected an intermediate position and eyed the magazines piled on a central table. The only English language offerings were two copies of *Drum* and a *Radio Times* for week ending 5th March 1955.

Soames had no sooner settled down to scratch a cluster of tiny, red-hot tents erected close to his navel by an exploring insect party the previous night, when one of the two waiting men shuffled over and addressed him.

'Is it my pleasure and fortune to be soliciting the two flying British who are transporting the magical scientific box hitherwards?' he enquired, in an English so elaborately broken that the two flying British were left rather in the air. 'Possibility that it can be no others makes a double delight.'

Always anxious not to make an inadequate response, Soames rose, bowed awkwardly, and said, 'How do you do? This is my colleague Mr Edward Templeton: my name is Soames Noyes.'

The stranger received these names with relish, repeating them to himself with his fingers on his lips, as if to get the feel as well as the sound of them.

'So!' he said. 'No meeting for me can be more too delightful,' and he announced himself with a flourish as José Blencimonti Soares. This done, he shook hands warmly and protractedly with both Soames and Templeton, producing a bandana after the operation, on which he thoroughly mopped his podgy hands.

He was a dumpy man in his fifties, dressed in a tropical suit, from the starched lapels of which burst a large flower like a geranium, its brightness in striking contrast to the grey jowls which brushed it during excessive outbursts of expressiveness.

'I am for long resident in Umbalathorp, sirs,' he said, 'and delighted to show you its attractions, if of convenience. I have the pleasure and fortune to be leader of local Portuguese community. We see few Europeans here: last one was an American called Mr John Gunther, and brand-new faces like yours always welcome, also pleasantness of visit very much agreeable. My residence, my wife, my food and my beautiful daughter Maria are open to you eternally.'

Ignoring the sly kick this last remark prompted Templeton to give him, Soames offered his thanks and enquired innocently if there were any Englishmen in the town. At this Soares' pudgy face clouded like a peke's with toothache, and he said, 'Only one outcast family,

28

señor, the Pickets, at whom you should be advised to steer clearly.'

Timpleton waved him nearer with two beckoning fingers.

'Here, Mr Soares, give us the lowdown on this dump. Never mind the English – what we want to know is, how about the women?'

The Portuguese laughed. Soames recognised that laugh; it had frequently been described in the literature of his boyhood as 'a greasy chuckle'.

'So you are what you call an old dirty man,' he said, nodding approvingly. 'In all the world is women to be had, and in Goya many good variety, what colour or size to fit the individual whimsy. Only one thing to be warned is of dreaded akkabaksi pox.'

'What the deuce is akkabaksi pox?' inquired Soames, alarmed and interested.

Soares rolled yellow eyeballs and puffed out yellow-grey cheeks expressively.

'Akkabaksi pox is very nasty local disease, misters, I telling you, cause much misery in the bazaar.'

'What is it?'

'Is caught from dirty woman, pfafft, just like that. After two days catching it, the victim finds hugest black scabs of matter at point of contact. Then he will pack up three days ration for food and water and will march off into the jungle.'

'What for?' Timpleton asked. He had turned an unsuitable shade of grey round the jowls.

'Is finished, sir,' Soares replied simply. 'Has no cure. Not Western medicine or witch doctor Dumayami can cure dreaded akkabaksi pox. In three four days, all the bones turn to jelly, the stomach will explode. Pfafft! Is finish!'

'Good God!' the two Englishmen exclaimed in chorus.

Switching his mood and expression from supreme dejection to extreme elation, Soares leant over and smacked them on the knee.

'But is no need for worry for you. Trust to me who can be your friend. Always I sell you good clean girl. Come to old Soares for priceless virgin flesh. Guaranteed no disease. Fresh as a sea smell.'

29

Changing this subject abruptly, he asked, 'Now you have an auditorium with President Landor, yes?'

'I suppose so,' Soames said. 'The arrangements seem a bit vague. We only got here last night, you know.'

'Any difficulties, come at a run to me, I insist,' Soares said, smiling winningly. 'Because I do much trade in Goya. I have pleasure and honour to hold ear of President.' He tapped his heart impressively as if he kept this presidential appendage in his breast-pocket.

'We're going to live in the palace,' said Timpleton. 'Is it OK here? Give us the lowdown.'

'Hunky dory,' Soares told him unexpectedly. 'All plumbing throughout by courtesy of José Soares and his company. All business here, my business.'

A palace guard entered and spoke briefly in Goyese to Soares.

'Now is time for my auditorium,' Soares said. 'Gentlemen, we are bounders to meet again.' Bowing, smiling, nodding, wagging one finger above his head, he left with the guard.

Half an hour later, the same guard appeared and beckoned to the two Englishmen. As they left, Soames glanced back at the other occupant of the waiting room. He was an ancient, white-haired negro with a battered cardboard box on his knee. Not once had he stirred since Soames had been there. Perhaps, like the 1955 *Radio Times*, he went with the room.

Soames hurried to catch up with Timpleton, who was slicking back his hair with a pocket comb preparatory to his audience with President Landor.

President Landor was worrying his hair with a pocket comb preparatory to his audience with the Englishmen when they arrived and bowed to him. He was a tall and splendid man just beginning to run to fat. His face creased into a broad smile when Soames and Timpleton entered, and he came across the room with outstretched hand, leaving the comb hidden in his crinkly hair.

'The geniuses from Unilateral Company, the splendid survivors of the air crash, the rescuers of my son Deal Jimpo,' he said easily, speaking in French. 'I regret that I have no English. Queen Louise, whom you will certainly meet, speaks it fluently, but not I, alas; a deplorable omission. I trust you both have command of French?'

Soames had, Timpleton had not.

'We shall get on splendidly,' the President said to Soames. 'You must tell your friend what I am saying. Sit down here and try with me some of this Canadian rye whisky which the all-too-capable Señor Soares has just left as a token of his esteem.'

They settled themselves in wicker chairs while an attendant filled their glasses and the President spread himself comfortably and looked them over. He wore Indian chaplis, white starched shorts and a white shirt over which latter was an unbuttoned brocade waistcoat, the magnificence of which robbed it of any incongruity it might otherwise have had.

'You do not mind to sit with me?' he asked.

'No. I'm sorry – should we – of course, we should have remained standing,' Soames said.

'No, no. That was not my point. I wondered if you subscribed to this popular thing, the colour bar.'

'The colour bar – is not reasonable,' Soames said.

'Possibly so. That does not prevent many millions of people being swayed by it.'

'Unfortunately people in the mass are swayed most easily by the unreasonable,' Soames replied, colouring slightly.

'You should have been a politician.'

'In England now, to be a politician one must also be photogenic, in order to appear on TV. My nose is too irregular for affairs of state, Mr President.'

'Just call me "President" – or "King" if you like it better, for I am both President of Goya and crowned King of my territories.'

'How unusual,' Soames said, smiling, for the President was also smiling. 'A surprising mixture of the American and British constitutions.'

'We try to retain here the best features of both great democracies,' the President said.

'What are you two on about?' Timpleton asked. He had finished his drink far ahead of the others. 'What's he doing about our rooms?'

'I'm just getting to that, Ted,' Soames said and then, tactfully, to President Landor, 'My friend is enquiring after the health of your son, Deal Jimpo.'

'His leg will mend. The witch doctor, Dumayami, has seen it and proclaimed the omens right. Jimpo is out now with the palace lorry and a host of porters supervising the transportation here of the all-important cargo of your plane.'

'My clean clothes,' exclaimed Soames gratefully.

'The computing machinery,' added the President gently.

He then pressed them for particulars. Timpleton agreed that when all the parts of the Apostle Mk II were brought to the palace he should be able to assemble them in three days, provided the parts had not been damaged in the crash. (Under the original contract, with the Birmingham man and Brewer to help, this process was only to have taken a day.) Two further days would then be needed to install the generator, which had also been flown in, and to carry out extensive tests, etc.

'Then *I* commence work,' Soames said. 'I will train the local man you have selected to operate the Apostle. There may be some difficulty in interpreting the results the machine gives, just at first. I shall be at hand to explain. These machines operate normally on the binary system, producing answers which only skilled mathematicians can comprehend. On your model, Unilateral have greatly modified input and output circuits, with the result that problems can now be typed out on an ordinary typewriter keyboard, whence they feed automatically into the machine on a roll of paper like pianola music; similarly, the machine's answers will be ejected, typed in English, from a slot on another piece of paper.'

'In English?' repeated the President.

'Yes, I hope that is what you wished? Your son, Deal Jimpo, was firm on the point in his contract.'

'Quite correct. Too many sons of guns, including myself, speak French here. But *English*, correctly spoken, is managed by but a very few. Therefore a mystery is created, and my people respect a mystery. Or rather – they fear enlightenment.'

'It is the same with the masses in England,' Soames said with unconscious priggishness.

'Ah, but their feeling is to be respected,' said the President, catching the note of condemnation in Soames' voice. 'Enlightenment is like a tearing down of old familiar rooms when we are left to squat in a desert of disbelief. What has education to offer but the truth of man's smallness and beastliness? What is knowledge but the gift of danger? – Did not one of your poets say that?'

'Pope said that a little learning was a dangerous thing.'

'Well? All learning is little, a block and tackle job of dismantling the gods.'

'Yours sounds a very disillusioned philosophy, President,' Soames remarked.

'Yes, it goes badly with this excellent rye whisky, eh? By tomorrow I shall probably have thought of a totally different set of things to say, thank God.'

'What the hell are you two jabbering about, Soames?' Timpleton asked.

'Be quiet,' Soames said.

'What I was going to say was to warn you,' the President told Soames. 'You more than your friend, for he is the hard worker and you are the talker on this job. Therefore my people will instinctively hold *you* responsible for any changes the machine introduces; they know – forgive me, but I am also in your category – that the talker is the curse of the world. The old mysteries are still here. Umbalathorp looks ahead, yes, but the jungle and the river are close, and the spirits of the jungle and the river are still strong. They look backwards, far backwards. Your machine will offend them. My witch doctor, Dumayami, will be offended. That is why you and the machine have been established in the palace. Not only is this a beautiful palace, but it is protected by guns and soldiers.'

All this was said lightly enough, but Soames was aware as he listened that the President was watching him searchingly, as if to see how he reacted to a hint of danger. While he was casting about for the answer which would create the best impression, Timpleton broke into the conversation in dog French.

'Où est la chambre pour nous dormir, monsieur Président?' he asked angrily. 'Vous et Soames ici sont parlent très beaucoup. Dernier soir, nous a dormi dans une – une, er, mud'ut très terrible, beaucoup de fleas, puces, très grands puces. Où est une belle chambre? Et avez-vous des femmes pour nous?'

President Landor rose, one eyebrow cocked at his visitors. He appeared more amused than put out.

'Désirez-vous une femme de plaisir noir?' he asked Timpleton.

'Oui,' Timpleton said emphatically, 'si vous n'avez pas les blanches. Toutes les femmes sont seulement femmes, après tout.'

'It is a thought which has echoed down history, though frequently better expressed,' the President said, as if to himself. 'If you will leave me now, gentlemen, I will attempt to see that your wants are attended to.'

Chapter Four

'With patient look, thou watchest …'

All men think alike; no two act alike.

In Umbalathorp there were, quite unknown to Soames, several people who considered themselves interested parties where he was concerned and who, from the moment of his arrival, vibrated with a passion of curiosity about him. In the thoughts of each, he appeared as a pawn merely, an object they could profitably, for one reason or another, incorporate into their own designs. But the ways in which they set about arranging a meeting with him were diverse; the meeting became, to one, an ambush, to another an attack, to another a lure, to another only a wary circling.

Timpleton also was under surveillance, but to a lesser degree. It was recognised from the start, in the uncanny fashion one does recognise such things, that Soames, of the two, was – in the expressive American phrase – loaded. Soames, though he would have shrunk from the idea, conformed to the slightly dated and therefore doubly appealing world-image of The Englishman Abroad to a remarkable degree. His indecisiveness, by which an inward panic frustrated all outward action, chimed curiously in all its external aspects with the British tradition for keeping one's head while all around are losing theirs; and the delicacy with which, on first riding through Umbalathorp, he had averted his eyes from its grosser squalors had easily been misinterpreted as the chill aloofness of a white barra sahib.

Eyes, hostile, friendly and calculatingly neutral, had read these marks upon Soames on his arrival and during his ride through the market, and had laid their plans accordingly. The first of these plans to develop from the theoretical to the practical phase was that of Queen Louise.

The Queen descended upon him while he was still surveying his room. Templeton had been shown by a servant to another, similar room down the corridor. Apart from the tropical generosity of window space, this might have been the cell of a top-brass priest on Mount Athos; it was of whitewashed stone, furnished only with bed, chair and chest of drawers. The bed was covered with a bright rug. The big brass bowl on top of the chest contained a handful of dead leaves.

The Queen knocked and swept into Soames' room, accompanied by a small, tittering maid, almost before he had time to cry 'Come in'. She was a large, ugly woman, with nostrils as mobile as gills and skin the colour of strong tea; when she announced herself, one heard the loud but inaudible fanfare of trumpets.

'You may kiss my hand, Mr Soames,' she said, in clear English, 'but otherwise no formalities. Kindly address me as "Queen Louise", as do my other subjects. Come, I shall be good enough to show you round the palace.'

Soames protested that his clothes looked too disreputable, that when the expedition to the plane returned he could make himself more presentable for such an honour.

'If I show you round as you are, that only makes the honour more great,' Queen Louise said. 'Please step along – I am, alas, not with much patience.'

It was difficult to decide what to say to this lady, Soames thought, as he followed into the corridor, jostling to get past the little maid to the Queen's side, for her manner was impersonal enough to make one wonder if she was being formal or friendly. In the end, he tried for common ground by saying, 'It is a pleasure to meet the mother of Deal Jimpo, whom I have grown to like very much.'

'Of course,' the Queen said. 'I shall not deny you any pleasure you ask. You shall see her copiously soon.'

This plunged Soames into eddies of confusion. He felt like a male Alice walking beside a composite of the Queen of Hearts and Humpty Dumpty. Either Queen Louise was referring to herself in the third person, in the manner of Caesar's 'Caesar is turned to hear', and offering to strip for him, or they had somehow come a cropper over the language barrier.

'You are Jimpo's mother?' he enquired hesitantly.

'Not I,' said the Queen. 'I am the mother of lovely, intellectual Princess Cherry, whom you shall soon meet. Jimpo is the son of the President's wife.'

'But you are the President's wife.'

'I am the King's wife.'

'But President and King are one!'

'They are held by one person, but they are two separate offices, each of which is entitled to one wife.'

'Oh.'

'I make bed with the King; that is fealty. I must not make bed with President; that would be adultery.'

'You must find these rather fine distinctions difficult to draw at times,' Soames murmured.

'It needs mighty discipline,' said the Queen with relish.

She swept him into an empty banqueting hall, clapped her hands and ordered him to sit down on a couch. She deposited herself beside him. When the gamelan-like harmonies of the springs had died, she began to interrogate him, first about England, then about himself. To excuse this interest, she claimed she had British blood in her veins, but did not amplify the point.

'The climate of Umbalathorp is good,' she said, changing the subject abruptly. 'You find it so?'

'I have no complaints so far,' Soames said, permitting a slight sulkiness to enter his voice.

'It is good,' the Queen said. 'Even the wretched Mr Picket thrives here, although he is an Englishman of another sort. I have read in a *Geographical Magazine* that the English race comes from the tropics, and Princess Cherry is also very educated, reading great many books. She will make somebody, some privileged personage, a good wife one day. No doubt you are eager to meet her?'

'Perhaps when my own clothes ...'

'She is engaged with her studies in the library now,' said the Queen, 'but it is possible to interrupt. Come, I know you will like her.'

Soames and the little black maid scurried after her, down a dark passage and into a room full of rickety shelves, on some of which reposed books and magazines. On a long cane chair lay Princess Cherry, heiress to her mother's estate and physiognomy. She wore a heavy, heavily flowered dress; a blue plastic bow slide was clipped into her tight curls. One pair of earrings adhered to her ears, another was clipped to the superb dihedral of her nostril flanges. In her hand, negligently, was a copy of Thomas Mann's *Buddenbrooks*; it was right way up.

'This is the Englishman, Mr Soames, Princess dear,' said the Queen. 'Get up and put your shoes on at once.'

The Princess complied and said, guiltily, 'How do you do? Possibly you like to sit down in my chair and read something?'

'Perhaps I might borrow something to have in bed tonight,' Soames said. A slow flush crept over his face, in case they should think he had been attempting an innuendo, but both faces were – features apart – blank.

'So you are a literary man?' enquired Queen Louise, looking at her daughter to prompt her to take over the conversation. 'The English are a great literary nation as well as conquering parts of Africa.'

'I read quite a bit,' Soames agreed.

'The English are a very great literary nation,' the Princess admitted uneasily.

'What do you read – besides *Buddenbrooks*?' Soames enquired. He would have enjoyed the conversation better had the Queen not been drawn up like an RSM behind him; she was breathing deeply, like a man receiving a VC at Buckingham palace.

'I read *Buddenbrooks* for a long time,' said the Princess sadly. 'The servants forget to bring me tea when I sit here in this room – library. Also I read John Keats' "Ode to Autumn", which I like. It is a poem. Have you heard of it?'

'Oh, yes, of course,' Soames said. They had swotted up the Ode for School Cert, fifteen years ago. 'For summer has overfilled their clammy cells.'

The Princess clapped her hands and smiled with delight. 'He knows it!' she said to her mother. Genuine pleasure filled her, she sat down naturally on the cane chair like an English schoolgirl, and Soames' feelings changed to liking for her.

'This is a sad poem,' she said, 'but for me mainly puzzling – for you see we do not have autumn in Goya.'

'Otherwise the climate is excellent,' said the Queen.

'Autumn must be so strange,' the Princess said. 'I wish John Keats had written a novel also. Will you perhaps explain the poem to me, line by line, if you are not always busy at your machine, for my English is so foul?'

'I should love to read the poem with you,' Soames said, 'but I assure you your English is very good indeed. Where did you learn it?'

The young girl's manner altered. The smile faded from her face, she turned her head away; she seemed to recall unhappy, far-off things.

'From Mr Picket,' she said.

'Come, we must leave the girl at her work,' said the Queen briskly, uttering a sharp word of command in Goyese to the maid. Before Soames was bustled out, the Princess rose and curtsied; a memory rose in his mind of a performing bear he had seen as an infant. It, too, could curtsy and look sad.

Outside the door, the Queen, drawing herself up to her full height and girth, surveyed Soames thoroughly. Under the glare of her eyes and nostrils, he felt like a man confronted by a bandit aiming a double-barrelled gun.

'She is sweet, the Princess, eh?' the Queen challenged.

Soames nodded once, saying curtly, 'I should like to talk to her alone sometime.'

For answer, he received a salacious wink. The password had evidently been given; the shotgun was lowered; Greek had met Greek. Queen Louise seized his wrist as they set off down the corridor again.

'You are staying here not less than two weeks, Mr Soames.'

'Probably.'

'That time must be enough for you to grow to love this country. We shall show you up all over it. Perhaps you will not like to leave it then. If it would be so, a very good job can be secured in the President's government; perhaps the post of Prime Minister could be found for you. I could arrange everything of consequence.'

'I don't doubt that, Queen Louise,' said Soames. 'But I must get back to England.'

'You are not married?'

'No.'

'You are single?'

'Yes.'

'A bachelor?'

'Yes.'

'Goya has many attractions for a young man, a single literary bachelor.'

'That I do not doubt. But I hardly think I shall stay, all the same.'

'Dumayami, the witch doctor, who is a clever man at reading the future, tells otherwise.'

Lunch was served in the banqueting hall. The small handful of people present huddled round two tables at one end of the room, under the only electric fan which was working. M'Grassi Landor with his two wives, Queen Louise and Mrs President, a buxom Goyese called Tunna, sat at one table with such of their respective offspring as were of manageable age (a category including

40

Princess Cherry and her younger brother Shappy), eating in almost complete silence. At the other table sat Soames with an assortment of black men who were court officials or government ministers. Since none of them possessed much English, silence fell there, too, when they had tried out the little they had. Templeton was not present, thereby missing an excellent Indian curry.

After the meal, the Indian chef came out of the kitchen to present himself to Soames. He was a slender man whose goat's eyes did not smile when the rest of his face did.

'My name is Turdilal Ghosti, sir. I am the head cook to this palace since three years, sir. Was the dinner exactly to your liking, I am hoping?'

'Excellent,' Soames said. 'I am very fond of Indian food. The chicken pilau was first rate.'

'Is the best, sir. How long you are staying here?'

'Oh, about a fortnight. I hope I'll see you again,' Soames said, shuffling his feet, preparing to leave.

'I am living in this bloody town, sir, since seven years. Is too long time for me. Here I am all alone with my old mother and my wife and my six little children and my brother and his family and my uncle and some of his relations and their relations.'

'I noticed there were a lot of Indians in Umbalathorp,' Soames said. He was cornered in an alcove, and the little chef was adroitly keeping him there. Soames could see that the inside of his mouth was bright with betel.

'Plenty Indians are living here, sir,' Turdilal agreed, 'and all are being so bloody unhappy, sir. This climate only good for black men. No other man is liking, sir. In the Japanese war I was cooking three years in Firpo's restaurant on Chowringhee Street at Calcutta; there I am learning all my culinary skill, sir. Perhaps one night you will come to honour my house with your presence? Then I am cooking for you a splendid meal, sir, and displaying to you my children.'

'It's really awfully kind,' Soames said, 'but I fear I'm going to be very busy during my brief stay.'

'I have very nice house, sir, half up Stranger's Hill. You will be having good entertainment.'

'Oh, I'm sure.'

'When I am in Calcutta I am having a white friend, sir.'

Growing more embarrassed, Soames attempted a feeble joke and said, 'I'd like to come. It's just that I think Queen Louise has my spare time pretty well arranged.'

'The Queen is a bloody old hag, sir, if you excuse the word,' Turdilal said, with no trace of anger in his voice. 'I think later you are regretting you don't come my house like I am asking, sir.'

He turned on his heel and snaked down the corridor. Soames sighed, abandoned his alcove, stuck his hands in his pockets and wandered down a flight of stone steps into the sunshine. Here, he was at the back of the palace; it was private and a rough attempt had been made at a garden. The trees were beautiful; big green lizards scuttled up them like rats as he approached.

Soames was enjoying himself. People are taking an interest in me, he thought self-indulgently; they may be no less self-seeking than my fellow-countrymen, but they go about the business with more originality, more verve. They are more amusing. The real reason for his enjoyment, however, was a deeper, sillier, better, less analysable reason; he was living in a strange land.

It was a different thing altogether from *holidaying* in a strange land. Here, although only temporarily, he belonged, was in touch. It was something, for all his excursions abroad and the brief business trips to Brussels and Paris, he had never managed before.

At the bottom of the garden flowed the river Uiui, only five feet below the brow of a tiny cliff. Soames stared down into the flood, its surface green and turbulent as it hurried along. A small fishing boat, manned by four negroes bent sweating over the oars, laboured against the current. A hill rose sheer out of the opposite bank, its jungle studded with jagged outcrops of rock. 'Africa,' whispered Soames to himself, 'darkest Africa'; and he exulted.

There seemed to be no reason why his stay here should not be entirely pleasant, despite the vaguely disturbing warnings of M'Grassi Landor about the witch doctor. Already, reports of the situation had been transmitted home from the wireless room in the palace. What had threatened to be a difficult monetary situation had also been cleared up by M'Grassi Landor and a gentleman grandly styled Minister of Finances who turned out to be manager of the Umbalathorp Bank. Both Soames and Timpleton had been loaded down with doimores, the local coin; twenty mores equalled one doimore, and one doimore was worth ten shillings at the current rate of exchange.

Feeling both at peace with the world and excited by it, Soames turned left and made his way upstream by a path along the bank of the river. It wound enticingly, hedged with flowers and sheltered from the piercing sun. Soon he had left the palace grounds behind; the growth on either side became thicker, the path more devious. He passed an almost naked hunter, who stood gravely aside for him without a word or gesture. The dappled shadows ahead, the silence, led Soames on as if under an enchantment; he walked dreamily, mind a blank.

When he reached a square-framed reed hut, Soames halted, telling himself there was no point in going further. Suddenly he was tired. The hut was empty, its interior cool and inviting. Inside was nothing but a bundle of rags in one corner and an old orange box in another; gratefully, Soames went in and sat on the box.

He mopped his brow, letting his chin droop on to his chest as he rested. Warm drowsiness overcame him.

A sudden sense of being watched jerked his head up. A man stood in the doorway, staring at him with unfriendly eyes; he must have come up with almost supernatural quietness.

'You frightened me for a moment,' Soames said, aware that his start had been observed.

'I am Dumayami, chief witch doctor of Umbalathorp. I want speak with you,' the stranger said soberly.

43

It invariably happens that in those parts of the world which, disregarding the opinions of their inhabitants, we call remote, the products of the white man are more welcome than his presence. They precede him, they succeed him. In the heart of Sumatra (as dangerous now to a pale-haired one as it was two hundred years ago), you may come upon old men drinking from little round tins which once contained fifty of Messrs John Player's cigarettes; the petrol can of the Occident is the foundation stone of the Orient; Coke bottles clog the very source of the untamed Amazon. Knowing this, Soames felt little surprise to find Dumayami clad in an undoubted Church of England surplice with, pinned to it, a badge saying 'I like Ike', just possibly a souvenir of the recent Gunther safari.

Apart from this, the witch doctor was an impressive figure, a giant feather nodding over his scaphocephalic skull, his face notched with tribal marks and wormed with wrinkles. An air of confidence and a whiff of rotten eggs surrounded him. Soames' alarmed thoughts took on a defensive tinge; alas, he was armed with nothing fiercer than a nail file.

'I am resting,' he said. 'What is it you wish to say?'

'I think you already know that,' Dumayami told him. 'The many spirits of Umbalathorp all speak out against your coming. They declare only ill will come from your visit.'

'What am I supposed to have done? Do the spirits tell you that?'

'Spirits tell Dumayami all things,' the witch doctor said, squatting for comfort on the threshold of the hut. The pupils of his eyes held a malevolent, tigerish glint. 'Spirits say you come with machine to make much trouble here.'

'Of course,' said Soames. 'The Apostle will trespass on your pitch in some respects, eh?'

'In Umbalathorp is room for only one law. Now you bring Christian devil box, cast wrong spells, make much trouble.'

'My dear man, the Apostle Mk II does no more than juggle with given data,' Soames said; this old man was clearly a bit of a

44

loon. 'You'd better come up and look at it when it's installed and set your mind at rest.'

Dumayami performed his own equivalent of crossing himself at the very suggestion.

'First Apostle Mark come,' he said gloomily, 'then other apostles, Luke, John, maybe Paul. You must not have success here.'

'Oh, how are you going to stop us? Burn cockerel feathers or something? Progress, Dumayami, has reached Goya at last.'

'Already spirits pull down your flying machine,' Dumayami said darkly. 'Next blow up Christian devil box machine.'

It was, Soames mentally conceded, a crafty point; some people might even have been impressed by it.

'And me? What's going to happen to me, Dumayami?' he enquired.

The witch doctor rose lazily, shaking his head as if to say that it was better for Soames not to know that. Groping under his surplice, he produced what looked like a sharp bone. With two backward paces he was out of the hut. He bent down and used the bone to inscribe a sign in the dusty earth of the threshold.

'If you do not step over this sign, you do not leave Africa,' he said. Raising one hand, he stepped from view and was gone as noiselessly as he came.

'Damned silly,' Soames muttered aloud. 'Of course I can step over it.'

He went over the doorway to examine the mark Dumayami had made. Before he got there, two little yellow and red birds had fallen squabbling and copulating on to the path outside. Their bright wings, fluttering in lust and anger, erased the witch doctor's sign. Soames stood there blankly, not heeding them as they plunged away.

At last, taking a long step over the threshold, he emerged from the hut and hurried back to the palace. Of Dumayami there was neither sight nor sound.

Chapter Five

'And now with treble soft ...'

Later that afternoon, the expedition to the wrecked plane returned. Wending its way through the corn patches and streets of Umbalathorp came a caterpillar of slow men bearing, across poles slung over their shoulders, the crates which bore the component parts of the Apostle Mk II, the generators, the cables. Leading this procession was the palace lorry, a dilapidated Dodge 3-tonner which looked as if it had just made the journey from Cape Town on foot. It was loaded up and weighed down with the heavier crates.

Grunting with disgust, it slewed round in front of the palace in a paddy of dust. Gradually it became motionless. From the passenger's seat in the cab climbed Jimpo, easing his broken leg down. The twelve guards presented arms to him, their umbrellas trembling above them.

Now disorder broke out. The bearers jostled and vied with each other to dump their burdens as near to the Dodge as possible. Scores of pot-bellied children cheered them on. When Soames appeared on the scene, attracted by the noise, he found the lorry had nearly disappeared behind a wall of crates.

Timpleton was there, standing back from the mêlée, regarding it with a seraphic grin. Following his gaze, Soames saw he was looking at the boxes themselves, and his own heart quickened as he read the words stencilled boldly on their sides:

UNILATERAL LONDON ENGLAND.

It was a pleasant reminder of home.

Going over to Timpleton, Soames said, 'It's good to see them here. None of them looks damaged.'

Timpleton smiled. 'Warms the cockles of your heart, don't it? That's what they need here, a spot of civilisation.'

Soames was about to enquire why the engineer should believe that something which had brought no happiness to Europe should work more beneficially here when he checked his tongue. No good would come of antagonising Timpleton. Already they had had a short, explosive altercation after the interview with King Landor, when Soames had protested against Timpleton's using the King as a common tout. At least Timpleton showed no sign of umbrage now, for which Soames was glad.

'Where were you at tiffin time?' he asked conversationally.

Timpleton's manner immediately became withdrawn.

'Oh, knocking about,' he said noncommittally. 'What have you been doing, Soames?'

'I, too, have been "knocking about",' Soames said, a little primly. Then he relented, and after a minute, told Timpleton of his encounter with the witch doctor.

Jimpo had now begun to restore order among the bearers, calling for Timpleton and Soames to help him. Skins of cool water having been carried out from the palace, the men refreshed themselves and then again shouldered their loads. The Dodge reappeared. The battleship grey boxes with their yellow, white and black stencilling were borne up the steps and into the building. Here, a large room facing out to the river Uiui had been set aside for the Apostle. Standing on the first packing case to arrive in this room, Timpleton began shouting instructions to the porters, cheerfully disregarding the fact that none of them spoke English.

'That's it now! That one over there, Johnny, that one over there. Easy with it, you silly sod – treat it like it was crockery. Now bring that one here. You! Bring it here. *Here*, you clot! That's better. Well, get your great foot out the way. Where are *you* going? Where are all them others? Come on, chop-chop, you black bastards, my grannie could move quicker. No, that's Number Twenty Crate, that goes right down that end. Further. Further still. No, not there. *There!* Good lad.'

The porters seemed to understand. They loved being sworn at. Grinning broadly, they parrotted Timpleton's words, calling to one another, 'No. Not dere,' 'You black basads.' Eagerly they fought for the diminishing pile of crates outside, in order to relish the joy of being cursed again inside. So forty-six grey boxes came to be strung out in line down the length of the room, in numerical order according to the stencilled numbers on their sides.

Timpleton rubbed his hands. He picked up a crowbar he had been using as a conductor's baton during the cursing operations.

'OK, Jimpo,' he said. 'Let's open a test case and see if anything's broken.'

Working delicately with the crowbar, he prised the lid off Crate Ten. Inside, packed tightly, partitioned with thick rubber, cushioned with foam rubber, each gripped in place by a spring clip, stood rows of transistors and valves as delicate as Fabergé jewels. The electronics engineer grunted, eased one of the partitions out and removed a valve from its clip.

It was pear-shaped, sixteen slender prongs protruding from its base. The lower half of it was silvered. Timpleton held it up to the light with a connoisseur's eye. Inside it was a lattice of wires and grids, a tiny structure as dainty as a fairy palace in a bottle, while through its interstices could be glimpsed the river Uiui, flowing darkly on.

'That's OK,' he said finally. 'And if a 10 CAAL 10 pentode has stood the journey, the rest of the equipment will be OK. I'll get started putting it together as soon as possible tomorrow morning, Jimpo.'

'Excellent, Ted,' Jimpo said. 'I will get down two of our radio engineers to assist you in any way.'

'Yes, they can help over things like bolting the main framework together,' Timpleton assented.

'I shall take this very good news to my father,' Jimpo said. 'Your personal luggage, by the way, is in the cab of the lorry. A bearer will fetch it to your rooms. Tomorrow the lorry will go back to the wreck and will transport the bodies of the dead men – so much as remains of them – here for burial.'

The last meal of the day was taken at sundown, and consisted chiefly of a porridgy meat mince which Soames did not enjoy. Turdilal Ghosti, the chef, was evidently off duty. None of the royal and presidential families was present except for Princess Cherry, who sat alone at the royal table, and Jimpo, who came down to the commoners' table to discuss computers and the wonderful science of electricity with Timpleton and his two radio engineers, Gumboi and L'Panto.

Eventually, Soames got up and left on his own.

The palace, which during the day preserved the quiet of a village church, was now as noisy as a village fair. From being nearly empty it had become nearly full. Thronging groups of black men and women made the corridors as unruly as hospital corridors at visiting time. Vendors descended on Soames, volubly offering him peanuts, cotton vests, sweets, drugged parrots and nicely shaped bits of old sardine tins.

Someone touched his arm and gently spoke his name.

'Come away from this maddening crowd with me, Mr Noyes. Outside it is pleasant weather before the rain breaks. We will find silence outside.'

An old Chinese with a dark skin and sleepy eyes stood there smiling, introduced himself as Ping Ah and repeated his invitation to the great outdoors. 'Who am I,' thought Soames, 'that all nations should love me?' He suddenly felt sour and suspicious, for the recent meal lay heavy on his stomach.

'I'm sorry,' he said, 'but I am tired. I don't want to walk tonight.'

'Then it would be very nice thing if you will come to my room here in the palace. Take a cup of tea with me, Mr Noyes. Discuss old times.'

'What old times?' (Even as he spoke, he was being manoeuvred down the passage, gently, celestially.)

'As a young man, my wife and I live in England five years,' the Chinese said. 'We make money there and enjoy. Liverpool very interesting city. You come from there perhaps, Mr Noyes?'

'No. I've been there, though.'

'Is very interesting city, no?'

'Very interesting.'

'In Liverpool are many Chinese men. This is my room now please.' Ping Ah seized Soames by the sleeve, opened the door wide enough to stick his head in, stuck his head in, and shouted sharply in Cantonese, whereupon there came an almighty scuffling inside, followed by silence.

'Just I call to see if my missus at home,' explained Ping Ah blandly. 'Please do me a favour of stepping inside.'

They entered what Soames soon found was the palace laundry; Ping Ah was in charge of it. The multitude who had scuttled into hiding had made an excellent job of it; nobody, as they walked through into Ping Ah's inner sanctum, was visible but his wife, whom he addressed as Rosie, pronouncing it Lousy. She came forward smiling through her rimless glasses, shaking her head, bowing, a little plump woman with dimples and a magnificent coiffure. She had no English.

'In Liverpool, she was always indoors, washing, ironing, seeing nobody, eh, Rosie?' said Ping Ah affectionately. She bobbed in answer.

They seated themselves round a scrubbed, bare table. Ping Ah clapped his hands, whereupon a girl hurried out to throw a pretty cloth over the white wood and lay out the paraphernalia for tea. As she did so, the Chinese talked.

'Anything you have for wash or clean,' he said, 'you bring down here, Mr Noyes, and we will attend to with greatest attention and lowest cost. No article is too small or too big for us. All notions of cleanliness admiringly observed.'

Was this pantomime, Soames wondered, just to solicit his custom? If so, very nice, very elegant. He felt suddenly indulgent as he covertly watched the girl preparing the table. To straighten a fold in the cloth, she had leant close to him; he had caught a tiny fragrance, at once soothing and exciting. She was dressed in green candy-stripe pyjamas; her figure and features were good. Soames became anxious to see her eyes, but she never looked at him. For a little while, Ping Ah talked on unheeded.

Now the girl brought in the tea things and a plate of diminutive cakes. Ping Ah poured Soames a shallow cup of sweet-smelling jasmine tea.

'And now let us talk of you, Mr Noyes,' he said, 'for the tales of travellers are always instructive. You have brought an interesting machine to Umbalathorp, but I fear it is too big and will not be used often.'

Soames, to whom this reflection had often occurred, carefully withheld agreement.

'Many disused things have similarly been brought here by our improvident King,' Ping Ah continued. 'Waste of money is cause for grief. Disused things fall to rust. Take more tea please, Mr Noyes. Pour, Rosie. I have many calculations to make for my work. I own not only this poor laundry but many stores in Goya. Each has one or two clerks calculating the books, making a mistake always. All waste of time and money, much grief. Your machine do all sums, hey presto, in no time.'

'A good idea,' Soames said. 'I'm sure King Landor would come to an agreement with you.'

'No, no, Mr Noyes!' exclaimed Ping Ah, slopping his tea. 'You do not understand the situation. The King is against me because I do not pay him squeeze. The Portuguese men pay him much squeeze. They can afford to do because they are big smugglers and rob the population. They are my enemies. Mr Soares particularly bad man. I am only honest trader.'

The Chinese paused here, looking searchingly at Soames over the cup he held between his two palms. Soames, saying nothing, took another sip of the fragrant tea; it was good, but he would have preferred a little sugar with it.

'In this republic is altogether too much intriguing,' Ping Ah continued. 'You would hardly imagine, coming from the peaceful cities of Britain. Because I do not have favourites, I am the victim of victimisation. Perhaps one day the Portuguese arrange for me to be killed.'

He paused again for so long that Soames was forced to say, conventionally, 'I am sorry to hear things are so bad.'

'You can fix help for me, Mr Noyes,' the victim of victimisation said. 'If you can arrange for me to have copies of all problems and answers going through your machine, then I can be forewarned. Nobody need know, only you and this person. You understand the machine, Mr Noyes. You rule her. You can fix.'

'I'm only here a fortnight, Ping Ah.'

'Still you could fix.'

'Sorry, Ping Ah. It's none of my business.'

'Please, Mr Noyes, you can fix.'

'I'm sorry, I can't help you,' Soames said. He was not annoyed; he had expected some such request. To soothe him, too, was the sight of the Chinese girl, who had seated herself on a low wicker chair near to them. She rested her head gently on her hand, her elbow on the chair arm, so that Soames, peeping down at her, could see framed between black hair and golden arm one subtle, appealing breast.

'All things and circumstances can be fixed in the world,' murmured Ping Ah, as if he were talking to himself. 'Men must be practical to gain their desires, else is no hope. For friendship sake I could fix my daughter Hwa to be anyone's room girl. Hwa!'

The girl stood up and looked at Soames. A python could hardly have done a better job of hypnotism.

'This daughter is a very good girl, Mr Noyes,' said Ping Ah. 'Very soft and gentle, also speak a little English. Address Mr Noyes, Hwa.'

'I can be useful in your room, sir,' the girl said seriously. 'Do all things. Good. Clean. Willing.'

Soames swallowed. He had no wish to be involved in local politics but he knew a bargain when he saw it; for Ping Hwa one might do wilder things than entering politics.

'Can make bed,' the girl continued. 'Make tasty dish. Show scenery. Also sing Canton song from opera, you like. Perhaps you also teach piece English poor girl.'

'You're getting your meaning over well already,' Soames told her earnestly, jerking at his collar. He was at a loss to think why he did not clinch the deal straight away; he could not imagine that the information passing through the Apostle would be particularly valuable. 'Who taught you English, Hwa? Your father, I suppose?'

'Father too busy work.' She lowered her eyes and said softly. 'Picket teach. He bad man. Daughter Picket also bad.'

'I keep hearing about this man Picket,' Soames said, faintly disgruntled that the only other Englishman in Goya should get so consistently bad a press. 'Nobody has a good word to say for him. What's he done?'

'Disgraceful thing best not to talk about. Enough said, nearly mended,' Ping Ah replied, patting his daughter's bottom gently, appetisingly.

Soames found the power to stand up.

'I'll think about what you say, Ping Ah,' he told the Chinese, who thereupon also rose, 'and let you know my decision in the morning. Thank you for the offer, thank you for the tea. Goodnight, Hwa.'

He felt nothing but a fool as he left the laundry and made his way up to his room. A stranger called him, placing a detaining arm on his sleeve, but Soames shook it off. He could not be too sure which scruples had made him refuse the offer. Ping Ah, as he had claimed, was an honest trader; the bargain had been attractive. Awakened lust bubbled in him like frying toadstools.

Moodily, he kicked open the door of his room and switched the light on.

Upon his bed, on the bright rug, sat a young, alert negress with eyes like a fawn. Her slender figure with its new breasts was startlingly black against the white wall. She wore two strings of beads and a scent of musk: a simple but effective costume. M'Grassi Landor had kept his promise.

'I suppose Picket taught you English too,' Soames snapped. It was, in truth, the only thing he could think of to say.

'How you know that?' the girl asked in astonishment, uncoiling slightly; her voice was soft and fluting.

'Picket must hold some interesting classes,' Soames said vulgarly, closing the door behind him.

Some long while later, Soames strolled on to the stone balcony outside his bedroom window. The cool sound of the Uiui came to him, and the cry of a night-bird. He glanced at the luminous dial of his watch. It was after midnight, but time no longer mattered. Unstrapping the watch, Soames threw it back into the darkened room behind him and heard it land on the now empty bed. Time was a European invention – or rather, Europeans had invented the idea of chopping it into busy minutes and seconds (what Powys calls 'turdlings of time') and tethering them on to the wrist. In Africa one need only live; as Princess Cherry had observed, there were no autumns – and with these larger punctuations of the year had gone the tiny ones, the seconds and minutes.

'Coitala,' Soames said aloud, savouring the name. The black girl had been aptly christened. At first he had been almost in awe of her, then he had not cared, then finally the awe had returned. He lay gazing at the burnished blackness of her. Seen so close, Coitala was a whole country, hills, valleys, plains, embankments, tumuli, every inch of it flawless. Soames touched the magnificent landscape with his fingers, with his tongue, marvelling. He found himself thinking, as he had done long ago before the plane crash, that this was another planet, that the creature beside him was of another species, quite alien. The only thing they had in common was a difference of sex.

54

A gentle wonder at what he had done filled Soames. It would have been unthinkable a week ago. Not only time and colour changed as one yielded up to the arms of the equator, but life itself, and one's attitude to life. Here, no withholding was possible. In the heat, the pores of the heart opened. One was an organism, involved in all the organisms around; the ability to be aloof was lost in Africa.

He saw the depths of Africa full of eyes and flowers and genitals and lizards and mouths and corn and mammals and leaves, going on for ever – individuals changing, types unchanging, parts fading, the whole always bright, something too rich to be grasped, a pattern of fecundity making the rest of the world a desert by comparison, a moon of a place with craters for breasts.

For their refreshment, King Landor had sent Coitala upstairs with a bottle of Portuguese wine. Slightly intoxicated with love and drink, Soames inhaled a great breath of air. It was laden with sweet and strange smells, even as Coitala had been. In her, Soames told himself – ah, tonight, now, *now*, he knew absolutely all that living implied! – in Coitala he had perceived not only the mystery of Africa but the greater mystery of womanhood. Right under the noses of men – even under their carcasses – women carried on their secret existence, their ambitions not man's, their responses not his. They were a captive race, for ever in bondage, a Chosen People whose superiority man dared only acknowledge singly, in secret. They were wonderful, in that word's literal meaning.

His thoughts grew as woolly as the clouds darkly gathering overhead. They shifted and spread until even Soames forgot about them, drifting through the embrasures of his brain, complete in themselves, patterns with a life of their own. Gradually, almost reluctantly, they formed round a memory of Sheila Thurston, and claimed Soames' attention again.

Sheila had been his great love. He had met her a decade ago, when he was twenty, a youth hamstrung by shyness and the sense of his own inadequacy. He had adored her, she had loved him; but inevitably she had been swept away by a brasher young man with a better line of talk; for he had scarcely talked at all. Soames now faced the fact that, at thirty, he would never love again with such whole-heartedness. This was something to regret, but it was after all only natural: the divine madness burns most strongly at the age we are given the vote; what he more seriously regretted was not that he could never love anyone as he had loved Sheila, but that he had not loved Sheila with the proper style, that whenever he looked back at that cynosure in his life it would be to see it badly flawed, and to wince at the timorousness which still dogged him.

He was down to earth again and it had started to rain. He went back into his room, undressing without putting on the light.

Chapter Six

'And sometimes like a gleaner …'

On the following afternoon, while most of Umbalathorp enjoyed siesta, the mortal remains of Wally Brewer, the engineer from Birmingham, and the pilot of the crashed plane were decently interred in a quiet grove near the palace.

'They were good lads,' Timpleton told Soames over lunch, in the voice of one reading from a tombstone. 'Real good lads. I'm proud to have known them. Wally Brewer was a proper bastard.'

Sucking a hollow tooth, he thought for a moment and then added, 'Old Wally would have enjoyed himself with me last night. I did a tour of the town with a friend – well, it was that Portuguese, Soares, if you must know.'

'Interesting?' asked Soames.

'I'm watching out I don't get the old akkabaksi pox, mate. I tell you! You must come down with us one night. Honest, the girls are okay, but the shacks they live in … lousy with cockroaches. One of them crawled over my bare arse. I'm fussy about that sort of thing, I am. It didn't ought to be allowed. It puts you right off your stroke. Now back in England a place like that would be properly disinfected and cleaned every day.'

'And closed,' Soames added.

Timpleton looked at him reflectively.

'What did you do last night?'

'Oh, I went to bed early,' Soames said.

'Not much of a one for the women, are you really?' Timpleton said sympathetically.

'They're all right on the whole.'

'After you with the hole,' Timpleton said.

'Excuse me, I must go and get ready for the funeral,' Soames said, rising from the table.

Lustful conversation was not what he wanted just then. It gave him too strong a feeling of life flowing remorselessly on. Although he cared little for the dead, he wanted to care for their sakes, shut away as they now were from all sun and flowers and flesh. Forgetting the way in which these elements were beginning to work on him, and little knowing how crowded his day would be, Soames resolved to preserve a proper mourning spirit until tomorrow, in honour of his defunct fellow countrymen. Thus pompously pious, he prepared for the funeral.

He found that the sad business had its amusing side.

The capital of Goya boasted a Christian priest, a Portuguese, but as a staunch Roman Catholic he refused to traffic with Protestant corpses. President Landor therefore took charge of the ceremony.

'Don't ask me to comprehend your religion,' the President exclaimed to Soames; he cheerfully announced himself to be of the heathen persuasion. 'With the mazes of politics I can, as a pragmatist, cope – but the mazes of religion – it is too much! If only the wretched Picket … However, never mind that; in the circumstances, as Head of State, I shall be delighted to read the last rites over these three servants of Unilateral.'

Soames attended the ceremony with Deal Jimpo and Prince Shappy; Timpleton, eager to get on with the job of assembling the Apostle Mk II, was not present. The only other people present were half a dozen blacks with nothing better to do, Tanuana, carrying his bicycle and smiling all the while to indicate his personal interest in the proceedings, and an aged Frenchman called Jules Michel – 'a Communist', Jimpo whispered importantly to Soames.

Despite this sparse audience, the President, resplendent under a tasselled umbrella held by two of his followers, did the honours thoroughly and, as the poor parcels of bones were lowered into the puddingy earth, broke into a valedictory oration over them.

'Let us not forget that speed brought these men to their untimely deaths,' he said in French. 'Speed is all that aeroplanes have to offer. To travel in them is to gain time and lose other more precious things. Any sensitive person is depressed by the draughty flatness of an aerodrome, and by its concomitants, the hours of delay, the yattering loudspeakers, the customs officials. To fly is to become denationalised; the thought revolving in our head in Durban is still there at Dar es Salaam; the tune we whistle at Leopoldville is still on our lips when we arrive at Marrakesh. We are always unprepared. These three men, my people, were unprepared.

'In the days of our fathers, their fate would have been different. They would have sailed from their northern island in a ship, with our red computer in the hold of the ship. The ship would have had great sails that would be steel blue by dawn light, grey by day, blood red by sunset; it would have seen many days on its journey here, and these unfortunate men would have had time to prepare. They would have understood then that this earth has only one sunrise which trails for ever and ever round the continents, from former ages into the future, and only one sunset, which trails after the sunrise like a dog after its master. Then these unfortunate men would come to understand how it follows from this that in all creation there is only *one* day; one day only, and however fast they travel back or forth, they can squeeze no more days, for there *are* no more days; time is indivisible and cannot be saved except by spending it in a leisurely way.

'According to the tenets of the religion of these unfortunate men, they are now enjoying another sort of life which goes on forever elsewhere. Those of you who have had the task of picking their festering bones and gristle from the smashed plane may doubt this. I doubt it too. I feel therefore that as fellow human beings who will some day be reduced to roughly the same regrettable state, we should hope charitably in our hearts that these three unfortunate men, during their lifetimes, interfered with their neighbours as little as might be expected and found leisure enough to relax, laugh, make others laugh, drink and enjoy. And let us hope further, for our own sakes as well as theirs, that if this hypothetical future life exists, it contains none of this world's sorrows and all of its pleasures, which are good pleasures indeed. Amen. No clapping please.'

The President, having finished his oration, accepted a fizzy raspberryade from one of his attendants and climbed into the Dodge which, with a wilting circlet of flowers draped over its bonnet, was doing duty as state carriage.

Soames turned to Jimpo.

'An ingenious speech your father made,' he said, since ingenious was the adjective he used for anything the point of which to some extent eluded him.

'One would never think to hear him,' Jimpo said, with a sad, abstract air, 'that he had never been up in an aeroplane.'

'That says all the more for the acuteness of his perceptions,' replied Soames, 'for there is much truth in what he says. Flying solves nobody's problems – it is merely taking refuge in flight.'

They stood silently together, watching the two black gravediggers enthusiastically belabouring the black earth flat with their spades, until Jimpo asked, 'You think my father speaks truth?'

'Do you mean just now, or continually?' Soames asked.

'Just now, of course. Nobody can speak it continually, least of all a man with a position to maintain.'

'I think,' Soames said, 'that what he said was mainly true, though whether he intended it for truth I can't decide: his speech seemed so impromptu it may well have come out accidentally.'

'Do you think he spoke the truth about being denationalised?'

This was asked so urgently that Soames instinctively gave an evasive answer.

'You will find as you grow older,' he said patronisingly, 'that one's instinctive enquiry after *the* truth softens into a lookout for some truth.'

'It may be so,' Jimpo admitted. 'What worries me more at present is this problem of being denationalised. In England, at school, I rejoiced to feel myself become English inside. In the holidays I travelled to France and Germany and Scandinavia and Greece, sending censored reports of my visits to my father, and then I rejoiced to feel myself become European. It is easy to become European: one has only to subscribe to *Le Figaro* and smoke American cigarettes. But now that I am back here, I find I do not fit. Nor am I sure if I want to fit. This must be because either I am denationalised or I am an existentialist; it is very worrying not to know.'

Soames scarcely heard Jimpo's last remark, for a previous one had started off a line of thought in his own head, and he said, wondering aloud, 'Do you think I might become an African?'

'It is more difficult than becoming European or English,' Jimpo said shortly. 'You could not do it. I am not even sure that I can manage it again.'

'But, you see,' Soames began, plunging into deep water, 'last night I had an experience for which I was, in your father's phrase, unprepared. It was as if a barrier went down within me –'

'I thought,' Jimpo said, delivering each word in an ice cube, English-fashion, 'we now discussed my troubles, not yours.'

Soames did not reply. He was not affronted; rather, he was glad that he had been checked before indulging himself in embarrassing confidences. Relievedly, he looked round to find they were alone. Even the gravediggers had left the burial site. A beetle the size of an ashtray hurried on to the arena of brown earth and commenced fussily to dig.

'Perhaps things will improve when the Apostle is working,' Jimpo said optimistically. 'Denationalised people may be needed to operate it.'

'From some of your remarks and your father's,' said Soames, 'I wondered if you were not already regretting the purchase; is not the Apostle an agent of denationalisation?'

Digging, scowling, into the pocket of his shorts, Jimpo produced an Italian ten lire coin and held it out on the yellow palm of his hand.

'This coin has two sides,' he said. 'On one is ear of corn, on other is plough. Now pretend one means denationalising and one means progress. When Goya goes shopping in the world market and gets this coin for her small change, how can she accept one side without the other? Is impossible.'

He hurled the coin into the bushes. It would be discovered two thousand years later by two Eskimo archaeologists, one of whom, extrapolating from this evidence, would write a learned paper entitled, 'The Extent of Italian Conquest in the African Continent Prior to the Immolation by Q-Bomb Warfare of All Land Masses Situated in the Temperate and Tropical Zones', which would sell nine copies in Peary Land alone.

'Why do you find it important to shop in the world market?' Soames asked.

Jimpo took his arm. 'My good humour with you is restored by that foolish question, which you would not dream of asking of your own tiny country, half the size of Goya. Come, before I go back to watch Timpleton at work, I will show you about Umbalathorp.'

Anyone seeking a physical model of the contradictions in the average human mind could have done worse than pick on Umbalathorp. Soames considerably revised his first impressions of it. There were good, even grand, buildings to be seen, often marred by pretentious fronts. Modern shops were surrounded by huddled shanties, as in the mind a little science may still be swamped by a lot of superstition. Paved streets petered out abruptly into muddy lanes, patios looked into pig runs, plate glass on to

62

jungle. Neurotic bantams foraged outside a white concrete clinic, while a contemporary style garage struggled for breathing space amid beehive huts and boxwood shacks. Tree lizards skittered up telegraph poles.

Leading Soames into a more prosperous road, Jimpo said, 'I do not wish your stay here to be without enjoyment. In this area live the ladies of pleasure. From my stay in your country I realise that the English are as amorous as any other nation, even when they pretend not to be. So I think you may like to pay a visit to some of these ladies, as relaxation after the sorrow of the funeral.'

Anxiety seized Soames immediately.

'That's very decent of you,' he said. 'But wouldn't it be a little – dangerous? What about the dreaded akkabaksi pox?'

His friend looked blank.

'This is something I have not heard of. Is it a disease?'

'A killing disease. Three or four days after contracting it, the victim's bones turn to jelly. There is no cure known to medicine.'

'How curious. I have not heard of this disease in Goya.'

'Oh.' It dawned on Soames that the disease was a mere fabrication of José Soares, designed to drive trade into his rascally hands. He was filled with relief.

'This is a good establishment. Let us go in here,' Jimpo urged, halting before a building on the verandah of which three women lolled idly, watching them. Over the doorway, written in several languages, was a notice with the bald announcement, 'AMERICAN MASSAGE'.

Instinctively Soames drew back.

'To tell you the truth,' he said, 'I have never consorted with prostitutes and I am reluctant to do so now. The business is too cold-blooded for my liking. You go in if you like, but I'll wait here.'

'You are a romantic and I honour you for it. But this is not England – and indeed in that sense many parts of the world are not England.'

'Oh, undeniable. But I am English.'

'Equally undeniable. And as my honoured guest, the benefits of my father's capital are doubly open to you.'

To continue this foolish argument, Soames had had to follow Jimpo, who was moving forward. They were now both on the verandah, where willing hands grasped them and pushed them inside. With twittering black girls jockeying for position about him, Soames was too much the gentleman to resist.

Jostled into a narrow and sweltering corridor on to which cubicles opened, he found himself cornered by a dark scrawny girl. She wore a crumpled cotton skirt and a blouse which opened wide enough to reveal the extent to which her pectoral muscles had let down her narrow pointed breasts. Their immense dark nipples stared at Soames accusingly.

Panting and tugging, the girl manoeuvred Soames away from the other females and into one of the other cubicles. Jimpo meanwhile was discussing prices in his own tongue with an enormous black man in jeans and a peaked cap.

'I'll be in the next cubicle,' he called as Soames was swept away by his fate.

A pleasant feeling of resignation overcame Soames.

In protesting, he had defended his scruples; in yielding, he had shown his adaptability. Nor was this determined young woman in charge of him exactly unprepossessing. Her breasts might look a little shop-soiled, but her face, with its copper sheen and wild eyes, was quite attractive – until she opened her mouth and smiled. To his horror, Soames saw that her teeth had been filed to points. An awful vision assailed him of being bitten on the ear; it might be as deadly as a vampire bite.

She motioned to him to lie down.

A hard couch was provided, covered with a sheet. It looked clean enough. At least there were no cockroaches in sight.

As he climbed on to it, Soames wondered to what race the girl belonged; ethnic groups meant nothing to his untutored eyes. Perhaps she was an Arab. He recalled the tale the recently interred

Birmingham man had related on the plane before they crashed, about the Arab girl who dug her heels into the small of her partner's back.

The girl was methodically undressing him, bending over him so that her long brown breasts swung before his eyes. Gingerly, he touched one. It was warm and felt like soft leather. The girl murmured encouragingly; she spoke no English. Feeling at once foolish and titillated, Soames allowed his shoes and trousers to be removed. He kept his shirt on.

'Have you tried the American Massage before?' Jimpo called over the top of the cubicle.

Wondering what extraordinary experience lay behind this euphemistic title, Soames had to admit his innocence.

'It's a great fashion here in the capital, since we got the electricity. Many men now like no other satisfaction.'

'Oh … I say, Jimpo, are you on the bed?'

'Yes. My little lady is just plugging in. Are you comfortably okay?'

'Yes, I think so. Good Lord, Jimpo, she's got a hand vibromassager!'

'Specially imported, very up to date. A modern sensation for an ancient region. All the ladies here are carefully trained to use them for maximum effect.'

'Mmmm. Now I begin to see what you mean …'

'I hear that your machine has started. Now mine also has started … Ah, capital, capital. The sensation is commendable, no?'

'My God … Yes, yes, highly commendable. My God … I didn't realise how far automation had gone. This is an absolute eye-opener for me.'

'As I told you on the occasion of our first fortunate meeting, here we are most progressive.' He rumbled on, developing the theme of Goya's march into the future.

It was, Soames reflected, a curious time and place to choose for an oration. He lay back, head propped on one bent arm, watching his girl devoutly at work. She knelt on the couch beside him, busily moving the vibro-massager a cunning inch or two, frequently looking up to smile at Soames with her pointed teeth.

'... Enlightened application of science, allied with enlightened application of politics, will give our people new liberty and pride in their work,' rumbled Jimpo, his voice rumbling over the top of the partition.

This girl with the filed teeth, Soames speculated, did she take pride in her work? Was there a union of vibro-masseuses in Goya? And why, after all, should he find that idea funny? This creature contributed as much to the happiness of man as any craftsman wielding a hand drill that she so resembled.

'We shall enlighten men and women to play their part. Our new programme of education will ensure that both sexes play their full role ...'

'So that you can shop in the world market?' Soames asked, interrupting.

But his mind was jogged off the subject by his body, his long white body turgid under those lean black hands. The little remorseless engine was working its wonders. Warmth spread, then gathered through his thighs. Yes, he thought, I'm a new man, a new vigorous man, big in big Africa, full of potential, full of seed, yes, bursting over, yes, yes, ah yes!

Ten minutes later, the two men were out in the dusty heat again.

As they walked down the chief street which, in deference to President Landor's policy of incorporating in his realm strands from both sides of the Atlantic, was called Main High Street, Soames and Jimpo discovered they were thirsty. Soames indicated the first café they came to, but Jimpo shook his head and walked on, later passing several other cafés.

'One has to be prudent,' he explained. 'The native cafés are not fit to use by your standards, and most of the others are owned either by the Portuguese José Soares or the Portuguese Lope de Duidos, who has a wooden leg much fancied by white ants; these two men are very powerful, and we at the palace must avoid showing preference to either one.'

Finally they came to a little, dark Chinese shop into which the princeling ushered Soames, remarking as they crossed the threshold,

'This place will be fine for us. It is called "The Fountain of One Thousand Appetising Intestines", but at least it is clean.'

'You speak Chinese?' asked Soames, surprised.

'No. But the name is not the sort you forget when you have heard it once.'

They drank two glasses of cold Russian tea apiece, Jimpo paid, and they emerged blinking into the daylight again. People were now about in the streets again, the hottest part of the day being over; the men divided, as far as outward appearance was concerned, into two types: the ordinary, unsophisticated Goyese, who looked as if he had just drifted in from the bush, and the Umbalathorp Slicker, in slash tie and angel blue suit with huge lapels, who pinned down an office job. Both groups acknowledged Jimpo politely as they passed, though the Slickers did so with greater enthusiasm, obviously recognising in him a man who had fulfilled all their own ambitions; Soames was reminded of a group of schoolboys greeting the Duke of Edinburgh.

'That's the Catholic church,' Jimpo said, indicating a weary-looking brick building with a corrugated iron roof. 'Several of our young men are Catholics. The building was formerly a Methodist chapel.'

'What happened to the Methodists?'

'They tried to address the people in the streets through loud-speakers, which was much resented. They were captured and tied to branches of a tree selected by Dumayami, hanging by the wrists with their feet just off the ground. At night come the floods and snip, snip, snip, crocodiles bite off the Methodists' ankles up to the waist, making them bleed to death. The Goyese are quiet people, but when roused are capable of great ingenuity. Now I show you the railway.'

They slipped through a narrow alley devoted to goats, past an Indian cinema and a warehouse, and came to the railway station. It was unmistakable. A tall palisade, some stakes of which had sprouted into good-sized trees, guarded it from the road. Boards running the length of the palisade announced in several languages: 'The Royal Umbalathorp State Railway. Comfort; speed; perpetual motion.' Jimpo put down his money at the booking office window, received two tickets, and led Soames on to the platform, which was crowded with people, many of whom obviously slept here, some of whom were already doing so.

'This place was the joy of my childhood,' Jimpo said, shaking hands warmly with a one-eyed porter who presented him and Soames with a leaf full of melon seeds. 'The line was then being built by Portuguese contractors. Instead of the little electric trains which English boys play at, I had a real train. The railway was planned to connect us with the up-country town of Uiuibursam, two hundred and fifty miles away. To do this, a bridge had to be built; unfortunately it never was built, and so the railway will never be completed.'

'What a pity!' Soames exclaimed. 'Why was the bridge so difficult?'

'It had to go over a tributary of the Uiui and be made of steel. A suitable German engineer was chartered to come up from Windhoek and achieve this thing. He travelled up the Congo and then overland, and was within twenty miles of Umbalathorp when he became killed beneath a herd of wild elephants. There are no elephants near Umbalathorp now, for the poachers have finished them all; so you see if we had had patience and waited, this bad thing would not have happened, and we would now have had our bridge.'

'Could you not now engage another engineer?' Soames enquired; he no longer hesitated about putting questions which seemed obvious to him.

'Now is fortunately no need for a bridge,' Jimpo said. 'Owing to failure of crops and baboon attacks, Uiuibursam is now deserted. Nobody requires to go there any more.'

'Yet the line seems very popular,' Soames observed, as a little 0–4–0 tank engine bustled into the station tugging two carriages. A good-humoured scrimmage ensued between those who wished to get out of the carriages and those who wished to get in.

'This is the most popular entertainment in the capital,' Jimpo said. 'Everyone likes to ride on it. Come on, Soames! Let us have a joy ride, man!'

Lowering his rugger-playing shoulders, Jimpo pressed forward and finally secured seats in a packed compartment for Soames and himself. A very fat lady wearing a palm leaf secured to her head with ribbon gave greyish nut kernels to everyone present, and the atmosphere became greasy with excitement.

'This line runs only to the slum part of our capital,' Jimpo said. 'You can almost see one end of it from the other. But still, who is doing any caring? The scenery on the way is good, and the government has profited from increased real estate values, since everyone fights to build a house on the trackside, in order to watch the train going by.'

The one-eyed porter thrust his head through the glassless window, speaking with extraordinary rapidity to Jimpo and employing great facial expression as he did so.

'I will be coming back soon, Soames,' Jimpo said, rising. 'My father wishes to correspond with me on the telephone. It should not detain me for a minute.'

He jumped off the train, following his porter friend into a room which evidently served as combined signal cabin, stationmaster's office and cloak-room. Soames could watch him through the window as he seated himself at a vast desk and spoke reverently into an instrument designed in gracious Second Empire style. The princeling's brow became overcast. He protested. He shot a glance or two at Soames. He remonstrated. He seized the telephone by its rococo throat. He listened again, and was convinced. He commenced a lengthy discourse. The train pulled out and he was still talking demonstratively.

This guileful move on the part of the train did not take Soames unawares. Indeed, he was given early notice of the manoeuvre by a jerk which caught his head a violent blow against the wall behind him – a mishap at which the other passengers, too experienced to be caught by the same trick, all laughed gaily; but he was too well wedged in by the fat lady, who had spread herself since Jimpo got out, to move quickly enough to dismount from the train. He consoled himself with the knowledge that the journey would be short.

Jimpo's point about the real estate was soon made clear. Little wooden houses, squeezed together like match boxes standing on end, pressed so close to the rails that their occupants could easily shake fists at or even hands with the train passengers. For Soames, it was as if they moved slowly through a cross-section, cut with a monstrous knife, of Umbalathorp, because the Goyese – even this upper crust who could afford to live right on top of the tracks – led such airy existences that no privacy existed in their homes. In one room they passed, a negro, his shorts supported by braces stretched to breaking point over a massive bare chest, was either kissing or biting his wife; in another, three naked children bounced up and down on a prone relation; in a third, a woman sat working a sewing machine with a babe at each breast. On one tiny balcony, a man had built himself a signal gantry; he crashed the signal arms down smartly as they chugged by, and blew a silver whistle.

Then the houses on one side fell suddenly away. The track swerved to run along one of the low cliffs hemming in the Uiui, hugging it so closely that some of the sleepers overhung the river. This perilous proximity continued only for some two hundred yards before the track swung inland again. Now the houses which had so closely parodied the suburban hutches conspicuous round Los Angeles or Birmingham were replaced by native affairs, Indian bashas, or mud, stone, straw and petrol can huts and shanties. The train stopped as violently as it had started. Soames buried his face in the loin cloth of the Goyese sitting facing him.

Jumping out, Soames saw why the abrupt halt had been necessary. Five yards ahead of the engine, the rails stopped. There were no buffers. Ahead, the tributary of the Uiui which had evaded bridging meandered amid marsh. Deep pits and gouges in the marsh seemed to indicate that the driver had not always been so successful in stopping his charge in time.

Only half the passengers alighted here, the other half sitting tight to enjoy the return journey. Soames found himself in what Jimpo had rightly designated slum. Fearing to lose face by climbing back into the train, from whose windows he was being watched with lively interest, he trudged off among the assortment of huts. Making his way through light mud and poultry, he came on to a low line of stalls, most of which, at first glance, looked to be selling nothing but flies. Several stall-keepers called to Soames as he went by.

Alas, thought Soames, his mind running in a familiar groove, I'm in this unpleasant little strait because of my parents; can a man ever have had such an ill-mixed bundle of characteristics wished on to him? The unseemly thrustingness of my mother made me jump off the train without due consideration, and the idiot timidity of my father made me too weak to get back on again when I saw what a filthy hole I was in. As if it were not enough for the sins of the father to be visited on the son, I have to put up with my mother's, too. If only I could shake myself free … At least it's not very far to walk back to the palace if I can only strike a road. A pity the only word of Goyese I know is the verb Coitala taught me last night: I'd probably get a thick ear if I used it here.

Continuing thus pleasantly to himself, Soames was able to ignore the vendors about him until he heard an unmistakably English cry of 'I say!'

Looking ahead, he saw a dusty convertible parked in the shade. A white man wearing a topi leant out of the window and beckoned to him. This was the first white man Soames had seen in a topi, although he had observed one or two Indians in battered specimens; he studied the face beneath this one with interest. It was the long, airedale-square countenance one generally finds in isolated places, lighthouses, Scottish moors or boxes at the Royal Festival Hall, definitely a British face; it bore the sad, tolerant look one sees in the faces of men of sixty and wonders whether it is of the world or of themselves that they have had to grow tolerant.

As Soames approached the vehicle, the wearer of the topi climbed stiffly out, observing Soames almost with anxiety all the while. He wore black shoes and a crinkled, cream, linen suit with a black tie.

71

He put out his hand and bared twin lines of false teeth in a welcoming smile.

'I can see you are English, sir,' he said.

Soames, of course, gave no hint of his inner reaction to this statement, but he was profoundly struck by several facets of it; to wit, its idiocy, its sheer beauty, in that it left no doubt that a type of Englishman was recognisable anywhere and that Soames was that type, its ambiguous note of welcome and warning, its brashness, and its subtlety in stirring instantly a corpus of British Empire myth: the Dr Livingstone complex, the Union Jack flying over lonely atolls, the sundowners, the chota pegs, Poona, the done things, the Khyber Pass, Victoria Peak, Noël Coward, Kipling, Douglas Fairbanks Jnr, Gilbert and Sullivan, Cable and Wireless, and practically anything and anyone else you cared or no longer cared to mention. It brought, unexpectedly, a lump to Soames' throat; but of this also he gave no hint.

'How do you do, sir?' he said, clasping the skinny hand, all his Englishness oozing to the surface. 'May I introduce myself? I am Soames Noyes, liaison manager for a London computer firm. My mother was inordinately fond of the *Forsyte Saga*, hence the unfortunate Christian name.'

'Oh, not much of a reader myself. I am Alastair Picket, late of His Majesty's Church of England. I was wondering when we'd see something of you. Do let me give you a lift, old man.'

Chapter Seven

'... thou hast thy music too.'

'Put those baskets of mine in the back. I always shop down this end of town; it's cheaper than in the flashier parts. Just come down once a week, do as much as I can in one fell swoop. The truth is, we share this horrible vehicle with three Portuguese families and only get the use of it on Tuesdays. Economy measure, you know. Not that I wish to imply that things are too tight in any way ...'

The voice of Alastair Picket died away as, with Soames beside him, he started the engine and coaxed from the gearbox a racket like the grinding of infernal dentures. They cantered unnervingly close to a stall full of brass utensils and headed towards Stranger's Hill. When Soames mentioned that this was not the quickest way to the palace, Picket placed a hand reassuringly on his knee.

'You must come and have tea with us, now I've caught you, Noyes. Mrs Picket would never forgive me, and of course I want you to meet my daughter, Grace. Nice girl. Very sensitive girl. Besides, we may not be down in town again till next week.'

Soames was silent. Although he recalled how often he had heard ill spoken of Picket, he was not one to protest sooner than necessary; indeed, the due time for remonstration was already past, for they were now zig-zagging up a dust track, as Picket flogged an unexpected turn of speed out of the communal vehicle.

'This is Stranger's Hill, up the top here, where the white colony of Umbalathorp is,' Picket said. 'It's supposed to be healthier than lower down, but what you lose in mosquitoes you gain in baboons. The damned brutes are always in the garden, can't keep them out. Traps don't seem to catch 'em.'

A panorama of the Goyese capital was now visible. Below them lay the slum end of the town; beyond the tributary which had defied the railway bridge, to the south of it, lay another congestion of huts. Wooden piers projected into the fierce flow of the Uiui, while on the opposite bank, the severe cliffs fell back enough to allow a line of huts along the margin of the river, their thatched roofs dwarfed by the enormous trees and boulders a hundred feet above them. To the north lay Umbalathorp proper, one corner of the palace just visible behind trees. It all looked very picturesque – that is to say, the discomforts of the environment endured by the inhabitants momentarily titillated the eye of the visitor.

'Terrible place, but it holds you,' Picket said, catching Soames' glance. 'God, how it holds you!'

The track up Stranger's Hill twisted through belts of thick, rhododendron-like bushes with zygomorphous flowers, past Nissen huts outside which black babies toddled and crawled, and deposited them before the Picket residence in an aura of dust.

The disorientation of *déjà vu* overcame Soames as he regarded the concave roof-tree, the deep eaves, the verandah whose rail had partly fallen away, the flimsy table and chairs on the verandah, the glimpse of mosquito netting through one window. He had seen this place often before. After a moment he recalled where he had seen it. This was the tropical residence par excellence depicted a thousand times in the *Wide World* and similar travel-minded magazines. Here, the grim-jawed men holding .375 magnum expresses faced the rogue rhino, the Zulu attack, the pride of pythons, the soldier ants, the horror from the mauve lagoon or whatever the anti-social threat might be, whilst in the dim threshold behind them, the blonde in jodhpurs clutched her baby, her breasts or her glass with terror on her countenance.

The blonde's place was usurped in actuality by Mrs Picket, who came forward slowly to greet Soames. She was podgy and pasty, with an ill look that her smile only accentuated. Her mouth drooped, the hem of her dress was uneven.

'Hot again,' was all she said to Soames as they were introduced, the two words forsaking her like a sigh. They all sat on the verandah chairs. ('Mind that bit of floorboard, Noyes; we suspect dry rot,' Picket said.) Silence fell.

'Well, go and get Mr Noyes some tea, Dora,' Picket said testily, drumming his fingers on the table.

'I'll call Pawli,' said Dora, adding conversationally, without raising her voice, 'Pawli.'

In the silence that followed, the darkest that Africa could do, a hirsute spider dropped from the rafters and alighted on Soames' neck, making off rapidly down his vertebrae. He was still fishing for it when a well-built young negress with a sulky expression, dressed only in headcloth and skirt, emerged from indoors and surveyed them. So intense was her scrutiny, so scornful the set of her thick lips, that Soames dropped his hand in embarrassment, letting the spider go its own way.

'Tea, please, Pawli,' said Mrs Picket despairingly.

'Get it yourself,' the black girl said, turning and disappearing slowly into the gloom from which she had come. Soames could hear her bare feet slapping on the boards.

'Terrible servant problem here. Bad as Britain, I believe,' Picket said with false cheerfulness, clearing his throat and looking fiercely at his wife. 'Will you go and get the tea, Dora, without further argument, and find Grace and fetch her here.'

'Please don't bother, Mrs Picket, really,' Soames said, alarmed by the ghastly look of her as she rose to obey. He reflected at the same time that she was the first person he had met in Umbalathorp who showed no disposition to talk continuously. She gave him no answer now, vanishing into the bungalow with soggy, uncertain step.

'It's no bother, old chap,' Picket said comfortably, patting Soames' hand. 'We're only too glad to have you.' Soames withdrew his hand sharply, employing it in a renewed hunt for the spider.

'I expect you're wondering very much how I come to be living in a place like Umbalathorp,' Picket said. 'Or have they been gossiping about me down at the palace? Hey? I shouldn't be surprised. Hey?'

'They hardly mention your name,' Soames said shortly, still offended by the man's treatment of his wife. He wondered if Jimpo was looking for him.

'Dora and I came here twenty-seven years ago. Twenty-seven years … It's a longish time, you know. That would be before you were born, I expect, Noyes?'

He waited so patiently for an answer that Soames was forced to say 'No.'

'Ah, then you'll be older than my daughter Grace. She was born in England – in Kent, as a matter of fact – before we came out here. She was just a babe in arms when Mrs Picket and I arrived here; the napkins were a trouble on the boat, I recall. We were missionaries. Missionaries! … Missionaries to Umbalathorp. Yes, His Majesty's Church of England, as I like to call it for fun, sent us out here with a blessing and a crate full of Bibles. And do you know what happened, Noyes? Do you know what happened? I took one look at Africa with all its savages and everything – and I lost my faith. Just like that!'

The airedale face screwed up in wonderment. After all these tropical years, it could still feel an immense surprise at the cardinal fact of its life, that faith had withdrawn as suddenly as a rat down its hole.

'I was in an awful fix,' Picket continued, drumming his fingers on the table again. 'I just couldn't square the Old Testament and the Hebrews and England's green and pleasant land and life Eternal and all the rest with – all this.' He waved his hand inclusively over the balcony rail. His eyes misted as the truth of his plight, overlaid by later accretions, pierced through to the surface once more; he retraced his mental steps and began to tell the story again.

'This was the trouble, Noyes, you see. Take a nice little English church in a nice little English town. You're friendly with all the people who matter in the town. The workmen salute you – or they did thirty years ago. You hob-nob with the squire and the squire's lady. You've got some nice, fresh-faced little choirboys all rigged out in surplices.' He sighed deeply. 'And what's in your heart, Noyes? You picture Christ as a white chap, don't you? Like yourself, in a sort of surplice himself, and with a trim beard, talking in English. Like that picture by that man Hunt, "The Light of the World". Then you get to Umbalathorp, swarming with natives. Have you seen their carvings of their gods, Noyes? You can buy them in the bazaar for a few coppers. They've got little squat, ugly gods, with big lips and bare bums and bones through their noses. Terrifying!

'Well, I saw these things when I first got here – twenty-seven years ago next month, it was – and I thought, "My God, they're right too, the Goyese are right, the gods are like that here. You can't preach Christ here." And I sat tight a bit and I thought, and the more I thought the less connection I could see between what goes on here and what goes on anywhere else in christendom.'

'But thousands of other missionaries –' Soames began.

'I know what you're going to say,' Picket exclaimed impatiently, 'same as John Gunther said when he was here. You're going to say if the others kept their faith, why couldn't I keep mine? Well, I don't know the answer to that. But I do know that at first I thought, "If I let this lot of niggers into the church, it means I'm letting them into Heaven, and nobody in England's going to like that, not even the bishops." I'm just telling you what I thought. Perhaps it sounds silly to you. Then I thought more deeply, and I began to see things from the native point of view, and the whole idea of Heaven seemed funny. It seemed so funny, I laughed all one day. I did! Mrs Picket was very upset. And after that, I just didn't believe any more, I couldn't. I had a bit of a temperature – it was like getting over the measles – but after that I was right as rain.'

The spider had eluded Soames; the conversation seemed to him to contain just the ideal mixture of foolishness and bad taste; yet it vaguely bothered him. Any sympathy he might have felt for Picket was still dampened by his treatment of his wife.

'So do you know what I did?' Picket said, switching abruptly from misery into laughter. 'I ceased to call myself the Reverend Alastair Picket from that day on. I flung my dog collar in the Uiui, I flogged the Bibles cheap to a French Jew, and I bartered all my cassocks and surplices to the local witch doctor in exchange for poultry, ducks and a cow. But the *funny* thing was – here, I'll show you!'

Laughing, he fished a wallet from a sweaty inner pocket and showed Soames an ancient cutting from *The Times*.

'You see, Noyes, a native five hundred miles down river fished my dog collar out of the water and took it to a Belgian missionary. The collar had my name on it, communications were bad – they decided I'd been speared by a hostile native. Hence this obituary notice! But that wasn't the end of it. The funny thing *was*, years later –'

His voice ceased, his laughter faded, he seemed to recollect where he was. His wife had returned to the verandah with a dark-haired, slender girl whose face, in its square, sad outline, ('good-looking in a doggy way,' commented Soames favourably to himself) bore a family resemblance to Picket's.

'Here's Grace,' said Mrs Picket, and sat down.

Picket jumped up and took Soames' arm. Soames released himself almost at once.

'Oh, Noyes, look here, this is my dear daughter Grace, the prop of my declining years, a very smart girl who ought to be in England. Grace, this is Mr Noyes, who isn't in Umbalathorp for very long. You two ought to see more of each other, really.'

'I'm happy to meet you,' Grace said. She gripped Soames' hand and looked into his eyes. He sensed instantly a tension about her;

it was not a nervous tension, for she was perfectly in command of herself, nor did it seem primarily a sexual tension, although she must have been as aware as he that they formed the only young English couple in Umbalathorp. Grace wore a crisp blue and white dress which very possibly had just been changed into; it looked as if she was wearing very little underneath it.

'Sorry to be so slow in coming,' she said almost as if she had read his every thought (but what else was there to think?). 'I've been putting on my nicest dress for you; we don't get eligible young Englishmen through Goya every day.' The remark was delivered as a statement of fact, without a hint of coquetry.

The frankness obviously infuriated Picket as much as it disarmed Soames, through whom a little warm trickle of interest began to flow.

'It's a lovely dress,' he said.

Grace smiled with genuine pleasure at this stagey remark – or was it relief more than pleasure? In the way she looked askance at Soames for a moment, he had the odd idea she might be frightened: not just shy of him, but frightened. Suddenly he could think of nothing to say; Grace was silent too.

'Where's the tea?' Picket snapped, breaking the awkward pause.

'Mother will get it,' Grace replied, whereupon Mrs Picket rose like a phantom and disappeared. Some of the tension went with her; Grace and Soames were soon chattering vivaciously enough about Umbalathorp.

Mrs Picket returned ten minutes later with a loaded tray, which Grace took. While her mother sat by, apparently preparing to faint, Grace arranged the cups and poured out tea. Her fingers touched Soames' as she passed him his cup; the frightened look slipped momentarily back into her eyes.

'So you're not staying here long, Noyes?' Picket said, after they had conversed on general subjects for a while.

'No,' Soames said, then, 'at least, I don't think so.'

Father and daughter looked sharply at him.

'I mean,' he explained, 'I shall leave in a fortnight if the Apostle is working satisfactorily, and if a plane then arrives to fetch me.' It seemed silly to want to mention Dumayami's prediction that he might never leave Africa at all.

'Yours must be a pretty good job, Noyes,' Picket commented, blowing covertly on his tea.

'This is my most interesting assignment to date,' said Soames, addressing his remark partly to Grace, whose eyelids fluttered once to acknowledge a compliment Soames had not intended.

'I meant in terms of £. s. d.' Picket said, staring moodily down at the patch of dry rot by his feet.

'Grace has never had anything to do with the young Portuguese fellows, Mr Noyes,' Mrs Picket suddenly observed, so surprising Soames that he could think of nothing to say. He need not have worried, for Mrs Picket, perhaps trying to mitigate the irrelevance of the remark, added, 'The Portuguese have dances every Saturday night and goodness knows what goes on there. They let the blacks in, too.'

'Twists and bossa novas,' said Grace, with idle envy. Silence fell with the boring completeness of bolsters dropping.

Soames, finishing his tea, suggested he should be going. Despite the usual protestations, he stuck to his point, promising he would visit them again.

'You could take me to the Portuguese dance if you felt like it,' Grace suggested.

'Yes, I shouldn't mind her going if you were there, Noyes,' Picket flattered immediately, patting his guest on the shoulder. 'Why not do that? You'd make a good pair. And don't heed anything you hear about any of us at the palace. Always remember, we're British and they're not.'

That at least was one religion the old man had never lost faith in, Soames thought. Yet Picket was only being logical: if he would not believe all men to be brothers under the skin, he had at least had the honesty to reject a religion which preached universal brotherhood.

The sky was dark overhead. As Soames moved down on to the verandah steps, the first drops of rain started to fall. He retreated; in a minute, a deluge of water fell like a curtain before them, hammering down on the earth in a fury of noise, turning the ground into a lake. They stared out at this inundation with Anglo-Saxon stoicism. Out of this solid yellow downpour, seeking shelter, came the native girl Pawli. She glistened with water, the rain bounded off her bare shoulders, her hair streamed, her long skirt clung about her legs. She took one quick glance at Soames from under lowered forehead, reminding him of a wild thing, something infra-human, not quite beast. As she jostled mannerlessly past them, one of her large nipples touched Soames' arm. Then she was gone into the house, leaving a wet trail behind her and Soames staring at a damp patch below his elbow.

'Have another cup of tea, Mr Noyes?' invited Mrs Picket faintly.

'I really ought to be going ...'

'Can't go in this confounded torrent,' Picket said.

'I'll drive you in the convertible,' Grace said. 'It's ours till sundown. Come on, we'll have to make a dash for it!'

Again father and daughter exchanged glances, then Grace was bursting across the open space, now no less than a muddy pond, to the car. Soames could see monsoon capes hanging on a peg in the hall of the bungalow, but since he obviously was not going to be offered one, there was nothing for it but to utter a hasty goodbye to his host and hostess and run after Grace.

They tumbled into the front seats of the vehicle together, laughing breathlessly for no reason and wiping the rain out of their eyes. Soames, pretending not to notice, noticed how tightly the blue and white dress now clung to Grace's thighs. The beads of rain on her face gave her a sparkle she had not possessed before.

'Of course, we're quite crazy!' Grace exclaimed, laughing again somewhat artificially.

Soames, humbly conscious of his own tedious sanity, did not reply. She started the engine and they slithered cautiously forward through the brown sea. The uproar on the roof was so colossal that it was a marvel how they could tell that an awkward silence had fallen between them.

They began to bump slowly downhill. The track had become a river of gurgling grit. When they reached the first line of rhododendrons, the wheel on Soames' side dropped abruptly, the engine roared, progress ceased.

'We've hit a pothole,' Grace said contentedly, cutting off the engine. She had slid somewhat towards Soames. 'We'll have to wait till the rain has stopped; there's nothing else for it.'

'I'll get out and push,' volunteered Soames, without eagerness.

'It will do no good. Half a dozen locals will be needed to push us out. I remember this particular pothole now, and it is extremely deep. I should have been more careful. I hope you're not too vexed with me?'

Soames laughed angrily. 'Not much good being vexed, is it?' he said, looking at her squarely. She bit her lip and laughed nervously back, the doggy planes of her face standing out appealingly. Suddenly, she struck the steering wheel with her fist, turning her head away from Soames.

'You somehow damn well *know* I drove into that pothole on purpose, don't you?!' she exclaimed, fierce tears in her eyes. 'Oh, my God, why aren't you a fool? I'm no good at pretending. I'm sorry, I've mismanaged the whole stunt very badly. You'll just have to put up with this now until the rain stops. It won't go on for long … I could *scream!*'

'I wasn't objecting,' Soames said.

'But you guessed, didn't you? You knew I drove into that hole on purpose?'

'All right, Grace, you've said you're sorry. Now relax,' Soames advised, eager to avoid a scene.

'I've *not* said I'm sorry! I was going to say it, but now I don't know. I can't understand you …'

'Naturally. You never met my parents.'

She sat in frustrated silence, balanced on an invisible knife edge, biting her lower lip, prepared to be pushed in any direction by one word from Soames. Soames said nothing.

'You're angry with me, aren't you?' she asked him finally.

'No,' Soames said angrily. 'Not at all.'

'Oh, stop being so negative, man!' she exclaimed. 'Put your arm round me, I'm wet and cold.'

'Cold in this heat?' enquired Soames sarcastically, but he did as he was bid and felt her soften against him, hardening his heart to a corresponding degree. He was perfectly well aware that to the Pickets he must represent both a potential husband and a free passage to England for Grace. His sympathy for her predicament as he saw it did not extend as far as that; nor did he intend to do anything now which would commit him later. This determination to act according to a cool appraisal of the facts was far from pleasing to Soames, who was not at heart a calculating man. Moreover, his blood and his head saw differently in the matter.

'You're trembling,' Grace said.

'Fever coming on.'

Silence.

'Listen to the rain,' she said dreamily, when they had been doing nothing else for five minutes. 'I've heard it rain like that for years and years and years. I lie on my bed and listen to it. It's surprising how much of it you can put up with ... I don't let myself get neurotic or anything, I just listen, and wonder how much of my life washes away in the rain. Sometimes I think listening to the rain is like bleeding to death ... That's a funny thing to say to a stranger, I suppose, but I just thought you'd be – well, interested. Or perhaps what I say is too trite? Perhaps whatever I say is trite. You don't know what it's like, Mr Noyes, to be born in a dump like Umbalathorp and have to live all your life here. It means you don't know what you are or anything.'

'Your father told me you were born in Kent,' Soames said, putting reproach into his voice to hide the insidious tug of sympathy he was feeling. How would Mother have coped with this situation, he wondered?

'Father lied,' Grace said harshly. 'Mother was pregnant when they got here. I've never even seen the sea. He's always lying – it's one of his few capabilities.'

'It must be very trying for you,' Soames said, marvelling as he did so at the lameness of the remark.

'Very trying indeed! Are all the English as formal as you, Mr Noyes? I don't want to be rude, but haven't you got any *feelings*? Do you ever *care* about anything?'

'For heaven's sake,' he exclaimed. 'I'm sorry about all this, but can't we just leave the usual social barriers up between us without trying to batter them down? You'll feel so silly about what you are saying afterwards.'

'Oh, perhaps I will, and I'll tell you something else that'll make me even sorrier directly I've said it. Father and I had a little plan all cooked up to get you *involved* with me, never mind why. Well, I should like you to know that I wouldn't get involved with you if you were the last man on earth.'

'Absolutely excellent!' said Soames angrily. 'In that case, please get your hand off my shoulder. You're pawing me worse than your father did!'

The fight went out of Grace. She collapsed limply into his arms, sobbing loudly. In the confined space in the front of the convertible, no hope existed of avoiding the duties of comforter. Indeed, it was not an unpleasant duty, as duties go. Gradually, under Soames' soothing, Grace quietened, nestling against him. It felt unexpectedly homely to have her there. The rain drummed down like war drums. When her lips came up to his mouth, they were as soft and hot as lips usually are. Her mouth was half open, her eyes closed. One of her arms went round his neck. With some surprise, Soames realised that his hand had reached the top of her leg unaided by anything but instinct. Grace opened her eyes as she felt him draw back from her.

'Not here, Grace,' he said, remembering his resolution. 'This is impossible here. Someone may come by.'

'Nonsense,' she said urgently. She tried to pull his head down to her face again; when he resisted, fear welled into her eyes like a spasm of pain; it happened so close to him, his attention was so closely focused on her countenance, that Soames also felt its hurt, though without correctly divining its source. He was aware, for a second, of Grace as a *person*, with importance, life and sensibilities in every way commensurate with his own – then the uncomfortable vision was gone.

'Please – now!' she begged, almost inarticulately.

'I can't,' Soames said, feeling a reasonless fright. 'I can't, Grace; I ...' But he could think of no sort of reason she could possibly accept.

'This may be my last chance,' she said. 'Look, it's not the sort of thing a woman likes to have to ask ... Oh God, oh hell ... please – what's your first name?'

'Soames. It was my mother's idea.'

'Please, Soames, for my sake. It's an awful thing to ask, but *please* do it to me, now, now. Another time ... No, it must be now. I'm not ugly. I'm not trite. Inside me, it's – there's a great thing, Soames, to be expressed. I can't tell you, but it's vitally important. Will you believe this?'

'I can't!' Soames exclaimed, struggling with her. 'Heavens, surely you can *understand*. It's not just something you *do* –'

'Don't say that! Listen, this isn't any sort of a trap, I swear; it's got nothing to do with Father's plan, and I swear I'll not hold you to it after or anything. All I'm asking –' She was working herself up into a frenzy now, talking wildly, trying to undo the white buttons at the shoulders of her dress until he seized her fingers.

'No! No, I tell you!' Soames exclaimed frantically. 'Cool down, Grace, will you? If you feel like that, why be so superior about the Portuguese? I'm not going to touch you.'

'You would have done if I hadn't wanted you to,' she said, half to herself. Again he had that disconcerting glimpse of her as a person.

85

'I'm sorry —' he began, then checked himself; he was not sorry.

The heat had left Grace, or she knew herself defeated; she drew back from him, sprawling awkwardly across the steering wheel.

'I thought perhaps they'd told you about me at the palace,' she muttered, 'but I see by what you say they haven't. I'm not repulsive, am I, Soames? You're *normal*, aren't you? Then I'm asking you still, please to take me. Just occasionally there is something vital one human can do for another; this is that sort of time. Some vital, imperative thing … Just *once* in your lifetime.'

'You make me sick,' Soames replied sulkily.

'Yes … I suppose I do,' she said thoughtfully. 'Oh, I feel like filth asking you. *You* make me feel like filth. You're —'

She didn't finish the sentence; instead, she flung open the car door and jumped into the rain.

'You filthy, smug, English swine!' she yelled. 'You're indecent!' Then, turning her distorted face away, she began to run back up the hill through the pouring rain. Instinctively, fearing her to be crazy, Soames jumped into the flood after her. He caught a glimpse of her flashing legs before he slipped and fell flat in the mud swilling round the car. When he picked himself up, he was drenched and Grace was gone.

His insides felt as if they had been churned with a stick. Without another thought for the convertible, leaving its doors swinging open, Soames started off at a jog-trot down the rude road in the direction of the town.

He arrived at the palace over an hour later. Although the rain still beat down, Soames hardly noticed it; nor did he give a thought to his bedraggled appearance. His mind gyrated like a labouring cement-mixer around the grey sludge disturbed by his brush with Grace. Never before had he been so conscious of his own inadequacies; his mishandling of the episode had been positively monumental. Of course she was a neurotic, but that in no way softened the beastly impact of the scene.

Trotting blindly up the stairs, he almost knocked Princess Cherry over. She jumped back with a little shriek.

'You get wet with rain, Mr Soames,' she exclaimed. 'I send up two handmaids for drying you, quickly at once.'

'No thanks,' Soames said, 'I'll dry myself. But do me a favour, Princess – come up to my room and talk to me.'

'*I* not dry you?'

'Indeed not. I must just talk to you.'

'Talk about autumn and John Keats? Not do any other thing?' she asked saucily, following him up the stairs and along the corridor to his bedroom.

'I want to *ask* you something, Princess. Nothing else.'

He pulled his wet things off and flung them distastefully on to the floor, while the black princess turned her back, covered her eyes and stood on tiptoe, possibly in embarrassment. When he had a couple of towels round him, he said, 'You can look now, Princess. I want to ask you about the Pickets. Nobody tells me anything about them. The Picket girl – Grace. What's the matter with her, what's happened to her?'

The princess had stiffened at the name of Picket. She pouted and walked about the room.

'Better for you to talk about autumn with me than this,' she protested. 'Pickets do bad things. Once in the years gone they have a small school for teaching English; I go there, and several other boys and girls go. Pretty soon, many complaints arise; my father, he close down the school. Pickets are not a good lot. Miss Grace – I do not know how to say this remark before you or you think me coarse girl – Miss Grace keep servant girls from slums, many of them, now have one called Pawli.'

'I saw her,' Soames said, remembering the feral eyes in the rain and the strong, bare shoulders. 'Go on, Princess.'

'Miss Grace go to bed with this bad Pawli. It is bad deed in Goya to be what you call a Greek girl, Lesbian. Make people very shameful, like me to have to tell you.'

Back to Soames, like a boomerang returning right in the eye, came the meaning of Grace's plea, 'just occasionally there is something

87

vital one human can do for another'; she had been trying to break back into the world of ordinary desires.

Coitala called at Soames' room that night; he repulsed her with such harshness that she never came again.

Only a quarter hour after the girl had gone, while Soames stood moodily watching a gecko chase its own shadow, Timpleton broke into his room looking wild and dishevelled.

'Boy, I've had an evening on the town!' he said. 'You should have been with me!'

Soames turned as the smell of strong spirits hit him.

'Ted, I've no wish to hear how the cockroaches crawled over your arse,' he said. 'Save that sort of local colour for when you get back home.'

Timpleton, steadying himself at the doorpost, surveyed his compatriot and said, 'You're not very interested in women, are you?'

'On the contrary. Today I have undergone an American Massage and have nearly been seduced by a lesbian. This climate is having a peculiar effect on me. I feel, to be candid, like a man slowly coming to face his destiny, and a man doing that hardly wishes to hear about cockroaches crawling over another man's bottom. No offence, of course.'

Dazedly, Timpleton shook his head.

'No offence, of course. I'm glad to hear you've been having a bit of fun.'

He left Soames to his unprecedented meditations.

PART TWO

Darker

Chapter Eight

'Conspiring with him ...'

The way the opposed forces of piety and wickedness have of inter-twining together like lovers has been remarked since the earliest times; good and bad, beauty and horror, comedy and tragedy – they walk hand-in-glove down the ages like the figures of an old morality. Only in our psychological epoch, with its emphasis on behaviourism, has this duality been forgotten, superseded by the dangerous theory that no motives are entirely black or white; we are left with the grey uniformity of compulsion, when frequently the old notion of human nature as a chequer board of black and white provides a far better key towards the understanding of our fellows – as far as a fellow may be said to be understandable at all.

In Umbalathorp, the powers of light and dark miscegenated with their traditional abandon. There they could be observed at work, not only in individuals, but in groups of individuals. The nucleus of the government, for instance, was a striking mixture of progressive and retrogressive elements. At the top of the scale, the enlightenment of President M'Grassi Landor was counter-balanced by the obscurantism of Dumayami, both men laying equal claim on the hearts of the people; while at the bottom of the scale, the blundering attempts of well-meaning clerks were matched by the corrupting influence of the wily Portuguese, as both groups vied for a dip in the purses of the people.

This conjunction of opposing forces, complementary but not complimentary, now became evident in another sphere. Under Ted Timpleton's expert hands, a considerable structure was growing on the floor of the computer room in the palace. Above a steel base measuring some forty-five feet by three feet, rose elaborate towers of relays; about them and from them ran wires, some no thicker than a strand of a spider's web, some sheathed in white insulation till they looked like squidges of toothpaste, some merging and running with scores of others into cables like frozen oil. The Apostle, plenipotentiary of knowledge, was growing cell by cell.

At the same time, a more sinister structure of suspicion was building up round Soames, intangibly but undeniably. It was something he did not know how to fight. Though its signs were several, its source was doubtful.

The uneasiness made itself felt on the day after his visit to the Pickets, when President Landor, Jimpo and Timpleton all showed degrees of reserve in Soames' presence. He found himself unexpectedly isolated. Soames could think of only two possible reasons for this new and unwelcome coolness. Firstly, a report of his excursion up Stranger's Hill had probably filtered back to the palace; this, because of the abhorrence in which the Pickets were held, might well have lowered his stock; yet this should hardly have affected his relationship with Timpleton, who was the last person to worry about moral standards. Secondly, his innocent invitation of Princess Cherry up to his bedroom might have been misconstrued; but this, too, would hardly worry Timpleton – nor yet Jimpo, who showed little regard for his half-sister.

Something, therefore, must have happened of which Soames had no knowledge. He suspected that the phone call which had detained Jimpo on Umbalathorp station might have something to do with the matter. Possibly Dumayami was at work, undermining

Soames' popularity in preparation for a countermove against the Apostle.

Looking for enlightenment, Soames wandered down to the computer room. Timpleton had shown no wish to fraternise all day, and was obviously keen to avoid anything approaching intimate conversation now. He stood in the middle of the electrical skeleton, testing a long narrow fuse box, not catching Soames' eye.

'Have a look on the jury board and see if Five-oh-Five's blinking, will you?' he asked curtly. Soames knew it for a gambit, a hint to him to be quiet, a reminder of his uselessness. His job was to wear lounge suits, talking about the general functions and uses of Unilateral machines to possible clients, ironing out any so-called 'consumer difficulties' which might arise; as such, he was an obvious butt for a technical man like Timpleton; what was more, he had no idea what the jury board was, or what a blinking Five-oh-Five might indicate.

Timpleton wore only mechanic's dungarees; his wiry, sweat-polished body was a startling mixture of white skin and black, prolific hair, so that he looked like a half-skinned animal trapped in the machine. Peering round an impulse switchboard, he noted Soames' hesitation with a heavy sigh of contempt and bellowed to his two assistants.

'Hey, L'Panto, Gumboi, run look-see bloody jury board, look-see number Five-oh-Five he go blink-blink-blink topside. He no do, you bolo me plenty loud and clear, savvy?'

'OK Ted, plenty bloody roger,' the young men called, darting eagerly to obey, bounding over the relay banks like salmon headed up-river. The amount of English, larded with technicalities and scatology, that they had picked out of Timpleton's home-made lingo was really astonishing.

Seeing his case was hopeless, Soames left them at it without a word, retreating under cover of their shouts.

His head ached; he had been roused early that morning by the shrieks of the birds in the creeper outside his window. Now the palace grew oppressive. The rear door of the computer room led straight out to the gardens at the back of the building. Soames walked through them and turned right, strolling by the river, his spirits reviving at the sight of the dark-flowing waters.

The path to the left, which he had taken two eventful days before, had led him to Dumayami. The one he was now on twisted and turned through maize patch and thicket and finally dumped him in Main High Street. Wandering aimlessly for a time, self-consciously the tourist, gazing in shops – some of which displayed the celluloid models of Donald Duck, the plastic ray guns, the useless china ornaments, the tubes of toothpaste containing chlorophyll, which may be purchased almost anywhere on earth – Soames bethought himself of the Fountain of a Thousand Appetising Intestines. A glass of Russian tea would be very acceptable.

On his way there, he passed a prosperous general store with a Portuguese name above its entrance. On the steps stood José Blencimonti Soares, a plump tailor's dummy whose grey cheeks shone like oiled putty; a red flower moped in his buttonhole.

Soames recognised him at once, though they had not met again since Soames' first morning at the palace.

'Good-day, Señor Soares,' he said, nodding.

'Good-day, señor,' Soares returned, with a curt wave of his hand, continuing to gaze into space. It was the snub direct, for Soames had automatically stopped for conversation, already deciding that if another invitation were issued to inspect the Portuguese's home, wife and daughter he would accept it. Affronted, Soames pursed his lips, then utilised the gesture to whistle to show he was not affronted; it was a second-hand gesture handed down to him from his father. Whistling, he turned into the Chinese café.

The interior was gloomier than ever, being well filled with several shades of people eating rice and, presumably, appetising intestines. Taking a seat by a window in whose meagre expanse a strip of Main High Street and an oleander on the other side of it were visible, Soames ordered Russian tea from a waiter whose bows were as violent as nitrogen bends. When the man had gone, Soames sat brooding over the snub delivered by the Portuguese. It was not that he cared much either way for Soares, who had as obvious an axe to grind as Ping Ah and Picket; but the man's behaviour was a straw in the wind. The wind was cold; today nobody loved Soames. It is never pleasant to find one's company shunned where it was recently sought, or to perceive that one's friends can vanish as rapidly as the snows of yesteryear, or the totalitarian politicians of today.

Dismally, Soames received his Russian tea and stared out at the lance-like oleander leaves across the road. The sun burnished them as they hung stiffly over a broken wall, until only a crazy painter could have determined whether they were dark green, black or a sullen gold. Against the imperfect wall, their perfection attained a hint of the uncanny; their shadows, pitched down on to the shabby sidewalk, were spear-sharp with menace. Behind the oleanders, behind all the other still foliage in Goya, lurked a storm whose violence could be felt but not described, just as, behind the insistent façade of sunlight, lurked utter blackness.

The view of the oleanders was abruptly eclipsed by the blue and cream bulk of an American automobile. Though its wings were buckled, its panels bent, it made an impressive spectacle in Umbalathorp; Soames remembered seeing it earlier in the market place. The driver remained in his seat when it bucked to a stop; the passenger climbed out, limped round the bonnet, and entered the Fountain of a Thousand Appetising Intestines.

Silence fell among the customers as the newcomer looked slowly round, spied Soames, walked over to his table and sat down facing him.

'You are Monsieur Soames Noyes, if I do not make mistake,' he said. 'I am Lupe Abonso Guidados de Duidos, senior member of Goyese Portuguese community. Perhaps my name is already familiar to you.'

It was the man Jimpo had mentioned as being José Soares' rival; Soames recognised him by the wooden leg Jimpo had spoken of, which, beginning below the knee, looked like a mahogany chair leg. Roses were carved upon it, and the name of the Holy Virgin. De Duidos was tall, thin and dark, as dry and wizened as Soares was greasy; he might have passed for a Chinese. He had none of the ingratiating airs of his compatriot; you would never imagine him in a drawing-room.

Soames sat tight and said nothing, accepting a small cheroot when it was offered. He recognised an air of menace when he saw one; it stimulated him not entirely disagreeably.

'You do not look happy,' de Duidos said, breathing smoke from the extreme corners of his mouth.

'The flies and the company bother me,' Soames said. 'What are you doing here? I understand you have a café of your own, Mr de Duidos?'

'Do you know this, Monsieur Noyes, that Britain and Portugal are very old allies in Europe, with never any trouble between, as between Portugal and Spain, or Britain and France? Here, when you come to Umbalathorp, is waiting a prosperous Portuguese community to greet you. But no, apparently for you Africa is not Europe; friends in Europe mean enemies in Africa. You avoid us. You speak only to this gangster man Soares.'

'You have rather the wrong end of the stick, I think,' Soames said. 'I'm a stranger here. I spoke to Soares because he spoke to me. If you wanted to fraternise, why not come to the palace, ring the front door bell and greet me properly?'

De Duidos smiled by the cunning expedient of drawing his lips back from his brown teeth.

'Things do not run on such smooth rails as that in Umbalathorp,' he said, 'as you will find if you live here that long. M'Grassi Landor is a dangerous man apt to side with the gangster Soares. Instead of myself, I send out my emissary to look out the ground. He reported to me you are not cooperative man or friendly with strangers, such as I like.'

'Who was this emissary, as you call him?' Soames demanded, gulping down the last of his tea and dropping three-quarters of the cheroot to soak in the dregs. 'Nobody has spoken to me of you, I am happy to say. Now I'm off, *Monsieur* de Duidos. Goodbye.'

'But I come too,' de Duidos said, following Soames into the street. He stuck a finger into Soames' ribs. 'And before I leave you, I tell you one thing and ask another. One thing is, that I enjoy company only of people with manners. Other thing, how you think you can make crooked deal with this Soares without other men find out? You think we are fools, eh?'

'What deal are you talking about?' Soames asked. 'I made no deals with anyone. It seems to me, de Duidos, you're running on the wrong track entirely.'

The Portuguese grabbed the cheroot butt from his mouth, came closer to Soames and said furiously, 'So, you pretend you know nothing about thousands pounds sterling of computer parts handed to this cheap crook Soares yesterday? You no longer are among bunch of softies in London now; you be a bit too funny and you are found only by hyenas dead in jungle, see?'

The information coupled with the threat did a wonderfully speedy job of softening Soames up; his semi-belligerent attitude vanished.

'I can assure you I know absolutely nothing about any such deal,' he said, 'but if one has taken place – if this isn't just an odd figment of your imagination – I should much like to know about it. I am officially in charge of the computer, as you may have heard. Please tell me what you know.'

'Not so fast, friend,' de Duidos said, smiling at his cheroot. 'Get in the car and we talk a little at my place all about the matter.'

'Where is your place?' Soames asked suspiciously.

'Not far. I can't offer you the bodies of my wife and daughter like that gangster Soares, but you will be OK. Get in! Your computer is worth a little ride, no?'

He held the rear door of the blue and white Oldsmobile open. Soames glanced up and down the street. Eyes watched from all directions. A native policeman in puttees leant against the Catholic church, smiling at them. Reassured by such a cloud of witnesses,

Soames climbed in; de Duidos eased in after him, slammed the door and they were off.

They hustled through the market with horn blazing, flashed past the palace gate, nearly stampeded a bullock cart, and wound up a road in a direction Soames had not yet explored.

The car fled through jungle and stopped at a solitary, neglected bungalow beside the Uiui. The cliffs were high here on both sides. As Soames climbed out, he could see, further downstream, the green water hemmed by a slender dam, above which stood a white structure, Umbalathorp's only power house. There was the contrast again: the ancient with the modern, order against energy.

'Come along in,' de Duidos said, uninvitingly.

They passed a muscular man lounging on the steps of the bungalow. He neither looked up nor spoke.

The bungalow was disorderly.

One big room served as bedroom and living quarters. Two refrigerators stood, disconnected, in one corner; a case of what looked like rifles lay under the bed. Boxes were piled beneath the table, while dirty cups and a sweaty shirt lay on the table. As a home, it was little enough; compared with chez Picket it exuded sweetness and light.

'Sit down,' de Duidos ordered, 'and say to me what you know of this swindle.'

A young Portuguese woman looked at them from the back room, peering cautiously round a curtain. De Duidos barked at her and she withdrew her head.

'I am sorry. A man's night-time recreations often trouble his daytime business, as perhaps already you find out. Umbalathorp is a dull town, monsieur, unlike our respective native capitals; a man turns naturally to all those things his mother once taught him to abhor. Proceed with your explanation.'

It took Soames about half an hour to convince the man he knew nothing whatever about any missing computer parts; de Duidos evidently had grasped this long before – perhaps before they entered the car – but was reluctant to accept it. Finally, he got up, lit another cheroot, and said, 'So. Then it is your friend Timpleton the culprit. He has made this villainous deal with Soares.'

'I suppose so: all the equipment is in his care,' Soames said. 'I want to get this stuff back, de Duidos. In that respect, I am with you against Soares, if Soares has it. I will check on what is missing as soon as I get back to the palace; meanwhile, tell me exactly what you have heard, then I shall go to the police.'

This made de Duidos laugh, a sharp, brown rattle of noise. 'Don't speak of police here!' he exclaimed. 'This is above police; they are only for keeping herdsmen and drunks in order. You do not read your excellent compatriot Graham Greene, or you will know these universal matters. No, do you not know Umbalathorp is Utopia, for here is crime abolished – rape and robbery and murder are reduced to private concerns? What we do in this matter is our own business.

'This is what I am able to find out by various emissaries. Your firm sent out this computing machine which is to transform Goya to Paradise packed in forty-one crates. Also, for preventing any delay here due to accident in transit, it sent in addition five crates of the spare parts which are sensitive to breakage.'

'Yes, that's correct,' Soames affirmed.

'It is correct; I tell you I find out,' de Duidos said. 'Nothing in all forty-six crates is broken, saying thanks to British factory packing, or maybe the gentle African tree breaking your plane's fall. But Timpleton sends cables to your firm of which you are not aware, saying all spare parts smashed and more required; my emissaries give me copies of these cables. Then Timpleton makes a deal secretly with this cheap crook Soares and the spare parts are smuggled out the palace.'

'How?' Soames asked. 'How could they possibly do that without being noticed?'

'My friend, in the laundry baskets of a laundryman without conscience called Ping Ah, who would sell his little daughter to a gorilla for two brass mores. So, all these delicate valves and so forth are taken out in the dirty nightdresses of the Queen – and that is a thought, monsieur, upon which we do not linger as we are pure men – and delivered to the hands of the ruffian Soares.

'Next act of the comedy, your man Timpleton takes a nice meal with this ruffian, is allowed to make the ascent of his mountainous daughter Maria, and is given nine thousand doimores as his payment. To consider that the parts are probably worth ten thousand pounds sterling in your money, or twenty thousand doimores in our money, Soares had ridden on a good bargain. All the same, nine thousand doimores is a princely sum. It can buy you half Umbalathorp and all the female population, if you should be so greedy to want them.'

De Duidos licked his lips sadly at this thought, rubbing his lighted cheroot between his palms.

Soames, after an outburst of anger against Timpleton, asked what good the spare parts were to Soares.

'Can you really not guess the little comedy?' de Duidos asked, raising a narrow eyebrow. 'Corruption is the great organ musicians like this villain Soares play all their life. When you English are gone, the two black men Gumboi and L'Panto are left in charge of the machine, and along come the snake and speak to them with a few doimores in his mouth.

'Pretty soon, one of these young men, perhaps Gumboi, perhaps L'Panto, kick in a precious glass valve and the machine does not work any more. The President, our King, sighs and says "Never mind, we get another valve from England, cost twenty pounds sterling." "Alas, that will take two weeks, maybe a month," sighs L'Panto or Gumboi. "Luckily we know a Portuguese with great presentiment who has a duplicate of this valve by him, which he will supply for only twenty and a half pounds sterling, with carriage free" …'

'I see,' Soames said.

A pause followed. De Duidos strolled over to a cupboard by the bedside, brought out a heavy revolver, and began ostentatiously to oil it.

100

'If *I* had these spares,' he said thoughtfully, squinting down the barrel at Soames, 'I should set up a proper firm called Computer Supplies and sell back to the government only at honest prices.'

'The parts must of course be retrieved from Soares,' Soames replied, hoping this sounded as if he were agreeing. 'You seem to know so much about the affair, perhaps you know where they are now?'

'My emissaries have informed me, by good fortune. You will go to any lengths to recover them, no doubt?'

'Er, a good many.'

'Splendid, monsieur. I will therefore sell you a revolver for a reasonable price and we shall discuss plans.' He brought cheroots from his pocket and gave one to Soames; pausing with his own gripped between his teeth, he added, 'You know, monsieur, I hope you are going to be more clever about this thing than your colleague Timpleton. He is a bungling amateur. If he had had the wits to cable your firm that the whole computer is lost in crash, insurance would pay up, and an entirely new computer would be sent; with that, we could do really big business.'

Chapter Nine

'Who hath not seen thee oft amid thy store?'

Soames returned to the Presidential palace in an ambivalent frame of mind.

The exercise in burglary he had planned with de Duidos for that very night caused him an amount of unease. Although on the surface it looked perfectly simple, he had a suspicion that de Duidos was secretly arranging a few frills of his own, even as Soames himself was. He hoped devoutly that the necessity for the whole venture might soon be removed.

On the other hand, he was considerably relieved to have an explanation of the coolness to which he had been subjected; the computer parts were undoubtedly at the bottom of it all. Soares was no longer interested in him, having gained his ends elsewhere. Timpleton's changed attitude was explained by the mixture of guilt and wariness from which he would now be suffering. As for M'Grassi Landor and his son Jimpo, their new reserve was also accounted for. Soames had by now accustomed himself to the idea that little was private which happened in Umbalathorp; if de Duidos had discovered the computer deal, so had the President and family. It was only to be expected that Soames should fall under their suspicion, as he had under de Duidos'. It occurred to Soames that the phone call Jimpo received on Umbalathorp station had been to acquaint him with the news of the theft; this supposition was later proved correct.

Going to the computer room, Soames exchanged an idle word with the taciturn Timpleton, surreptitiously counting the number of crates at the same time. There were only forty-one of them; de Duidos had not been indulging in fantasy. Unexpected rage filled Soames, a blend of moral anger (to think that Unilateral had been so calmly duped) and personal affront (to think that he, too, had been duped).

He went, therefore, straight to the President in his private chambers, telling him briefly that he had discovered the fraud, and omitting all reference to any part the Portuguese were playing in the matter.

Landor, who sat with his wives, Mrs President Tunna and Queen Louise, heard Soames out in silence. He fingered a strip of pasteboard which, after a long pause, he passed to Soames. On the pasteboard was the slogan:

DEAL JIMPO FOR PRESIDENT.

'Neat but effective, I think,' the head of the state said. 'I am tired of the Presidency and the people are tired of me; now my son must run for office. By springing the elections in three days' time, and making my son the only man in the running, I can ensure he is the successful candidate. Our elections here are very peaceful.'

'Sir,' Soames exclaimed angrily, 'did you not hear one word I said?'

'I have some madeira presented by my loyal subject de Duidos this morning,' said Landor. 'Would you care to join the three of us in a glass?'

'I would much prefer a straight answer,' replied Soames.

'Very well, you shall have one. You will naturally forgive us while we drink our madeira. Please sit down, Mr Noyes; even at moments of crisis, let us not forget that man is a sedentary animal.'

Soames seated himself unhappily and waited while the President poured drink for himself and the ladies, afterwards settling down in leisurely fashion on a cane chair before addressing himself again to Soames.

'The British, Mr Noyes,' he said in French, 'are not a race which inspires love wherever it goes. Indeed, its peoples seem often not to love each other much; only street accidents, boxing matches or conscription can call them together. In their own land, I hear, they prefer not to speak where possible; I suppose it may be this boredom with each other which has distributed them all over the globe. Only the mosquito can rival the British in ubiquity.

'*But*, and it is one of the world's great buts, if they have no love, they have justice. They are honest. You may deal with them as one's left hand deals with one's right. So it has always been, and all men have known it – except within this last generation. Always before, they were trustworthy; now, *voilà!* they are not! I do not believe in sudden changes in human nature, Mr Noyes, but I believe that slow changes make themselves suddenly manifest, and that a rotting apple which decays imperceptibly may nevertheless be held good one day and bad the next. I believe this applies to Britain and to its representatives here.'

'I, too, hold many beliefs,' Soames said, angrily answering in kind, 'among which is the conviction that verbosity is not a sign of wisdom, but of wisdom's opposite. Another is, that, like all novelists and some psychiatrists, you read your own illnesses into other people. I have no intention of listening to any more diatribes against my country, whose faults I am happy to know at first hand.'

'You are above yourself!' exclaimed Queen Louise.

'And you, madam. What is more, I have not finished. I came here only to ask you that Timpleton should be put in custody until he can be taken back to England; I shall naturally cable the facts of the case to Unilateral at once. Also, I have discovered the whereabouts of the missing computer parts. When I take you to their place of concealment, you can recover them and

104

you will then have concrete evidence against Timpleton and his Goyese accessories.'

'That will not be possible,' President Landor said. He rose and walked quietly round the room, speaking without raising his voice, for he was that rare type of man that can face the anger of others without becoming angry himself. When Tunna interrupted with a burst of Goyese, he silenced her with a mild gesture while continuing to address Soames. 'When I told you something of the way we shall conduct the forthcoming election, you credited me only with irrelevance. I was trying to hint that our methods differ. They differ in every way, more drastically than you may imagine.

'You should therefore not be astonished to learn that we knew of this little plot concerning the Apostle almost from its inception. It happens that I pay well an informant who is already well paid from two other sources; indeed, Ping Ah must be at once the richest and least reliable man in my country. Just as when a man doubts everything he will believe anything, so there is a stage beyond corruption where a pseudo-loyalty exists. In that sense, Ping Ah is our most dutiful of servants, and Liverpool's loss is Goya's gain.

'We did not interfere in the plot when he learnt of it. Why should we? It is, after all, convenient that we can obtain replacements for the computer locally.'

Soames exploded. He could hardly believe he had heard aright.

'And you have the cheek to lecture me on justice!' he exclaimed. 'This is the most barefaced …'

'You find an anomaly somewhere?' enquired the President blandly. 'My position is, simply, that I am displeased with you two British and delighted with myself.'

Soames began to laugh. Something had happened in his stomach over which he had no control, causing him to utter the short, sharp bellows we recognise as signs of amusement. He fought to stop the undignified sounds, but they flowed the louder. Though he was still more angry, the funny side of the situation had intruded itself.

Pale, choking, he rose finally and bowed to the three Goyese, who had been watching him with interest and some sympathy.

'Then I take it that any cables I might send informing Unilateral of this matter would not leave Goya?'

'Your assessment of the position is swift and accurate,' said the President. 'As I believe I remarked once before, you should have been a politician.'

Still feeling somewhat confused, Soames left them. He was no sooner out of their presence than a thought occurred which sent him hurrying back into the room. M'Grassi Landor and his two wives were already talking volubly together in Goyese.

'I'm sorry to burst back like this,' Soames apologised. 'I find there is one other thing I must ask. You tell me you watched this unfortunate affair from its beginning; if so, you must have known all along that I had nothing to do with it. Why, then, have you – and Jimpo – treated me so coldly since supper last evening? What have I done to offend you?'

'Excuse me,' Landor said gravely. He turned and spoke to his consorts. After a short, angry-sounding confabulation, these two ladies left the room by a rear door, whereupon the President turned back to his guest.

'I take it that you would prefer me to answer your question straightforwardly,' he said, in a prefatory fashion, looking slightly away from Soames. 'Some crimes rank less highly in one community than in another. The matter is interesting, and would repay study. We have before us this example of what you would call the theft of the computer parts. In the land of the have-nots, theft is the Exchequer's left hand, a device to keep wealth circulating, or poverty on the run. Similarly, murder, which in the Western world is reckoned the king of crimes, exciting much interest, is here only a by-product of the sun, like heat exhaustion. But you have one habit, prevalent at all times and sometimes fashionable, which in Goya is accounted the foulest and most unholy of all vices. I refer to a person's preference for his or her own sex with which to obtain sexual gratification.'

106

In a cold voice, Soames asked how this affected him, although he could almost guess what was coming.

'The Pickets, Mr Noyes, father and daughter, are both addicted to this badness. It is for this reason I have forbidden them entry to any part but the slum end of town. It is for this reason Dumayami has placed a severe tabu upon their loathsome persons. And it is for this reason they, and the few base wretches who still consort with them, are shunned by all my people.

'Yesterday, Mr Noyes, you were observed to fondle this monstrous Picket girl in a car. That is the only reason why we no longer greet you with our former warmth. You are contaminated.'

'Another hateful habit which you seem to find a virtue, is spying,' Soames declared angrily. 'I am afraid I must insist on being able to choose my friends. Good-day.'

He left the room with burning cheeks.

Lying on his bed a few minutes later, Soames began to cool down. Rain was falling again; a boat shooting down the Uiui was filled with little crouching, gleaming figures.

He was full of uncertainty. He saw the restoration of the computer parts as one of his responsibilities; Landor had unintentionally reminded him of another: Grace Picket. Soames could not avoid feeling that he had somehow committed himself to helping her by his failing her (as he now thought of it) the day before. He was acutely aware of the way he had misunderstood and humiliated her, aware too, even, that others in his place might have used a little intuition.

Unfortunately, he was as much baffled over his own behaviour as over Grace's. He was baffled also to know how she could best be helped. He only knew that someone had to help her; since she wanted help, she could not be beyond it. Perhaps the next time they met, they could avoid her dreadful father – and there was a certain curious attraction in the thought of seeing Grace again.

That problem, however, had to wait. The threat from Dumayami, which now seemed nebulous, was also thrust into the background

107

at present. First of all, Soames intended to retrieve the spare computer parts. What Landor had said about the decline of British integrity had stung Soames more than he had shown. There was nothing for it but to get back the spares, put them down before the President with a fine gesture, and say 'There you are! Don't lose them again!' Which meant Soames had to go through with de Duidos' plan as prearranged – at least, de Duidos' plan with the few variations Soames had already thought of.

He needed an accomplice.

There was nobody in whom he could trust. In his mind, he ran through everyone he knew, from Timpleton – to all intents and purposes his enemy in this matter – to Ping Ah's lovely daughter, Hwa, and even Tanuana Motijala, the man with the green bicycle. But of course he needed someone who could speak English.

Once more Soames felt he was stranded in an alien world, but now despair rather than elation filled him. Eventually he decided only one person could help, a man who stood between the two worlds: Deal Jimpo Landor.

Getting off his bed, Soames went to hunt the princeling out. Jimpo's stiffness of manner soon melted under Soames' persuasiveness; he was more tolerant than his father of the vice that Goya so condemned, thanks to his liberal education. Indeed, it was obvious from his questions that he wanted to know more about what Grace Picket said and did than Soames was prepared to tell.

'Never mind that now,' Soames said; 'there is something more urgent to be coped with.'

And he told Jimpo all he knew about the five crates of computer spares, including the roles played by the rival Portuguese, which he had omitted when talking to M'Grassi Landor. When he went on to deal with the projected raid on Soares' property, Jimpo became positively enthusiastic.

'Yes, sir!' he exclaimed, his rather heavy young face lighting up. 'I am a man of yours, Soames. I understand your feeling as my father cannot. The spares must be reclaimed to satisfy you and your honour. Then, since other spares are on the way from England, we can sell them to de Duidos.'

'Well …' Soames said, marvelling that he had once believed only the Americans saw all the possibilities of a business deal.

'Tonight I am my father's one-man Scotland Yard,' Jimpo said excitedly. 'My last fling before I become President! I only hope my leg isn't a nuisance.' The local hospital had sunk Jimpo's damaged leg a foot deep in plaster of Paris. He pulled a card from his pocket and said, 'Looks good, eh, Soames?'

The card read: 'Deal Jimpo for President.'

'It's real good prose,' Soames told him, and they both laughed.

Just outside Jimpo's door, Soames ran bodily into Turdilal Ghosti.

'Excuse, sir,' said the Hindu painfully. 'I am coming only as humble faithful chef to wish Deal Jimpo all hearty good bloody old wishes for being the President.' He bowed and entered the room Soames had just left.

Soames ate well at sundown. He observed that Jimpo talked as amicably to Timpleton as ever; perhaps those who knew of his deal with Soares regarded it merely as a neat bit of self-help. After the meal, Soames retired to his room, examined closely, anxiously, the revolver he had purchased from de Duidos, and settled down with all the patience he could muster to wait for the Portuguese's 'emissary', who was to lead him to a hidden lorry.

Not until one o'clock in the morning, when the customary mêlée downstairs had dispersed and the rain had ceased, did there come a tap at Soames' door. It opened and Turdilal Ghosti, the chef, smarmed into the room.

'Sir, greeting. I am pleasing to find you alert,' the Hindu said, smiling. 'There is a truck-ride been prepared for you, and now I am coming to say is time come for go.'

The sight of the chef did not please Soames. He saw instantly that if his double-cross succeeded, it would be only too easy for the other side to settle the score with a slice of toadstool in his next curry. That, however, was a point which must be settled later. He rose and followed the Indian down through the palace, and out into the grounds at the back. Two sentries, easily distinguishable, walked up and down with rifles slung over their shoulders, talking together. It was a simple matter to dodge them.

Straightening up, Ghosti took the left-hand turn by the river bank.

'Be careful of all the bloody old puddles, sir,' he cautioned. 'This land is a terrible land for making water.'

They came so suddenly upon another man that Soames jumped.

'Here is your driver, sir,' Ghosti said. 'A man of reliance called Eekee, sir; he is not speaking English but he has many instructions to take care of you. To follow with him you are ideally safe. Now I will return in secret to my home, for my part in this matter is now finish. I wash my hands at it! In my heart I am wishing God's bloody good luck for you always, sir.'

'Thank you,' Soames said.

'To be kind, sir, is exquisite pleasure for me. I am simple, faithful man. I wait for your safety home-coming with tainted breath, I assure. In Calcutta also I have good white friend.'

Any further bursts of good nature on Ghosti's part were interrupted by Eekee's suddenly heading into the bush. It was very dark, the moon having yet to rise; Soames had to follow him at once or lose him. They moved rapidly down a narrow path, the bushes on either side yielding up the rain they had hoarded from the last downpour. In no time, Soames was soaked.

Eventually they emerged on to a shabby bit of pasture, about which cattle lay like discarded suitcases. Brushing his hair out of his eyes, Soames padded along through dung balls, over a tiny bridge, and so among a maze of mud huts. Ahead of him, never looking back, a mute, inglorious Virgil, strode Eekee. Still there was no sign of the lorry de Duidos had promised and Eekee was supposed to drive.

The huts were of many shapes and built with varying degrees of competence; representatives of many tribes had drifted to Goya, eager to settle in this black African republic. Sudanese were here,

Kikuyu, Kavirondo, the Mongolian-cheeked Masai, the Samburu, the ferocious Somalis, the beautiful Cyallas, the Zulu, and many others. Although the night was half gone, people were awake, some smoking, some talking; fires still burned, palm oil lights gleamed here and there from a low entrance. Quiet muttering and laughter surrounded Soames, a rat scuttled under his foot. All these shadows, awake or sleeping, about him were real people, their lives in many particulars more vivid than his, their ways as remote from his as a bull's from a bee's; yet from them rose a force which affected Soames strangely. The low noises, the strange scents, the glint of light on a chest or a crooked leg, even the rhythm of his own uneven walking, produced in him a heady exhilaration. The force nuzzled his temples, his loins, made his glands chime, made him walk with his mouth open and his ears pricked. The force was an appetite, all belly and organs and no mind, a brontosaurus. His belly spoke to the belly of Africa.

When they finally emerged from the kraal, Soames was trembling. He tried to dismiss the notion as nonsensical, but could not avoid feeling that something vital had just happened to him, oddly transforming him. That anonymous, transcendent *appetite* still rumbled inside him; he could not tell what it was, or what it was doing. He wanted to stop and think, to puzzle things out, as a pack of cards must do when, having been reshuffled, every value lies against a new value, but Eekee still pressed voicelessly on and Soames was compelled to follow.

A plump moon was now rising. Soames recognised their whereabouts. They had made a wide arc round the outskirts of Umbalathorp and were now at the top end of the market place. An electric light burned in a window of the hospital opposite, native butchers slept on their slabs, a beggar rested by the central well. Somewhere afar, a hyena urged a pack of jackals into hysterics.

Halfway down one side of the wide square, Eekee stopped, turned for the first time, and beckoned Soames. Between two wooden buildings, a small fifteen-hundredweight truck was parked. This

111

was the 'lorry' de Duidos had promised. They climbed in, Eekee taking the driving seat, Soames the other. The noise of the engine starting cut through the stillness like sharks' teeth through vellum. As Eekee crashingly sorted out gears, they began to move. They rattled down the market place, turning right towards the station.

Soares' warehouse, in which de Duidos' emissaries reported the stolen parts to be hidden, was a large building standing next to the station. It had been intended originally as an engine shed, until the supply of railway lines had given out. Indeed, had they given out any sooner, they would not have stretched to the end of the station platform. Making the best of a bad job, the construction gangs erected buffers where the line tailed off, filled up the open end of the engine shed, and sold it cheaply to Soares as a warehouse.

Outside it, blocking the doorway with an ancient charpoy which looked as if it had been dragged all the way from Simla, lay an ancient Sikh. A small lantern stood on one post of his bed, a burning stick of agarbatti was wedged in another. Eekee reversed the truck and drove it backwards, stopping it within ten yards of the Sikh.

Soames and Eekee here changed places, so that Soames climbed out of the driver's seat and stood by the open cab door. He called to the Sikh, asking him the time, the way to Uiuibursam, the date of the next eclipse of the sun. The Sikh appeared to be very deaf and very stupid. It took considerable prompting on Soames' part before he lowered his feet to the ground, took up his lantern and shuffled forward.

As he reached the rear of the truck, Eekee materialised round the tailboard, slipping a scarf over the old man's head and across his mouth, so that he could not cry out. With four leather thongs he was bound and then stretched quietly beside the truck. Soames had insisted on this harmless procedure rather than the more reliable and colourful cosh on the skull favoured by de Duidos.

Running forward, Soames pushed the charpoy out of the way, and unbolted the large door set in the front of the store. With Eekee at the wheel again, the truck was backed down until its canopy was just inside the entrance. Having switched off the engine, the negro now hurried forward some yards to take up his post as look-out, as prearranged.

Flashing the gigantic torch de Duidos had lent him, Soames crossed the obstructed floor of the warehouse, piled high with miscellaneous lumber. This was where his own private arrangements came in, and he was momentarily glad that the Portuguese was not man enough to be present at his own operations. Reaching the only window in the building, he found the catch and opened it. He was facing down the length of Goya's solitary railroad; the tracks glinted in the moonlight. As Soames' head appeared in the opening, a shadow moved from the shadow of the station platform and Deal Jimpo came quietly forward. Climbing on to the buffers he was able, with Soames' aid, to clamber into the window. He paused, gripping the flimsy frame, swung his plaster-encased leg stiffly over the sill, and dropped into the warehouse.

'Everything all right with you?' he whispered.

'Fine,' Soames replied, clapping Jimpo's shoulder. He was still gripped by the kind of exultation which had seized him in the kraal. 'Have you seen anyone hanging about who looks as if he might be an assistant of de Duidos that he did not bother to tell me about?'

The princeling shook his head, and Soames began at once to search for the computer spares, flashing his torch industriously among the bales and boxes. He was still hunting when the drums started. They sounded close, beating against the ear like moth wings.

'What is that?' Soames asked. 'Not anything to do with us, is it?'

'No. It is drums from the other side of the river,' Jimpo answered. 'A party of hunters celebrates killing a leopard.'

The sound was as thick and warm as a bloodstream. Soames stood where he was, listening. Now, added to the ensnaring thud of hand against skin, came the chant of voices. Insistently the words were reiterated, coming clear across the Uiui:

I kumma jum
Kumma jum
Kumma wumma jum
I kumma jum
Kumma jum
Kumma wumma jum …

'What does it mean?' Soames asked.

'The warriors sing that the old man had lost his gourd,' Jimpo explained, limping back to the window. 'The black leaves fall from the blue-gum tree and his gourd is gone beyond the river where no man may go. The river is deep and one becomes exceedingly wet in it. The old man is sad and beats his smallest son because the gourd contained a month's supply of mepacrine tablets. Now the old man beats his head in sorrow against the blue-gum tree.'

The first box of spare parts was discovered beneath a stiff and stinking lion skin, the transistors neatly embedded in moss and grass. Soames set it gently into the back of the truck. He then found that the rest of the contents of the original five crates were cached in a formidable number of cardboard boxes labelled 'Slazenger Tennis Balls'. Removing his jacket which was already soaked in sweat, he commenced to load these boxes into the truck. He worked automatically, inundated by the stifling heat in the store and the plud-plud of the drums.

An urgent call from Jimpo, keeping a watch by the window, interrupted Soames. Hurrying over to the princeling, he stared into the darkness where a dark finger pointed.

'Something going on down there,' Jimpo muttered, 'down at the slums end of the town. A new fire burning, and people crossing it.'

Soames found it hard to see anything distinctly. The moon had shaken its cloak loose off the hills and rode high, calling a meaningless pattern of glints and shadows from the earth. Soames was unimpressed.

'Call me if anything exciting happens,' he said, returning down the length of the store to his loading. They could be away in a few minutes now. When the truck was stacked with all the parts, he would whistle to Eekee, who would return to receive at Jimpo's hands what he had previously meted out to the Sikh. Jimpo and Soames would then drive like hell and in triumph back to the palace with the booty, de Duidos and Soares would both be discomfited.

The scheme was simple, workable. Soames' spirits rose under the extra dash of adrenalin supplied by his glands for the venture. The diminishing pile of Slazenger boxes twinkled into the truck to the rhythm of the chant.

> I kumma jum
> Kumma jum
> Kumma wumma jum

'Soames, man!' Jimpo bellowed.

Surprised, Soames dropped a box. He turned in his friend's direction – and the reason for the shout was apparent to him from where he stood. Soames remained transfixed, staring through the square of window framed in the blackness of the warehouse.

The railway engine was speeding up the single line, speeding towards the station. It pulled no carriages, and appeared to be going flat out. The close-standing houses near the track were illuminated one by one by the ruddy glow from its firebox, as it flashed past them, trailing smoke. Now the clamour of its progress was audible above the sound of drums.

Something frighteningly unlikely hovered about the spectacle of that little iron demon hurtling up the dark track; it was as if Turner's 'Wind, Air and Steam' had been repainted by Francis Bacon. Soames was reminded of an old play called *The Ghost Train*. He thought, 'If it doesn't slow down, it'll overshoot the station,' before realising that whoever rode the footplate had no intention of stopping.

'Run, Jimpo, it's coming!' he yelled.

Over the charging engine rode a great sock of smoke, transformed to orange just above the cab. As Soames called out, a piercing scream came from the whistle, enough to rouse all Goya and the lands beyond. Jimpo, who had stared from the window petrified at the sight, turned to run. His plaster cast snagged him even as he swung round, and he fell full length.

Yelling with all the power of his lungs, as if in an attempt to quell that paralysing whistle, Soames ran back to the princeling. It was like running at a charging rhino, for the front of the engine was clearly framed in the window now. He snatched Jimpo's forearms, pulling him frenziedly to one side; the walls were only lath: if he could break through them –

But the terrible monster had breasted the final rise, was clattering through the shuttered station. At the last moment, two maniac figures, golden for an instant, flung themselves off the footplate towards the platform. Then their charge, screaming still like a dying boar, flattened the buffers as if they were dough and burst insanely into the warehouse. It ploughed into crates and cartons, grinding into the concrete floor, belching smoke, sparks, and steam. Everything flew. Noise was like chopper blows on the ear.

Fighting its way blindly ahead, the engine struck de Duidos' truck and mangled to a catastrophic halt. Flames instantly burst out, engulfed the truck canopy, sprang to the roof, flooded the interior. Smoke filled the building, illuminated as if it too were burning.

Soames, who was hit and knocked down by a flying plank of wood directly the iron monster burst in almost on top of him, scrambled up dazedly. In the growing brightness of the flames, he could see Jimpo a few feet away, tossed into a crazy attitude over a pile of broken timbers. With a last splurge of strength, he got the princeling on to his back and dragged him out the only possible way: through the gaping hole by which the engine had entered.

Outside, his knees buckled and he went down. When they were discovered, they were lying there together, unconscious.

Chapter Ten

'For summer has o'erbrimmed their clammy cells.'

Of all the miscellaneous structures in Umbalathorp, the one which most closely obeyed the architectural precept that the appearance of a building shall be related to its function was the prison. It could be mistaken for nothing but what in the States is called colloquially 'the jug'. A low, one-storey erection of brick, with nothing but bars to enliven its façade, it seemed to wear its roof like an exceptionally low brow, so that written all over it was the same look of miserable stupidity as might be found on most of the countenances of its inmates.

Another American phrase applicable to such institutions, 'the clink', fitted Umbalathorp's jail excellently. Perched perpetually on its roof were a half dozen white, bloated, carrion-consuming birds with scarlet wattles like turkeys, who sharpened their beaks with nicking, clinking sounds against the ridge of the roof, or rolled the gritty pellets of their droppings down the runways in the corrugated iron.

Only the slang term 'the cooler' would have been inappropriate here. Under the iron roof, the cells twanged with heat. Soames lay miserably on a board bed, holding his forehead. Tenants of nearby cells were singing convivially, but he did not join in. He counted out his life in beads of sweat.

It was well after noon, when Soames had been locked in his cell for seven hours, with only a jar of stale water smelling like urine for company, that his door was unlocked and two negroes entered. One was a handsome young Samburu of the flashy tie brigade, clad in a grey and yellow lounge suit with impossible shoulders; the other was an older, tired man, with a wise, monkey face, dressed in crumpled reach-me-downs.

The younger man bowed and introduced himself in fluent English.

'I am appointed your defending lawyer, Mr Noyes,' he said. 'I shall handle your case with great ability, that I promise. Having been a resident for some long years in South Africa, I am proficient in all legal matters. My name is Assidawa Obendsi, at your service, and here allow me to present my first assistant, Ladies Only, who is fluent in Afrikaans but not English.'

'An unusual name,' commented Soames grumpily.

'Surely not, Mr Noyes, in your country? My assistant, being a Christian, chose this name especially for he understands that before it white men fall away; he is hoping to create a similarly immense impression on the world.'

The older man, knowing himself to be talked about, said 'Laaa – dee sonli,' and laughed sadly and silently, his mouth open, his head nodding.

'Well, I hope you're soon going to get me out of here, Mr Obendsi,' Soames said. 'Just what is the situation? Hasn't Deal Jimpo been able to explain what happened last night to his father yet? Once that's done, I should be able to walk out of here a free man. I've done nothing.'

Obendsi smiled, sitting down by Soames and interposing his briefcase between them. Ladies Only leant against the wall, beginning to bite his nails with melancholy vigour.

'That is not quite so, Mr Noyes,' Obendsi said gently. 'The matter is not really simple. Deal Jimpo, the President's son, lies still in the hospital senseless, and in consequence, ipso facto, cannot say

118

anything to anybody. When you will walk out of here a free man I cannot commit myself to say exactly. There are three grave charges brought against you by three different parties.'

'How absolutely absurd!' Soames exclaimed. 'What are these three charges?'

The lawyer ticked them off on flexible fingers; Ladies Only nodded his head to keep time with the ticking.

'First, the Portuguese de Duidos brings action against you for theft and total damagement of one fifteen-hundredweight lorry valued at twelve hundred doimores, plus value extra of four new tyres to be decided later. Second, the Portuguese Soares brings action against you for total destruction of one warehouse by means of deliberately aimed railway express engine, said warehouse containing goods valued at one hundred thousand doimores. Third and last, the Royal Umbalathorp to Umbalathorp State Railway Company brings action against you for the theft and ruination of one 0-4-0 tank engine named "M'Grassi Thunderbird".'

'That's absolutely crazy!' Soames exclaimed, jumping up. 'Complete nonsense, the lot of it!'

'On paper it looks quite sensible and formidable, Mr Noyes.'

'It's crazy, I tell you!' Soames said agitatedly. 'All three charges are perfectly ridiculous. If you're going to defend me, you'd better know what really happened last night.'

He told Obendsi the whole story behind the night's activities, ending by saying, 'Whoever set that engine on to Jimpo and me, it was neither of the Portuguese concerned, since they stood to lose by the smash-up. Has anyone questioned the driver and fireman yet? de Duidos, of course, is framing me; that's obvious enough. If you could find this man Eekee, the driver of the truck, and get him to talk, that would squash the first charge.'

'I will certainly look for this man,' Obendsi said doubtfully, making notes. 'As to the fireman and driver of the engine, the Chief of Police, *more suo*, has already asked questions of these unhappy men. It is their custom to drive the engine at night, when the railway closes down, to the slum end of the track, whereby they have their place of habitation. During the last night, they were set upon in their rest by persons unknown, who tied them and then stole the engine.'

'Well, that proves it wasn't me, surely. Did they see these attackers?'

'One attacker was observed to wear a white face and an English bowler hat,' Obendsi explained. 'He was presumed therefore to be you.'

'For God's sake, I haven't got a bowler hat!'

'You suggest someone impersonated you in a cunning disguise?'

'I suppose so,' Soames replied. 'If only Jimpo would come round … was he badly injured?'

'Very badly; he is senseless all the time.' The lawyer rose, handing his notes to Ladies Only, who during the conversation had been staring boredly at the roof. 'We will do our very best for you, Mr Noyes,' he said, 'and hope your truth will prevail over the other. Tomorrow I come early to see you again. Sit tight in your comfortable cell and do not despair.'

'Wait! Will you let me write a note to be delivered to President Landor? Will you see it gets to him?'

When Obendsi agreed and produced paper and pencil, Soames wrote: 'As British subject, I demand reliable lawyer from London, who will perhaps impress the court, though I doubt anyone could be more efficient than Mr Assidawa Obendsi. Also beseech personal interview with you, to convince you that British justice and Goyese injustice lead the world. Noyes.'

Obendsi scanned the message, beamed at the passage inserted especially for his benefit and pocketed it.

'You know I can pay appropriately for your very best services?' Soames asked, anxious to detain Obendsi as long as possible.

The lawyer translated Soames' remark into Goyese for the benefit of Ladies Only, who again laughed his dry, monkey laugh, clicking his tongue at Soames.

'I must not be paid twice,' Obendsi said. 'Here is a letter for you explaining how my stipend comes.'

He presented a folded sheet of paper to Soames.

The letter was brief, and read:

Dear Soames,

Whatever have you been up to, has the sun got you or something? Everyone has a different version of what you have been up to, but I hope to get you out of the lockup soon. I am paying this lawyer chap a large sum of doimores I happen to have handy to frame things your way.

Apostle on last lap.

Cheer up.

Ted Timpleton.

Well, thought Soames, the blighter certainly has a good heart. He recalled his first morning in Africa, when he had climbed out of the plane to find the engineer frying eggs, and a wave of nostalgia swept over him.

As the two lawyers prepared to leave the cell, there were handshakes all round. Then Ladies Only opened the door for his superior. As Obendsi's back was turned, the older man, one finger to his lips, extended a much folded spill of paper to Soames; still with the bored look of a tourist on his face, he winked once and then tailed quickly out after Obendsi.

When the door had clanged shut, Soames opened the spill, carrying it over to the tiny window to read. The schoolgirl scrawl inside said:

Keep hopeful for immediate release sooner or later. I will see you are set free, do not fear. But mind what things you say to lawyer Obendsi who is one of witch doctor's friends, who has no love of you.

I have,

Cherry.

At least it was good to know that he had friends. Somewhat stunned by a feeling of helplessness, Soames gazed from the window. A ragged man was sticking posters to suitable buildings; on the poster was the legend: JIMPO FOR PRESIDENT, in several languages.

'I'm sorry, I can't start this ruddy thing up without Soames,' Timpleton said decisively, folding his hairy arms across his chest.

Queen Louise, who was acting as interpreter, repeated this remark to the President in Goyese.

'Tell him he is talking entire nonsense,' Landor said briskly to the Queen. 'Say I know that Noyes is only a mouthpiece, and that if the Apostle is now ready to run, he must make it run without Noyes.'

'The King and President condemns your line of gibberish, insisting you wake the machine now. Noyes is only an official for show, who can be done without,' the Queen said in English.

'Avez-vous ever écouté de "protocol", monsieur Président?' Timpleton demanded. 'It's more than my job's worth to start this valuable baby without official OK. Get it? Le OK official, n'est- pas? Le monsieur Soames seulement peut le donner. You tell him, Queen.'

'You are being obscurantist,' hissed the Queen.

'The three figures stood before the great dull hulk of the computer. The blood-red matt-surfaced plates which protected its delicate insides had now been clamped into place. It was ready for action. Twenty-five feet long, seven feet high, three feet deep, the Apostle Mk II was a splendid sight, enough to fill a Unilateral man's heart with pride or send terror into an infidel soul. The long row of dials, one set in each panel, stared out like octopus eyes; they, and the formidable array of indicators on the control block at one end, silently awaited the pulse of life.

'You are not fulfilling the conditions of your contract,' Landor told Timpleton through the Queen. 'I shall cable your firm and tell them so.'

'What? When I've worked like a black – better than a black to put this thing together? Be reasonable now!' Timpleton said. 'I can't get it straight from anyone what Soames is supposed to have done, but I know jolly well he wouldn't meddle in anything that didn't concern him. He's not the type! If you let him go free, we'll check this thing over and have it going in two shakes.'

The Queen and King argued together in Goyese.

'The King and President declares it is none of your business,' Queen Louise finally said, 'what Noyes has committed. Even he cannot yet comprehend exactly what happened last night; that is why there must be court thrashing out. Valuable public property was destroyed last night.'

'You mean the railway engine that was busted up? Crikey, Queen, you don't seriously believe poor old Soames did that, do you? Don't you know him better than that?'

'All men in Umbalathorp have anger in their hearts at the destruction of a fine public entertainment,' Queen Louise said. 'They demand somebody to be punished.'

'Why pick on Soames! Even if he was hanging about there, I'm damn sure it wasn't to jigger up your mouldy little railway.'

'The King and President – and I too – declare you to be a man without understanding. We command you to start the machine to work.'

'The three of you can go to hell in a bucket,' Timpleton said, dashing down the cigarette he was smoking and grinding it underfoot. Without waiting to hear any more, he strode out of the room.

At first he wandered aimlessly about the grounds in the rear of the palace. Then, reaching a decision, he set off along the river bank, walking upstream. If it was no good appealing to the head of state (using, at the same time, a little leverage), he would appeal to the biggest crook in the state, with whom he had already had dealings: José Blencimonti Soares. For Timpleton had misgivings already about the efficiency of the black lawyer, Obendsi, whom he had hired directly he learnt that Soames was under arrest.

Timpleton had never thought deeply on any matter outside his own profession, for which he cared passionately; he regarded anyone who sought to impose an intellectual pattern upon their life as a crank, a fool; his own – totally unconscious – modes of behaviour were dictated, like those of many of his social level, by a wish to project the irrationality of adolescence as far into middle age as possible. He had no love for Soames: their natures were totally dissimilar. What he did have (and what Soames, in his place, would have tended to despise) was an urge to help out a fellow countryman in a tough spot. To do this would be to assist Timpleton as well as Soames, for his simple, unchangeable, irrational creed was that he was superior to anyone with a coloured skin – just as he was superior to anyone born in Italy, Spain or Germany.

He had gone only a short way down the riverside track when the rain began. Sprinting, Timpleton ran for shelter in a small hut he had passed before on his way to Soares. He dived into its dark cover, to glare morosely out at the sudden shower, cursing the climate. In thick jungle, this rain would scarcely have reached the ground, being absorbed by the mat of foliage overhead, but here it soaked down in random leaks, as if the heavens were a giant colander.

To Timpleton's pleased surprise, the downpour began to slow after five minutes. He did not know it, but this final errant douche represented the end of a brief wet season; the skies would now be cloudless for several weeks. As quiet fell again, he heard a sound behind him; turning, he found two pairs of eyes regarding him intently from the rear of the hut, one pair belonging to a man stretched on a skin bed, one to an old woman who squatted naked beside him, tending him.

The man on the skins had evidently been wounded. His body was smeared with dung and a white, chalky substance, and dotted with omens of recovery: a lion's hair, a tiger's tooth, a festering wing of a bird, berries. By the feet of this much decorated invalid lay a bowler hat.

'My crikey, they're crazy, these people,' said Timpleton, noting this last incongruity as he plunged out of the shelter. Turning up his collar, he trudged doggedly on to Soares' place.

A wrought-iron gate set in a white wall gave access to the white-walled Soares home. The half-caste gatekeeper recognised

Timpleton and let him in. Soares himself sat morosely on the verandah, talking to three Goyese in suits; he looked up and saw the engineer, waving without rising as he generally did.

'Ah, great pleasure and honour as always to seeing you,' he called, as Timpleton mounted the steps. 'Maybe you hear today I become Number One Ruined Man, all my hard work gone for a wind. Just now I consult, but please to go in and make free with my house and daughter while they are here. Tomorrow, all may be swept right away with debt.'

He turned and said something in the native tongue at which his three companions laughed.

'I'm sorry to hear the bad news, but I didn't come to see Maria, José,' Timpleton said, not pleased by laughter he could not comprehend. 'I came to see you. You seem to be able to swing most things in this town; I want you to get my pal Soames out of jail.'

'Wha-a-at that you saying?' the Portuguese asked, his plump face slowly turning dark red. 'You come to me and talk about your friend Soames? Your *friend*! Madre dios! You give me too much insult. Are you not know this scab-devouring, double-deal-addict Soames run down my first, Number One warehouse in just this last night? If they fling him in the jail house, don't I want anything else in the whole world except maybe shoot him? Now you come for ask me let him *out*? You crazy? You got touch from the sun? Or maybe you take too much bad palm wine? Which it is?'

Timpleton climbed slowly on to the second verandah step. Anger in others always infected him with anger, as simply as we yawn because we see others yawn.

'Shut your greasy trap,' he said. 'I asked you a civil question and I expect a civil bloody answer.'

'Then go elsewhere!' Soares shouted. 'I am finished man through this fellow Soames. All my assets destructed! So you can clear out; our deal is finished and no more business to make. Go on, hop off!'

'OK, you stinking little ...' Timpleton said. Jumping up the steps, he kicked the bamboo table aside and grabbed Soares by

125

the fat bundles of breast under his shirt. Ignoring the Portuguese's struggles, Timpleton brought one fist back – and then the three Goyese gentlemen, hitherto sitting politely in their places, joined the exchange. They were big and bony, with disinterested attitudes towards pain. In a confused fashion, Timpleton was aware of being lumped and battered towards the garden wall; next minute, he was tossed over it, to sprawl hard in the tall grasses outside.

If the most typical English smell is the refreshing tang of wet pavements, the most typical central African one is a sharp-sweet spicy aroma, as of cardamom inhaled from a mighty armpit. Timpleton lay idly savouring this odour for some while, until the sound of a car engine roused him enough to make him sit up.

The car drew level with him and stopped. When the dust had settled, much of it over him, Timpleton perceived that the driver was Assidawa Obendsi, the lawyer; beside him slumped his assistant, Ladies Only.

'Do you wait for anyone, ceteris paribus?' enquired the lawyer politely, fitting his wide shoulders into the wide window and leaning out to inspect the Englishman.

'Gimme a hand, will you?' Timpleton said thickly, pulling a lump of mud off his ear.

Obendsi gestured to his assistant. At once, the little monkey-faced man scuttled round the battered bonnet of the vehicle. With much grunting and clicking of the tongue, his mouth hanging open, Ladies Only managed to help Timpleton into the back seat of the car. There he sat, cradling the engineer's tousled head in his lap, muttering words of comfort to him in Afrikaans.

'Wisest course is to take you into the hospital for treatment,' Obendsi said, looking round contemptuously at Timpleton. Taking silence for confirmation, he started bowling down the dusty track again.

'Any news of Soames? Did he send anybody any notes?' Timpleton managed to ask, as they finally slowed down in the market place to get past three home-going bullocks.

126

'No notes, no nothing,' said Obendsi positively. 'My client is very low in spirit, but I cheer him up. Here is the hospital. Here they give you a really thorough treatment and make you never wish to visit there again.'

Ladies Only helped Timpleton into the foyer, where white-clad negroes took over; he produced a sad, simian smile of farewell and returned to the car. Timpleton was then as thoroughly, as efficiently, manhandled as he had been at Soares' home. For half an hour he was probed, X-rayed, massaged, plastered and disinfected; he had his eyeballs examined, his chest thumped, his knees tapped, and the cavities between his toes examined for foot rot. It was dark when they released him with no more serious an injury than a wounded pride.

As Timpleton lingered on the gritty hospital steps, staring out at a hundred tiny lights, the palace lorry drew up outside. Cushioned benches in the back seated five personages who now disembarked in the sort of profusion one usually associates with three times that number: President M'Grassi Landor, Mrs President Tunna, Queen Louise, Princess Cherry and Princeling Shappy. Timpleton stepped uneasily back into the foyer, uncertain of his reception, but the President gave a friendly nod as he passed; had the engineer but known it, M'Grassi tolerated anger and insult almost cheerfully; the people he disliked were those who perpetually showed him an imperturbable front; he had long ago realised that self-control is a prerequisite of the assassin.

Princess Cherry stopped and seized Timpleton's sleeve.

'You have been here to see Deal Jimpo?' she asked.

'No,' Timpleton admitted. 'I tripped up and had to have a bit of plaster on my knee.'

'Then come with us to see him; we go to his room now. If he is conscious, he will welcome. In fact, the more the merrier.'

'Well, thanks, Princess, but … it's none of my business to tag along with you.'

'No? I think it is business. This I must say to you, that though you do not feel a friend inside, you must act in friendship with

127

me. You are a recessive man, Timpleton, I tell you; but here is no staying neutral. Not even trees stay neutral in Umbalathorp. You must be on one side or the other. Why not be on the winning side?'

'It's not a question of sides,' Timpleton said uneasily.

'I am saying it is so,' Princess Cherry insisted. 'Come on. If you stand for your friend Soames as I do, you stand for Jimpo. Therefore you come to see him. Just follow me.'

Shrugging his shoulders, Timpleton allowed himself to be dragged on by the young princess. Walking rapidly, they caught up with the rest of the royal party on the stairs. Thus they were in time to see, as Jimpo's ward door was opened by a curtsying matron, that Dumayami squatted on the bed, crouching over the prone body of the prince.

Chapter Eleven

'While thy hook spares …'

The witch doctor adheres to a rule followed instinctively by the practitioners of all schools of physical and mental healing: he strives through visual display for mental domination of his patient. The ornate robes of the High Anglican church, the frock coat and top hat of the market-side quack, the faultless tailoring of your psychiatrist, right down perhaps to the anxiously hurried air of the average GP, all strive to strike awe in the beholder through his optic nerve. Dumayami went one – or rather, two – better: he also attacked through the aural and olfactory nerves, by rattling bones and burning bat dung at the bedside.

He squatted astride the blanketed body of Jimpo, leaning forward to insert pellets into the prince's nostrils, with his great haunches rising on either side of his arched body like wings. The electric light had been switched off; in its stead rush lights by the bedside cast great devil shadows on the ceiling, transforming a hospital ward into a cave. Timpleton gasped involuntarily at the sight. For a moment, something inside him communed with ancient European memories of vampirism, black mass and the joyless junketings of Walpurgis Night; then the President turned the electric light on.

In a flash, Dumayami was just a dirty old man in cassock, Ike button and grey flannels, with painted face and bloody hands. He was also an angry dirty old man. With ferocious agility, he jumped from the bed and confronted the royal party.

M'Grassi Landor was no less angry.

It is a distressing trait in human nature that we tend to underestimate the good in others when circumstances are against them; if we intercept a couple creeping out of a single bedroom in a hotel, we are more prone to suspect them of having indulged in the emptiness of lust, than to reflect that they may have found that beauty and goodness which we ourselves have previously discovered in a similar situation. It never occurred to M'Grassi now that Dumayami was merely doing his best to succour a sick man.

'This is damned interference,' he said thickly. 'Since when have you been on the hospital staff, Dumayami? Who allowed you to come into this room?'

'I ask no permission of anyone where I go,' Dumayami replied; 'I go where the need for me exists.'

'You dare to carry out your beastly rites here!' M'Grassi exclaimed. He seized the bag of pebbles, the green bones, the dung pouch, the carved horn, from the bed, and flung them out into the corridor. 'Get your insanitary relics away from here, Dumayami, and take yourself with them. I don't want you near Jimpo again.'

'You offend every tabu in Umbalathorp!' the witch doctor screamed. His face twitched like a mask, the wearer of which is convulsed by sneezing. 'By this deed, you have roused your father from his grave; your grandfather and great-grandfather also wake to curse you. Now the lines of the dust will rise and trip you, and the grey grains of shadow fill your eyes with sand. When the hands of the dead come for you in the night-time, your screams shall curdle in your belly. When the horse-headed gods – Arghhh!'

He drew back with a withered hand raised to his cheek. M'Grassi had struck him across the face. For a second, the two men looked

130

at each other with mutual fear; both knew that the long, uneasy peace they had kept was broken, both feared the unknown future.

'I regret doing that,' M'Grassi said, half in a whisper.

Dumayami gave no sign of having heard. Hand still raised, he skirted the party, who shrank back from him, and went quietly through the door. Little Prince Shappy burst into tears.

A jangle of incoherent concern shook the royal party. They were brought back somewhat to themselves by the realisation that Deal Jimpo was watching them from the bed. The matron, who had hovered anxiously in the background during the foregoing scene, hurried over and smoothed his brow, afterwards collecting up the little guttering rush lights and carrying them from the room. By the time she returned, the royal family had clustered round Jimpo's bed; M'Grassi was pulling a grey pellet from his son's nostril.

'Nobody is to blame for this,' the matron said humbly. 'The man Dumayami forced his way in here declaring that the Prince Deal Jimpo had need of him. We did not like to oppose him.'

'You may forget the matter, matron,' the President said, with more sharpness than graciousness.

'Thank you, sir, Your Majesty. Might I also suggest that you all left the Prince now? His condition is still critical, and the scene in here will not have improved it.'

'We will be as brief as possible,' replied M'Grassi, 'but I have questions which must be asked. Kindly leave us, matron.'

When the woman had gone, he leant over the bed, examining Jimpo's eyes. Truth to tell, little but Jimpo's eyes were available for examination. The rest of him was swathed under lint bandage; both his legs were in suspended splints and a rib cage protected his trunk. He hardly had a bone not fractured or a stretch of skin not burnt.

His cracked lips moved in their white frame as he greeted his father.

'To see you like this brings us very great distress, son,' M'Grassi said, speaking in Goyese, as Mrs President Tunna pressed forward to clasp her son's hand and shed a tear on his sheet. 'We wish to

131

know what happened, that the malefactors may be punished at once. Can you tell us briefly what occurred?'

'Soames is in the jug, Jimpo,' Templeton said urgently. 'You've got to help us get him out. They're saying the whole shindig was his doing.'

The dark eyes in the mask switched to Templeton's face, as if the sound of English was suddenly very refreshing.

'None of this was Soames' fault,' he said in English. 'Soames was a hero. Soames saved me ...' He paused, fighting for breath; his eyes closed. When he resumed, he spoke again in Goyese, evidently finding this easier. Princess Cherry translated into English for Templeton's benefit as they went along, much to Templeton's discomfort; as he began to gather that Jimpo and Soames had been involved in stealing back the computer parts he had illegally sold, a strong desire to sink below the floorboards assailed him.

M'Grassi Landor heard his son out in silence. Then he paced beside the bed, arms akimbo.

'You must by now, Jimpo, be too thoroughly aware of your foolishness in joining Soames' escapade for me to need to dwell on that aspect of the matter,' he said. 'What disturbs me more – I mean, quite apart from seeing you so injured – is that you should have sympathised with Soames' wish to recover the computer parts when you knew I did not; for this means we think very differently, and I had hoped you would grow up to be of my mind in affairs. The futile and contradictory wish of fathers is always that sons may share their thoughts and avoid their sorrows. However ... Soames' psychology eludes me, but at least it is clear that he was trying to make amends for what others had done. I see I have underestimated him.'

Templeton, at this point, braced himself to meet M'Grassi's eyes, but the President continued to pace with downcast glance, closely watched by his family.

'Soames must be released from his incarceration,' he went on. 'That much is obvious and does not bother me. What I do find bothersome is the fresh problem which now arises. Who launched the "M'Grassi Thunderbird" on its last run? What were their intentions? Could it possibly be that –'

'They were trying to assassinate my poor Jimpo,' Tunna said, stroking his bandages with her plump black hand. 'They were trying to kill him, that was their intention.'

'That was not what I was about to say,' M'Grassi said, turning to stare through the mosquito screens, 'but nevertheless you may be right. A simple mind often tracks down truth where a more devious one cannot follow.'

Walking in an excruciating mockery of prostration, the matron re-entered the ward and ushered them back into the corridor. Jimpo's eyes had already closed.

'You will make him better again, won't you?' Shappy asked tearfully.

'We are doing all in our power,' said the matron.

'Let us control our weeping until we get home, Prince Shappy,' Queen Louise said regally. 'Seize his hand, Cherry, and see to it that he does not cry.'

'If the rest of you will sit in the lorry, I will phone the prison Governor at once from here,' M'Grassi said. Catching Timpleton's eye for the first time, he added curtly in English, 'Goodnight, Mister Timpleton.'

'Tell him I'm sorry about all this trouble, will you?' the engineer asked Princess Cherry.

She did so. When her father had spoken in answer, she translated with a slight smile on her ample features.

'The King and President regrets that this has been such an unprofitable transaction for you, because you gave the money you took from Soares to Obendsi, and no change will come from him.'

His lips tight, Timpleton nodded to her and passed out of the building. He walked slowly back to the palace, reflecting how simple and happy was life in London.

M'Grassi sought out the matron's room, picked up the telephone, and was eventually put through to the Governor of the prison, to whom he spoke earnestly for some while on the subject of Soames.

'The railway company will drop their charge against Noyes directly I inform them that new information has come to light,' he said, 'which leaves only the charges brought by the two Portuguese, de Duidos and José Soares. Perhaps when I have rung off you would get your secretary to contact them both, inform them of what has transpired and warn them that Noyes will very probably sue them for defamation of character unless these charges against him are squashed at once.'

'Very good, President Your Majesty,' said the voice at the other end of the line. 'And Noyes shall be freed as soon as these charges are dropped.'

'I think we can do better than that, Governor. I confess to a certain liking for Noyes; or perhaps I am merely sorry for him because I feel that in his heart he still has not decided what his life is. Therefore I am prepared personally to stand bail for him to the extent of twenty thousand doimores. Will you kindly release him at dawn?'

'At the very first crack of it,' cried the Governor smartly. 'You may rely on me to be thorough, but first' – he added, replacing the bedside phone – 'I shall be thorough with you, my little popsy python-chicken,' and he planted a resounding kiss on the lips of his latest and in all senses greatest mistress.

The circumstances under which Soames passed the night beneath the Governor's roof differed considerably from those enjoyed by the Governor; nevertheless, they, too, had their happier moments. A villainous blanket and a vaguely inedible bowl of food were handed to him early in the evening. Shortly afterwards, three negroes were herded into his cell.

The cell was already small; now it seemed smaller. These boys were obviously here for the night. Trying not to make his actions too obvious, Soames hurriedly staked himself a sleeping position on the floor; he was too exhausted by the heat to fancy passing the night standing up. The three negroes beat dust from their clothes and also settled down on the floor, their backs to the wall, their knees drawn up. Unlike Soames', their ankles were shackled together. They were members of a working party which spent its days repairing roads or quarrying stone.

Time passed with the unsure gait of a sad reveller returning home. The full moon hung like an undescended testicle in the belly of the sky. A pack of jackals laughed with the shrill abandon of schoolgirls reading de Sade.

Soames' mind drifted on an uneasy tide of heat and worry, staying in the cell but leaving his body behind. As through the dark glassily, he recalled the splendidly defiant words of an artistic acquaintance, who had once said, 'I never change my socks until I can throw them against the wall and they stick there.' It seemed to Soames, in his dreamy state, that the humidity and temperature of the cell had knitted themselves together to lie pressed over all his apertures with the exact consistency of tacky sock; so that he had but to take a handful of air and throw it, and it would adhere luxuriously to the walls of his prison. This idea insidiously wove itself into a rhyme, 'Stone walls do not a prison make nor sweaty socks a pair; from foot to mouth my sweat doth fake a suit for me to wear'; but the rhyme was a dark streamer of which Soames grasped only portions at a time, and those portions began to weave deliriously with foot and mouth disease, and then with a Scots town called Lossiemouth. Lossiemouth, as a word and as a picture – an ultra-hirsute Lassie sheepdog, wearing lipstick and gleaming false teeth, supporting droves of little kilted figures – assumed in Soames' brain such gigantic proportions of hilarity that it was only when three pairs of hands shook him urgently that he realised his sense of humour had carried him into shrieks of inane laughter.

'I am so sorry,' Soames announced into the darkness. 'I hope I did not disturb you. Perhaps I have a temperature.'

The Englishness of these remarks comforted him greatly.

After a little while, just when his mind was beginning to wander again, a tin cup was thrust into his hand. Surreptitiously polishing its lip with his sleeve, Soames raised it to his mouth and drank.

This time, the three pairs of hands shook him to break him from a terrible spasm of coughing and giggling. He could see or feel nothing but the fiery sword, garlanded with nettles, which stretched from his throat to the pit of his stomach. When its heat at last faded, Soames faded with it into a deep sleep. He was roused by the singing of his cell mates. The night was wearing thin, for the moon rode high, throwing a pebble of light between their bars. Outside, a foolish bird called tirelessly, 'Crippen! Crippen! Crippen!' Doubtless, Soames reflected muzzily, it was a jailbird.

The singing grew round him, nourished by voices from other cells. It seemed to become a creature in its own right, independent of the singers. Soames was much affected by this sound, which seemed to contain so much beauty and sadness. He could not help comparing it with sing-songs he guessed they might have at Brixton and Dartmoor prisons, where staple offerings were no doubt 'If You Were The Only Girl In The World' or 'Mademoiselle from Armentières'. This singing here reminded him of his walk through the kraal with Eekee; the same, dark African appetite was nuzzling him.

When finally it died away, he began without premeditation to sing himself.

Now I am a bachelor, I live with my son,
And we follow the weaver's trade.
And every, every time I look into his eyes
It reminds me of that fair young maid.
It reminds me of the summertime,
And of the winter too,
And the many, many times I held her in my arms
To save her from the foggy, foggy dew.

Soames knew no more of the song than this. When, rather surprised at his own temerity, he paused and found the silence plainly straining for more, he sang this verse over again. When he had sung it four times, another voice, one of his cell-mates, joined him. Soon other voices, deep and true, entered; soon the whole jail was singing the ballad.

The night turned grey and dusty round the edges like an old sandwich, dawn broke, colour was violently reborn. With a crash, Soames' door was flung open, and a guard entered to march him before the Governor. When he was set free twenty minutes later, the prison still reverberated to the strains of 'The Foggy Dew'.

PART THREE

Darkest Africa

Chapter Twelve

'As the light wind lives or dies ...'

M'Grassi Landor was not a man to trifle with time. On a wall in his private study hung a portrait of the negro Henri Christophe of Haiti, who had also been president and king during his few years of power – though not concurrently, as M'Grassi was. From 'L'Homme', M'Grassi drew not a little strength and much of his dislike of wasting a day.

Accordingly, he was now, after breakfast, dictating to one of his secretaries instructions on the official opening of the Apostle, which he had decided should take place that very afternoon. A list of the guests to be invited to the ceremony had already been compiled; M'Grassi hesitated over it and then added Dumayami's name. He could not afford to antagonise the witch doctor further. The old man was powerful and dangerous. M'Grassi might rule over the upper half of his people's heads, but Dumayami held sway over the lower part of their hearts.

At the same time, Soames was upstairs being bathed by two of Princess Cherry's most muscular hand-maidens. Indeed, Soames had been hard put to it to dissuade the Princess from adding her exertions too; her sympathy for his prison ordeal was deep and muscular. When Soames finally returned, bruised but refreshed, to his bedroom, it was to find her and Queen Louise sitting on the bed, awaiting him. Their greeting when he had first arrived back from prison had been hearty, and was as clamorous again now. As always, Soames felt slightly apprehensive under their friendliness.

The twin cannon of the Queen's nose swivelled round drawing a genial bead on Soames.

'You know we are regretful for your staying for one day in our jail, Mr Soames,' she said. 'It is a major mistake.'

'Don't worry about it,' he replied lightly and evasively. 'At least I've been getting a bit of local colour.'

He saw instantly that he had somehow said something to offend them.

'You know what "local colour" is,' he explained. 'It means the typical and exotic wherever you happen to be.'

At this their brows cleared, and the Queen said, 'It is a sign of favour that His Majesty does personal bailing for you. He admires you for an individual. I feel you should live in Goya now and …' She paused for a long while before finding the word she needed: 'Ratify.'

It seemed to Soames that if she required this word, he did not. He stared rather blankly at them until the Princess said seductively, 'There are suitable positions for such men as you, Mr Soames.'

Soames, still slightly light-headed, laughed coarsely.

'We forgive you for going to see the Pickets, Mr Soames,' Queen Louise said. 'We hope you now realise that all requirements are available in the palace.'

'Thank you very much,' Soames said. 'You are very kind. You almost make me wish I was not going home in a few days.'

They left shortly after that; Soames was free to go down and test out the computer with Timpleton, while Gumboi and L'Panto looked admiringly on. When the two Englishmen realised that neither intended to say much about the recent past, they relaxed considerably, becoming almost genial with one another. The standard trials of the computer went smoothly; without hesitation, the Apostle Mk II put out a tongue of paper with neatly typed answers to all the key tests they ran through.

'Is a number one class job, crikey,' L'Panto said warmly. Each in his peculiar way, they echoed those sentiments.

The tests lasted for two hours, after which the computer was roped off for the afternoon's ceremony. Shortly after four-thirty, when the greatest heat of the sun had slightly abated, the first few of the President's guests arrived, and began to mill with open mouths along the Apostle's imposing façade, over which was draped a banner bearing the one word 'Bakkuds', which is Goyese for 'Progress'.

Soames experienced a certain reluctance to meet people. This, he realised, might be partly due to the drugs he had taken to subdue his slight fever; it was also connected with his visit to jail. He had to take himself firmly in hand and realise that a prison sentence in Umbalathorp did not bear the same social stigma it did in England. Even the scum of the Western world become little lords when they get East of Suez or South of Casablanca; and although this situation is not as extreme as it was even ten years ago, it is still extreme, representing, sociologically and historically, one of the most curiously interesting problems of the world's myriad curiously interesting problems. If only one could go back in a time machine to that distant point in prehistory when an ancestor decided he should split his offspring into different colours – if only one could return to that point and talk him out of the crazy idea, the human race would be much less interesting today. Nonetheless, as matters have turned out to date, the idea of incarceration in black minds frequently goes hand in hand with the idea of white authority; to have incurred one is often to have defied the other; what then is a prison sentence but a token of the free-thinker?

Indeed, everyone was so extremely nice to Soames that he hastened to climb on to the specially constructed platform of honour to avoid them. In the large Portuguese party, both de Duidos and Soares were present, the latter with his daughter Maria; from the grotesque succession of winks, nods and smiles

143

they shot at Soames, it was obvious the winds of their cordiality had changed again. Had not Maria, before Soames scrambled to safety, touched his arm with a white lace glove and said, 'Now we achieved dislodging Mr Timpleton from following us, we hope we have the honour and pleasure of encouraging you to see us in our agreeable house?'

This was something Soames meditated on now, for as a man of judgement who knew a good thing when he saw it – and could still, moreover, feel the touch of its lace glove on his arm – he could not but see that, prised away from her parents, Maria Soares would be welcome to be as encouraging as she pleased.

Also in the crowd was Ping Hwa, slender and self-contained, holding over her sleek head the sort of parasol Soames had thought existed only in picture books. He was looking idly from her to Maria, as a man may hesitate between a whisky and a gin and lime, when his coat was tugged from the rear; glancing back, he saw Ping Ah standing behind the platform.

'Perhaps you look see my Number One daughter, Ping Hwa, Mr Noyes,' he said, with an expression far from inscrutable. 'She much regret no chance to talk with you privately. I too have expected you would wish to condescend to talk with me.'

'I don't think I've much to say to you, Ping Ah,' Soames replied.

'The question, Mr Noyes, I made mention of. The secrets going into your computer machine …'

'I had not forgotten. But from what I hear, you have enough contacts inside and outside the palace not to need me at all.'

'Contacts I have, yes,' Ping Ah agreed, still scrutably, 'but not enough. With delicate art of contacts, saturating point is not reachable. Perhaps I send my daughter tonight to reveal certain things to you, yes?'

Possibly he read on Soames' face the battle between the desire he undeniably felt for Hwa and the dislike he had for treating her as an article of exchange. He slid away ambiguously, leaving Soames considerably uncomfortable. Soames, indeed, had a habit of being unhappy about himself; he thought again of Sheila Thurston, the one girl he had really lost his soul to. Yet he had swilled about like an old maid in a pig trough and lost her. Now women were being foisted on to him from all sides; although he conceived it his duty as a man to accept them, a nervous fastidiousness kept him away. With Coitala it had been different: her unexpectedness had stormed the barriers of his delicacy.

Now the royal family was making its way to the platform of honour, Timpleton trailing aimlessly in their wake. The platform creaked heavily as they boarded it. M'Grassi Landor was dressed in a Western lounge suit; the Mayor of Umbalathorp, who also climbed aboard the swaying deck, was draped impressively in a red and purple blanket. He was Mayor Wabe, and he spoke first – in Goyese, while three interpreters standing safely on the ground floor below shouted out translations phrase by phrase in Portuguese, French and English. This rendered it difficult for anyone to hear anything.

'My people,' the Mayor said expansively, when the clapping and drumming which greeted his attempt to stand upright had subsided, 'my people, today we become citizens not merely of Africa, but of the world. We have got a computing engine which really … (cheers). Next year, if we are lucky, we will also have some hydrogen bombs which work. (More cheers). In five years, perhaps we will have artificial satellites. (Cheers.) Then we can defend ourselves properly, and perhaps one day … moon! (Cheers and laughter.)

'This computing Apostle comes from England, where many good things come from and go to. Among my many activities of office, I may tell you I am also a Member for the Preservation of Epping Forest. (Cheers.) You think of England as a land of factories. I … know better. England is like Africa, covered in forest. My English friends here on this platform will tell you just the same. Great forest and lake everywhere, Forest of Dean, Sherwood Forest, St John's Wood, Pinewood, Elstree, Shepherd's Bush, also Blackpool, Liverpool and Bayswater. (Prolonged cheers.) Also we now have computing engines like England, binding the two countries. Here is His Majesty, President Landor to say something …' (Cheers.)

M'Grassi rose slowly, unbuttoning his jacket so that all present should see his magnificent brocade waistcoat.

'My beloved subjects,' he said, 'it is not my custom to speak where I can act. If you know me as a plain, blunt man, it is because I have thought deeply enough to doubt … words. No man utters a sentence without excusing and at the same time condemning himself. This may seem a strange thing to say to you, who are avidly availing yourselves of the best education our schools can offer. (Cheers.) You are trying to learn … All I am trying to imply is that man's wisdom is not infinite; no, not if you read and remember the contents of every book in the world. For one thing, as soon as you become literate, you lose the precious wisdom of the illiterate which – like innocence once it has gone – can never again be recaptured or imagined. The man who steals his friend's only blanket may still regret to see that friend shiver, but he does not suffer with him as once he did. The man who has committed adultery may still love his wife, but he cannot love her as he did. The man who secretly ruined our railway may consider himself still our friend, but we regard him differently than we did before he committed this act. (Cheers and howls.)

'All I am attempting to tell you, my dear subjects, is that the brains of all of us are finite in their capacities. When we take a step forward, we have to relinquish the step behind. When we try … like … down a stream. That is why our two English friends have brought us this computer. It is a mechanical brain, not subject to the weaknesses of our brains of flesh. In its cells lies the capacity to think of everything we cannot. Nothing in Goya can be hidden from it! Not only can it think a thousand times *more* than any of us, it can also think a thousand times faster! Woe to the man who yesterday thought himself clever or great in magic, for today this thing towers above him as the mountain towers above the lake! (Uneasy cheers.)

146

'I now call upon Mr Soames Noyes, the inventor of this wonderful machine, to address a few words to you.'

This last sentence acted like a jab of anaesthetic at the base of Soames' spine. No warning of this had been granted him – indeed, he suspected that M'Grassi, carried along by his own eloquence, had only just thought of the idea. Prodded violently by Timpleton and Queen Louise, who sat next to him, he found himself on his feet, with the crowds waving before his eyes like a desert islander's shirt from a palm tree.

'Er, of course I'm not really the inventor of the Apostle,' he began. 'I'm just a, well, an, er, entrepreneur, but we'll let that go. But one thing I would like to say …' ('Speak louder,' someone in the crowd called, although the three interpreters were bellowing so loudly the noise seemed to numb Soames' faculties; he wondered if the rubbish he was talking sounded any better in Goyese.) 'I'd like to say how kind everyone has been, and to take this opportunity … if you'll bear with me … I ought to, er, explain that unaccustomed as I am … er, my time in Goya and in particular in your lovely capital of …' ('Umbalathorp,' Timpleton growled) 'Umbalathorp, how very pleasantly and also how very fruitful my time … I mean, it has been given to few Englishmen – few Englishmen have been given such a, er, such an opportunity …'

Suddenly Soames noticed Dumayami in the crowd, surrounded by a few choice cronies. The witch doctor's eyes glistened like gristle, while a faint, malevolent smile moved over the notches and tattoos of his face. The sight did much to pull Soames together.

'But perhaps I had better say a few words about the Apostle Mk II,' he said, and heard Queen Louise give a gusty sigh of relief at his side. 'This machine we are celebrating this afternoon is wonderful, yes, but it will not perform magic. It is no more than an agent of progress. Its function is chiefly mathematical, though by its ability to differentiate between alternatives it is possible to coax it to answer general questions superficially unrelated to mathematics – questions of probability, for instance. This is something we in England have been trying to make quite clear to you since we were first notified of your desire to possess such a machine.'

'Is it any good or isn't it?' called a voice from the crowd, which had been listening to Soames in stony silence. The speaker was Obendsi, the lawyer.

'That's a silly question,' Soames replied. 'You must realise that any machine develops in the context of its own civilisation. You do not get ocean liners till you have compasses to guide them with. You do not send up artificial satellites to girdle the earth until you have in your country many thousands of men engaged in rocketry and electronics. Everything has to come in its context. These computers have their origins in punch-card systems which have been in use for a long time, but they come into full being only when many of the complex mathematical problems of a technological culture cannot be handled except by computers. The need for them exists – so they are invented.

'That explains why the Apostle Mk II is out of context here. It's like giving a blind man –' (Soames stopped abruptly. He had been going to say 'a pair of high-powered binoculars', and then realised how unflattering this comparison was) '– a guide dog which is so powerful it is apt to pull him over,' he finished weakly and sat down.

In the puzzled silence which followed, one or two hand claps sounded like exploding airguns. Not only had they not understood him; many had misunderstood him.

'Christ, you bollixed that one up proper and no mistake,' Timpleton said, sotto voce. 'They'll start slinging things in a minute. You're a bloody fool, Soames; why didn't you stay in jug?'

'It's the truth,' Soames said defensively.

'Of course it's the truth. That's why you'd have done better to sit on your arse and say nothing.'

Through the crowd, now splitting into little groups, Dumayami was thrusting his way. When he got to the platform, he half-turned, so that he was addressing both people and personages. He spoke in his lopped variety of English.

'We must not spoil festivity with criticism,' he said, 'but if a sadness occurs – such as waste of public fund – wise man turns and faces that fact soon as possible.'

Roars of approval greeted this when it was translated. M'Grassi stood up, and the noise died like wind among straw.

'What do you hint at, man?' he demanded, glaring down at the witch doctor. 'Innuendoes are the weak man's currency. Speak out straight.'

'I am not weak man,' Dumayami said, unperturbed. 'I issue challenge to this Apostle Mark, to see if he can work properly or not. Let him answer a problem and I will answer also, and we shall see who is right. Make a test!'

'A test!' cried several throats.

M'Grassi looked at Soames, who immediately gestured a frantic 'No', whereupon the President looked away again.

'We accept your challenge,' he said in Goyese.

The witch doctor, lifting the hem of his cassock, climbed nimbly on to the platform.

'Hear then Dumayami's test,' he said in a ringing voice. 'Your son, Princeling Deal Jimpo, Next-for-President, lies in a bed with much injury. Let the Apostle machine say if he will recover.'

'My God!' Soames exploded to Timpleton, 'we can't tackle anything like that. I tell you, these people don't understand –'

'We'll *have* to tackle it,' Timpleton said. 'It's just a matter of getting enough factors together to make an accurate prediction.'

'But don't you see, Ted –'

'Spit in it!' Timpleton stood up and said in a grave, official voice, 'Thank you, the Apostle will be glad to accept the challenge, Mr Witch Doctor. We will deliver our verdict on the Prince by sunset.'

A mutter of excitement ran through the crowd but Dumayami quelled it.

'If you need so long, take it,' he said contemptuously. 'What poor, slow magic! I can give my prediction now.'

149

'Then give it,' M'Grassi said, 'so that all may hear.' The silence was now almost bullet-proof. Dumayami, for the first time, looked uneasy. He fidgeted, while the crowd stared mercilessly at him. Every eye prodded him, until finally he said in a low voice, 'Prince Jimpo will die before tomorrow's sun goes down.'

Chapter Thirteen

'How to load and bless with fruit ...'

The perfectionist dreams of, and the humanist dreads, the day when all things may be reduced to equations. Take the case of a sailor floating in mid-ocean after his ship has sunk. Could we know certain vital details about his psychology and physiology – his stamina, health, swimming ability, age, will to live, prospects on land – plus certain external conditions such as state of wind and sea, temperature of water, possibility of predatory fish in the area, proximity of shipping – could we gather together all these many details, it would be comparatively simple to predict precisely the moment at which the sailor will drown. Until our sciences reach this pitch of excellence, it is simpler to throw the man a lifebelt.

Jimpo, as far as the problem confronting the computer was concerned, was now in the place of the sailor. Soames and Timpleton went to the hospital as soon as the meeting at the palace broke up, in order to gather as many imponderables as they could. A helpful doctor, a graduate of Achimota, painstakingly gave them full details of all the injuries Jimpo had sustained and all the treatment he was receiving. This information then had to be sorted, coded, and fed into the big red computer.

It was growing late when they did this; the mosquitoes were singing outside the mosquito screens. The machine hesitated only for a second before sticking out a white tongue of paper at them. Soames and Timpleton snatched at it together. On it were the two words INSUFFICIENT DATA.

Soames groaned.

'I knew it,' he said. 'The problem's impossible.'

His face hard, Timpleton went over to the keyboard and typed PREDICT ON DATA GIVEN.

After another minute pause, another tongue of paper appeared. On it was typed PATIENT WILL RECOVER.

'Well, there you are,' Timpleton said. 'That's what we'll have to stick to. Come on, it's getting dark; let's go and take it to the adjudicators.'

'I'll stay here, if you don't mind,' Soames said. He took out his cigarette case, gave one to L'Panto, who had been helping them, lit one himself, and watched through the door as Timpleton crossed into the gardens. At a table lit by a lantern, Mayor Wabe, who was acting as judge in the trial, sat waiting with Dumayami and a couple of his followers.

Sweat poured down Soames' forehead, through his eyebrows, into his eyes.

'Why's it so hot?' he asked testily.

'Rain go, Jack, rain bloody go gone,' L'Panto said in the simple phrases he had contracted from Timpleton. 'Switch to dry time. Dry time up, roger now. All bloody thing sun now work OK, chop-chop, strength five. All indicator say rain go, cloud bugger up, dis, u.s., flesh, gone, roger, out. Sunshine testing loud and clear.'

'You make it sound very convincing,' Soames replied straight-forwardly, mopping his face.

Timpleton had reached the Mayor's table. He plonked the note on the table and returned without stopping or speaking to the computer room.

'I'm going to get bloody drunk,' he announced, picking up his jacket and hanging it over one shoulder with a thumb. 'Come on, L'Panto, you can help me. More elbow up-down, quick time, plenty glass.'

'You'll regret it in the morning,' Soames said, half-jokingly.

'So what? My job's over now. I'm time-expired now, I'm just waiting to shoot off home. This place is a crazy place. Nothing fits.'

'Such as?'

'Oh, anything,' Timpleton said grumpily. 'Look, witch doctors and computers, engineers and bullock carts: it's all looney. This place is like a sort of junk shop, Soames. Hasn't that struck you? They've got real proper pull-chain water closets, but there's no water in 'em, so a chap comes round each morning with a bucket to empty 'em. It's screwy, it makes you want to drink! And yesterday I saw a nigger lying on a pile of dirty rushes with a bowler hat hung over his bed. It's just little things like that —'

'Wait a minute,' Soames said. 'This bowler hat – where was it?'

'Never mind *where* it was, that's not what I'm telling you.'

'I know, Ted. But whoever drove that renegade engine the other night was reported to be wearing a bowler hat. Now, I'd like to investigate this one you've seen. It may be the same one – there can't be many bowlers in Umbalathorp.'

Timpleton described the position of the hut in which he had sheltered from the rain shower, without showing any great interest in Soames' theory.

'It sounds like the hut in which I first met Dumayami,' Soames said. 'I wouldn't mind betting this was all his doing – the engine episode, I mean. If only we could pin it on him … See you later, Ted, eh? Go and get drunk.'

'Where are you going?' Ted asked suspiciously.

'To visit the English colony,' Soames said.

Soames caught a rickshaw outside the palace gates and was duly pulled up Stranger's Hill. When he had paid the man and watched him go away, Soames still lingered by a group of trees near the Pickets' bungalow. A light burning miserably on the verandah threw a cold glow out into the darkness. The mission

153

that seemed clear-cut to Soames a few minutes ago had developed a lot of misty corners; his determination was slipping. He told himself he had come to investigate bowler hats, but he knew it was impossible to go to the bungalow without resuming some sort of contact with Grace Picket. Grace had to be faced eventually, but for preference not just yet.

Human relationships are sticky as spider webs. We run into them cheerfully enough, then they stretch a mile rather than break and let us go free. If we poor flies were not also spiders at heart, the matter might be easier.

While Soames hovered in true Noyesian indecision, cursing impatiently once more the fact that his parents had been as opposite in nature as they were in sex, another rickshaw drew up a little further down the road. A figure climbed down, gestured to the driver to wait, and began to walk moth-foot along the road.

'So – I'm being followed!' Soames exclaimed, shrinking against a tree trunk. The figure, without noticing him, chose the adjoining tree trunk and peered towards Picket's bungalow.

'Nice view,' Soames said angrily, recognising his neighbour.

'Oh … oh, sir, such startlements are greatly harming to the constitution,' Turdilal Ghosti exclaimed, for – in the Victorian novelists' phrase – it was he. 'Each and every beat of my poor old bloody heart is missing in surprise, sir, to cause much anguish.'

'Serves you right,' Soames said. 'I don't suppose you will bother to deny you had come up here to spy on me?'

The yellow goat's pupils surveyed him widely through the gloom.

'I, sir? A spy, sir? I make a protest! I am the palace chef, with much long years' training behind me at Firpo's, also other reliable restaurants. How I am knowing you are up here creeping in the trees, sir? My innocence is entirely a full hundred per cent.'

'You must think I'm a fool,' Soames said. 'Of course you were spying. Come on, I'll show you back to your rickshaw.'

As he went over to the Hindu, a little knife appeared in the other's hand. Soames paused thoughtfully.

'Forgive that I accidentally am bringing a kitchen blade with me,' Turdilal said evenly. 'Sometimes where I walk are snakes. Am not liking to make any bloody old trouble, sir. Goodnight, sir.'

With that, he was gone. He took a few paces into the night and vanished. Soames felt quite certain he could not be far away. Not being particularly anxious to be seen entering Picket's home, for fear of again incurring royal disapproval if the matter were reported back to the palace, Soames accordingly skirted the area, looking for a rear entrance to the bungalow.

The ground to one side of the Picket home was rocky, studded with pot-holes and low bushes; to cross it in the dark was a slow, painful business, but Soames finally reached the wooden fence which marked the boundary of the back garden. He attempted to climb the fence. As he straddled it, a ghastly indeterminate thing descended all over him, and a heavy object struck him on the temple. Pitching forward, he sprawled full length into a garden bed, while the world receded from him.

It receded to a distance which he blurrily estimated as about five miles. There, on its tiny surface, three figures ran about with tiny shrieks; after some gesticulation, they picked up a slumped object, which they carried between them into a building. Light and sound were bad; Soames could make no sense of what was happening; it was like watching a television play the minute before the cathode ray tube explodes.

Gradually, however, he began to identify himself with the object dragged into the building. This process was assisted by their both having similar pains in the head and right kneecap. The other figures, too, grew more comprehensible. One in particular, stuck in the foreground, had him on a bed and was massaging his limbs with a certain amount of personal satisfaction. It was a man. The realisation dawned on Soames that it was Alastair Picket; what he could not understand was why Picket seemed to be repeating the word 'baboon' over and over.

'Eh?' Soames gasped at last, breaking surface as the world returned to its proper distance. The syllable cleared his head and vanquished the last of the cotton wool. M'Grassi should be informed of this instance of the power of words; it would interest him.

'I said I was very sorry that this happened to you of all people, my dear boy,' Picket replied, looking into Soames' face and continuing to rub, 'but unfortunately you ran into one of our baboon traps. The cursed creatures get into the garden and pinch all the fruit, don't you know? Great big baboons, can't keep them out. You are actually the first one we've captured. You got a net and an old flat iron on top of you.'

He rubbed his hands in satisfaction and said, 'Not too badly hurt are you? You're beginning to look better.'

'I don't know,' Soames said thickly, 'but I'd be obliged if you'd keep your hands off me, thank you.'

'No offence meant,' Picket said blandly. 'No offence meant at all. You surely don't think –' He chuckled throatily without completing the sentence.

Grace came forward with a tray of tea which she set down on the edge of the bed. Seating herself on the bedside chair, she poured Soames out a steaming cup. When she offered it to him, her hand trembled slightly. Her face was set in doggy lines; Soames feared to meet her eyes, but when he did so it was to find none of the shame he had expected; the shame was in his own eyes and she, immediately comprehending it, dropped her gaze with a tiny moue of vexation.

'How's the tea?' she asked flatly.

'Splendid,' he said, drinking in frequent tiny sips to cover a surprising disinclination ever to speak again. He supposed the suppressed feeling in the air was causing a neutral bloc.

Bringing another generous load of silence with her, Mrs Picket entered the room. Her little plump face seemed to hold all the chubby dustiness of a puff-ball; if anything, she looked sicker than before. Soames instinctively tried to move his legs to allow her to perch on the bed, there being no more chairs available, but a flash of pain in his knee-cap warned him to keep still.

'We thought it was a baboon,' Mrs Picket said faintly.

'And was it?' Soames would have liked to ask. Instead, he kept silent, sipping his tea and thinking, 'It now only needs Pawli to complete the gay family circle. How the other half lives ...'

'Well, nice to see you, anyway, old man,' Picket said abruptly. Perhaps he could no longer bear the noise of Soames' sipping. 'Forgive the unconventional style of greeting, eh?'

'Yes, of course,' Soames said. He could not bring himself to make the effort of explaining why he had been climbing over their fence, nor did they seem very curious about the matter. He changed the subject. 'Mr Picket, isn't there some British authority you could approach out here who would arrange for you all to have a free passage home to England?'

It was Mrs Picket who answered.

'They think we're dead,' she said, wandering out of the bedroom as if she was going to see whether they really were.

'Dora's right,' Picket conceded. 'I told you – *The Times* announced that we were dead twenty-seven years ago. I've been through all this, Noyes ...'

'But surely –' Soames began.

'Besides,' Picket interrupted. 'What the hell do you imagine an old man who has acquired a taste for black boys would do in England?'

A look of bitter weariness passed over his face, speaking volumes, saying nothing. He got up and blundered from the room, exclaiming indistinctly as he went, 'It's only for Grace I'm interested ...'

Soames' dismay at this outburst was keen; he sensed that – for the first time in his sheltered life – he was witnessing the disintegration of a man. Then a hand touched his wrist and Grace said, 'Don't be too upset, Soames; I've heard father deliver that line a dozen times, I should think. It satisfies both his sense of guilt and his sense of the dramatic ...'

The loathing in her voice silted up the end of the sentences. Soames experienced the selfishly intense desire to run a mile. In an urge to get the visit over as soon as possible, he said, 'I actually came about a bowler hat.'

Then he burst into wild laughter. He hooted with merriment at the incongruity of bowler hats and steamy emotions – and when he turned to look at Grace, she was quietly crying without spilling a tear.

'I'm sorry,' she said, searching herself hopelessly for a handkerchief. 'Obviously, you can't be expected to appreciate how – how howlingly ghastly existence here is, or you'd never laugh.'

Ashamed of his outburst, Soames fished out his handkerchief and obligingly mopped her dry cheeks. She had the rare ability of looking attractive when dishevelled. By the time he had dried her face (for at his touch, she had summoned a few real tears), he discovered, with surprise and some admiration, that Grace was now lying on the bed beside him. It was basically the same tactic she had worked on him in the convertible the night they had first met. Now, as then, Soames could not refuse. The point of refusal was a slippery thing which he never grasped; in the new warmth flooding them so invitingly, it slipped constantly away and was lost entirely. Not even the cries of an irritable knee-cap could call it back. So it was that Soames and Grace underwent that curious and revelatory experience often represented typographically in novels as …

Finally, Soames sat up. Again his fastidiousness, his moral code, had let him down; he began to worry about it at once. He could not even argue that he had done what he had done on humanitarian grounds, for Grace's sake. He had done it for sheer enjoyment – and that was surely wrong. When he turned to look at her, the expression of peaceful pleasure on her face banished many of his doubts. She gave a long, greedy groan of delight.

'Snuggle down here with me and let's talk about bowler hats,' she suggested.

For Soames, however, it was over. He sat primly on the side of the bed, patting her hand absently, trying to dismiss the idea that her previous practices had contaminated him, wondering at the obscure spiritual link he had with Pawli.

'I don't know,' he said. 'I just can't work things out. Perhaps I missed learning something as a kid I should have learnt. I don't seem to get things right. No, that's not quite it. It's just – well, there seem to be two standards to everything – to every aspect of everything. I mean, what's just happened with us: was it good or was it bad? I'd say it was good – almost unreservedly. But lots of people – people you'd think should know – would say it was bad. And then again, is it important or unimportant? There, I can't even tell which I think it is. It *ought* to be a natural, spontaneous expression of something – youth or good will or something – and yet at the same time, well just at present anyway, it feels a cardinal event in my life … No, not quite that, (is there any tea left, darling?) but what I mean is, well, we did transfer something to each other. A sort of cloud of ripeness, of hope. My father and mother were very different people. Perhaps it's the mixture of them in me that makes me always feel two standards, my father is horrified at what I've done, my mother's delighted.'

She handed him a cup of lukewarm tea.

'There are probably more than two standards for everything,' she said. 'As long as you are quite clear what you feel about it yourself, you must not let the rest matter.'

He was about to ask her how she felt, but an unusual wisdom warned him of the instability beneath her surface calm. He told himself thankfully that he had got off lightly so far, and the best thing was to beat a hasty retreat. Such a reflection, if it was typical of Soames, was not one over which he had a monopoly.

'About the bowler hat,' he said. 'Did your father ever have one?'

Grace's eyes narrowed at mention of her father, but she said merely, consigning the subject of love regretfully to silence, 'He had one, but got rid of it when he turned heathen. I've heard him tell how he gave it to Dumayami when he sold his cassocks and stuff. Apparently Dumayami went off wearing it, proud as punch. Why are you so obsessed with bowler hats this evening?'

'I just wanted to know,' Soames said evasively, testing his leg and finding it good.

A quarter of an hour later he was walking fast and alone down Stranger's Hill. Once more, he told himself that he had got off very lightly.

Chapter Fourteen

'… warm days will never cease.'

One major difference between life as lived direct and life as sampled through books, which are perhaps the most vital way of retransmitting experience, is that while literature can at best show us only a pair or a group of people at the centre of the stage at one time, in reality everyone has star billing, or so it must appear to them. This is the great fault of an undiluted diet of art, that it insensibly foists upon us the illusion that we are more centrally important than is actually so; which is why dilettanti, or undergraduates first coming into full contact with Great Authors, are at such pains constantly to emote: they are trying to live up to that consciousness which doth make Hamlets of us all.

The more balanced of us, however, remind ourselves, or are painfully reminded, that in this lurid pickle called 'real life' we are, to everyone else, attendant lords merely, extras hanging about in the wings of their progress. Whatever happens to us, the world goes on. Say we should die, will even those whom we made laugh find time to cry?

Though this inescapable contrast between art and nature was apparent to Soames, he had forgotten it as he walked back through

Umbalathorp to the palace, his head being too full of his recent scene with Grace Picket to contain much else. He was dimly aware, it is true, of turbulent crowds in the market place, of the sound of drums from the kraal, of an old man scraping down a poster saying JIMPO FOR PRESIDENT, but these registered simply as irritations: it never occurred to him that he might be as irrelevant to their mood as they were to his, that for them he did not exist, even as an extra waiting in the wings.

He was fully aware only of the fact that, in doing something Grace had set great store by, he had acted spontaneously, rather than performing a duty for which she should be beholden to him. The pleasure he felt about this was nullified by the perception that it was partly pleasure in his own responsiveness, for whenever Soames detected virtue in himself he became uneasy, condemned himself for conceit; though this was not to say by any means that he was not conceited. Unease also filled him when he reflected that he had gone to the Picket place without any conscious intention of seeing Grace at all; for now a small voice, whose source he could not trace, told him that the subconscious motive for his visit all the time had been, simply if not purely, to take what Grace had already offered him. This, of course – because he was a painfully conscientious creature – led him to call his whole nature into question.

'You've no self-discipline,' he muttered. It had been a favourite phrase of his father's.

It was not surprising that, in this muddled state of mind, Soames could not sleep when he went to bed. Long after midnight, he was still awake, so that the tap at his door was a welcome distraction. He sat up eagerly.

'Come in,' he called, suddenly remembering Ping Hwa, and wondering what he should do about it if it were she.

But the figure which entered had at least three times the mass of the Chinese girl. It was Queen Louise. She bore a small oil lamp, which she set down on the bedside table after closing the door.

Around her bulky body, like the ice round Everest, was wrapped an enormous white crêpe-de-chine shawl, which seemed as if it went on forever, in the manner of saris and Mobius strips.

'Now I have found you,' she said. 'Before, no one is finding you, and this is a great relief.'

'I have been out,' Soames replied. 'Do sit down.'

She sank heavily on to the bed. Soames moved his foot just in time, wondering what all this might be about, but too polite to ask; Queen Louise was overpowering, but he respected her unconventionality.

'This moment, I feel, is made for you,' she said.

'Blimey!' Soames exclaimed to himself.

'The climate of Umbalathorp is good,' she said.

'Admirable,' agreed Soames, 'except for the heat and rain.'

'Except for some heat and some rain,' agreed the Queen comfortably.

She paused. She seemed to gather herself together like a tatty old windjammer before the hurricane bursts upon it.

'I will not thrash round the bushes with you, Mr Soames,' she said. 'That is not attractive for me. For people like us of intelligence, plain speech is the alternative. Only this difficulty of language barrier please excuse for making my talking less than natural. This is what I must say that my husband and I feel affectionate for you. Despite misconstructions of no consequence, we grasp you absolutely in our esteem.'

'Even after that awful speech I made today?' Soames enquired, turning cold at the memory.

'Most especially after that,' the Queen said. 'For this we ask each other, "Who excepting Mr Soames will rise at this boastful moment and instead for boasting at his mighty machine to make all apologies for it?" And we answer each other, "Nobody: for nobody has this modesty; though he does not make a good speech, he makes a good impression." Therefore, now this great sadness has happened, I think at once of the part for you to play in days immediately to come.'

'That's very handsome of you, Queen, but what great sadness are you referring to?' Soames enquired.

'You do not hear already? My dear, I am sorry; then I tell you wretchedly that the Prince Deal Jimpo is dead.'

'Oh no …' Soames groaned. 'Jimpo … he was a great chap … and he was only a youngster.' He recalled the hubbub in the market as he returned from Picket's, and realised now what it had been about. 'I'm terribly sorry about this, Queen Louise; Jimpo, you know – I felt he was a real friend, and indirectly I am to blame for all this.'

'That is not to be said. Circumstances are always more entangled than we realise, as to make blame something nobody can distribute. Jimpo was Jimpo, making his end self-contained, as all our ends are self-contained. This is why I come to you. Somewhere at your target centre, not meaning to be personal, you have not committed yourself. You are a man undecided of his true role in life. Now we ask you to do this decision in our favour.'

'Er … I don't quite see …'

'Mr Soames, to the gap left by Jimpo, you can fill it. You would be a steady man for my husband, as Jimpo would be. Stay in Umbalathorp, that is what we – I – beg you to do. All you need shall be able to be found for you, in the nature of all interest and security, as far as it is in our power.'

Soames propped himself against the wall in the semidarkness. He knew all too well what she meant by saying he was not committed; and an unreasoning fear of committing himself rose at once in his breast; what we want is always what we fear. The Queen seemed to sense something of this.

'Think without forcing, sleep,' she said, rising. 'Stay five years, three years here; only think well about it. Be assured you are welcome.'

'Yes,' Soames said. 'You've been so frightfully good to me, Queen Louise. I'm very grateful …'

'If you stay, we are grateful.' There was a note of disappointment in her voice, perhaps because he had not at once taken up her proposal. She returned to the door, a crêpe-de-chine mountain which had just visited Mahomet without profit.

'Wait,' Soames said. 'What's going to happen here now? – I mean, the Apostle was unfortunately wrong about Jimpo; it slipped up on this prediction and Dumayami has won the contest. No doubt many people will be impressed by that. How is that going to affect local affairs?'

'For once Dumayami has put his feet wrong,' the Queen said, with satisfaction. 'This has not added to his power but subtracted. Dear Jimpo had mighty popularity, especially in the city. Now our people think, "The witch doctor said he will die and he has died; therefore the witch doctor make this happen." Therefore they have wrath against Dumayami, for this is the way our people reason. Dumayami is very unpopular tonight. But ...'

'But?' Soames prompted curiously.

Queen Louise sighed.

'I feel as our people feel. Though we have anger with Dumayami, he has the ju-ju, and always in the end he is right.'

'That's nonsense,' Soames said. 'It's just luck; after all, he had a fifty-fifty chance of being right about Jimpo; it wasn't very long odds against him. You're educated, Queen Louise, you know a man can't foretell the future and all that sort of stuff.'

She picked up her lamp, creating shadows that turned her face into meaningless planes through which highlights seemed to twinkle.

'No?' she said sombrely. 'I have not the great faith in education which I should be having. For me, education only means a system in logic. Your machine works by another system in logic. Dumayami works by a third system. His system is not bounded – binded? – by common sense, which is a limitation; so he gets farther than we can. This is difficult to explain to a non-African. You must become African, Mr Soames. Goodnight.'

As she closed the door behind her, Soames thought, 'And believing this of Dumayami, she believes I shall stay here, because he said I should not leave Africa. Well, perhaps I shan't.'

And instantly he fell deeply asleep. It was like dropping down a tall cliff face.

Soames, in the morning, was up betimes. After breakfast, he went to hunt out Ted Timpleton, whom he found in the computer room, sitting on a crate and enjoying a smoke. L'Panto and Gumboi were already at work, pumping problems through the Apostle. They had rapidly mastered the idea of breaking questions down into a form the machine could digest, and were now practising on some of the queries the local government offices had sent in to them. These were mainly questions of the order of 'Would it be profitable to pay our school teachers one extra more per month, if we cut down their numbers by five per cent?' All that was required was to telephone to the Mayor's educational department to find out how many school teachers were being paid how much already, and the result was a sum so simple that the Apostle Mk II seemed to snigger as it spat out the answer. Yet L'Panto and Gumboi grew more and more impressed. Timpleton had already realised that in this operation the phone would really be more important than the computer, and was having additional lines run into the room.

He greeted Soames equably, and they talked of Jimpo for a while before drifting on to the subject of the computer.

'My boys say,' he remarked, nodding to the two black operators, 'that if private clients were allowed to submit problems for the Apostle at the rate of two mores a time, they could easily make a profit by flogging the answer slips in the market as charms for three mores a time! Crazy world, isn't it? We'd better fix up something with old M'Grassi, legalise the racket, and make ourselves a fortune. What do you say, Soames?'

'Sounds reasonable,' Soames agreed and, taking the engineer to a corner of the room, began to tell him a little of what he had learnt at Picket's bungalow the night before.

'So it looks,' he finished, 'as if this old bowler hat proves Dumayami was responsible for the runaway engine; it must have been one of his men, wearing the bowler in order to look like an

Englishman, who leaped from the footplate at the last moment. But as well as this circumstantial evidence, I think we now have a motive.'

'Dumayami has plenty of motive for knocking you off,' Timpleton said. 'You're the big white god of the machine; that's quite ruddy sufficient.'

'That's what *I* thought once,' Soames said. 'And meanwhile everyone else believed the Portuguese caused the accident for their own dark reasons. Suppose we are all wrong. Suppose the whole object of the affair was to kill Jimpo?'

Timpleton mulled this over, then shook his head.

'Nobody knew Jimpo was in the go-down with you until after the smash-up,' he objected.

'I told myself that until last night, when I ran into Turdilal Ghosti up on Stranger's Hill,' Soames said, 'and then I suddenly remembered: as I came out of Jimpo's room after fixing up the details of our proposed robbery with him, I banged into Ghosti. He had some excuse or other that I thought at the time was a bit pat, but I wouldn't mind betting he had been listening at the door to what we were saying. He's a little snake. What's the betting he didn't sell that information to Dumayami?'

'Sure. Sounds likely enough. But what had Dumayami got against Jimpo particularly?'

'You've already told me, Ted. If he was against me, just because I came out with the machine, how much more would he be against Jimpo, who brought me and the machine into the country?'

Timpleton whistled a few bars of 'The Policeman's Holiday', lit a new cigarette from the butt of his old one, and said, 'Soames, my boy, forgive me if I've sometimes had my doubts about you. I reckon you've hit it there, smack on target. And of course if Doctor Dum-Dum knocked you off at the same time, so much the nicer, eh? Two birds with one stone. You know, it's a wonder I haven't had snakes in my bed; after all, I put the Apostle together. Still, my turn may come. Well, where do we go from here?'

'You've seen how the law works here, Ted,' Soames said. '"Every man his own bobby" is the motto. I think we ought to go and see if the chappie with the bowler is still lying up, licking his wounds in Dumayami's hut; if he hurt himself badly, jumping from the engine, he should be there. If he is, we'll collect him and bring him back here to M'Grassi for questioning.'

'Fair enough. And if he isn't there any longer?'

'Well, we'll have to tell M'Grassi what we suspect. But obviously it'll look better if we have some evidence.'

'Too bloody true,' Timpleton said. 'Righto, then. Do you want us to go now?'

'The sooner the better, I think,' Soames replied.

'Then I'll just get my two boys, L'Panto and Gumboi, in on this. They can come along in case there's any trouble. You never know, you know!'

He went over to the two negroes and began talking to them in his extraordinary brew of pidgin and blasphemy, with gestures thrown in. Soames walked up and down outside the room, along the cloister which faced out across the garden to the Uiui; tension piled steadily up inside him, he could scarcely say why; no doubt it was something else he had inherited. After some while, Timpleton came out to him.

'The boys aren't happy,' the engineer announced. 'They say it's safer in the palace just at present. Odd patches of trouble keep breaking out outside. Old Dum-Dum has stirred up plenty trouble for himself, predicting Jimbo's death. Seems like his faction and the royalist faction are clashing. L'Panto thinks we might get stuck in the middle of a clash. Can we hang on for a bit?'

'We aren't going more than a mile,' Soames protested. 'It should be quiet enough by the river, surely. Let's get it over with, Ted.'

'I'll fetch 'em out,' the engineer said.

He went, returning almost at once with the two negroes, looking sheepish.

'These two boys'll lose their cushy bloody job on the Apostle if they don't come along us pretty chop-chop, won't they, Soames?'

Timpleton said, winking at his fellow Englishman. They set off at once.

They strode silently through the gardens, turned left, and followed the path upstream. Nothing moved. The sunshine was as solid and silent as felt. Such noises as they could hear were distant. Twice, L'Panto halted, begging them to go back, whereupon the engineer cursed him and hustled them on.

'What's the matter with him?' he said irritably to Soames. 'I'm getting jittery myself, damn it.'

At length, round a bend of the track, the thatched hut came into sight. This was where Soames and Dumayami had first come face to face. The place looked innocent enough, half-buried in the shadow of the trees beneath which it stood. Only for an instant did Soames suffer the illusion he had first experienced in the Chinese café, sitting looking out at the oleander bushes: that the sunlight was just a flimsy façade overlying impenetrable blackness. Then the four of them moved forward and came level with the entrance.

The wounded man still lay at the back of the hut on his pile of skins. He was just visible between the legs of a dozen warriors, standing there quietly in battle array. These men were bedaubed with ochre and white and held spears. Dumayami, a pair of great eland horns on his head, stood in their midst.

For a long, entrail-twisting moment, the two parties faced each other without movement. Then L'Panto turned with a cry and began to run back down the path the way they had come.

Everyone was in movement immediately.

The warriors shouted like one man, rushing to get first through the doorway. Soames swore to think he had not brought the revolver de Duidos sold him. The first man out on to the trail raised his spear and hurled it past Soames' ear at the fleeing figure of L'Panto. Timpleton jumped on him. As they went down together, rolling in the dust, half a dozen men piled on top of them, spears ready to strike when they got the chance. From the middle of the mêlée, Timpleton gave a high scream like a wounded horse.

169

Soames' wrist was grabbed. He was dragged backwards. Someone was bellowing at him, the words indistinguishable. He was running back down the trail, still firmly held. Gumboi was leading him, yelling like a maniac in his native tongue.

'Stop, you fool!' Soames shouted. A spear hurtled between them. They nearly tripped over it as it quivered angrily in the dust. Shedding all instincts bar self-preservation, Soames bounded down the track with Gumboi beside him. The bushes whipped past them, the earth thudded to their steps. Behind them, all too close, came the shouts of the pursuing party.

His mouth open, Soames ran for his life. Another spear slashed by overhead, impaling a low branch. Another whipped waspishly into the thicket.

'God!' Soames was afterwards aware he had muttered, 'God! God!' Nothing more: his own god, Picket's god, an African god, any god, any god that would grant him breath and speed and get him out of there.

Gumboi suddenly screamed and stopped still. A spear had pierced his upper arm, hanging there now as he struggled with it, muttering savagely at it.

'Come on!' Soames gasped. 'Run, man!' He did not pause. He had one glimpse of the greasy eyeballs of Dumayami's party a few yards away and redoubled his speed. Gumboi dropped behind; a roar of delight announced that the warriors had got him.

Another glance over his shoulder told Soames he was still being pursued by about half the party; the others were flocking round Gumboi. He ran on, his heart knocking, his head bursting, sure every step would be his last.

So he burst into the palace back gardens, cursing the fact that there was no guard here by day. Under the full morning heat, the grounds lay empty of shade or people. Bounding madly across flower beds, Soames ran up the shallow stone steps, into the computing room and across it, like a hunted fox, to the inner door; he dragged at the handle. It was locked. Hopelessly, he recalled this was Timpleton's idea, to prevent disturbance now that Apostle was functioning; Timpleton would have the key.

Outside, clearly outlined against the Uiui, the witch doctor's posse burst from the trail and into the gardens, still in pursuit. Soames had a minute left at the most. Irate shouts told him that people in the palace had seen this invasion – but they would be too late to save him now the warriors' blood was up. They would tear him to chops before help came.

Frantically, he dashed behind the bulk of the computer. An inspection panel behind the control column stood ajar. Without pausing to think, Soames flung himself into the concealment so offered; tearing wires and relays madly away with his hands, he made enough room to turn round and slam the door shut behind him.

Heat and fatigue rolled over him, encasing him in a snowball of fire. Soames leant against a panel, cooling his forehead, gasping painfully for breath. Never, never, never had he run like that before. All the spunk went out of him; he began to tremble and feel sick.

Above the knocking of his own heart, he heard Dumayami's posse burst into the computer room. They beat about the place, shouting their frustration at having lost him, angrily, loudly calling his name, 'Soom! Soom!' Nobody even thought of touching the mighty red machine; it was tabu.

Soames lost interest in what was going on outside until his circulation slowed and he recovered some of his normal senses. Then he realised simultaneously that it was very hot inside the Apostle Mk II and that a considerable argument was going on outside. Just in front of him was a narrow slit of light through which outgoing messages left the computer. Peering through this aperture, Soames saw that Dumayami and his party were being confronted by a group of palace guards with M'Grassi Landor voluble in their midst. He settled down to watch without being able to understand a word, irritably wishing they would all leave so that he could get out.

171

What was in fact happening was ominously simple. M'Grassi, thunderously, railed against Dumayami for breaking into the palace. The sweating witch doctor, almost as thunderously, declared that he had come merely to protect the august body of his King and President from the white man Noyes. This white man, he declared, was the author of all past evils, including the death of Jimpo – and would be the author of many more, were he not destroyed. His life spelt ruin for Goya.

M'Grassi denied this. Condemning the witch doctor for a mischief-maker, he asserted that Soames was merely the servant of the machine. But, said Dumayami, the machine was evil, therefore its agent also was evil. Arrant nonsense, M'Grassi declared roundly. Very well, Dumayami said craftily, aware he could not gamble on the royal patience lasting much longer, let there be a test. He was asked to describe the test.

'This machine,' Dumayami said, raising his fist to the Apostle, 'this machine, in which you trust and in which the power of the white man resides, shall make the decision here and now, before us all, of what shall happen to Soames. By its reply I swear to abide, and you must abide too; but if its reply is inadequate, or if it fails to reply, then the man Soames shall be handed over to me as soon as he is found.'

A rumble from the crowd – the great room was now packed with people – told M'Grassi that this challenge sounded fair to them. They appreciated and understood such contests. To back out would mean, not only that he would lose their confidence, perhaps for good, but that the computer would also be discredited; they would take it that he had no faith in his machine.

For the first time, M'Grassi looked at the great bulk of the Apostle with clear eyes. Being an honest man, at least in private, he admitted to himself that its installation here had been nothing more than the vainglorious gesture of an ambitious man, a sort of grandiose attempt to keep up with the Joneses. He did not flinch for a second.

172

'I accept the conditions of the test,' he said firmly. 'Ask the machine your question, Dumayami.'

The knot of people round the witch doctor gave way as Gumboi was dragged forward, bleeding generously and clutching his wounded arm. He was the only man present, except for the hidden Soames, who knew how to operate the machine; the sight of him dispelled M'Grassi's hope that the test would be cancelled for lack of an operator.

Prodded from behind, rolling his eyes, Gumboi came reluctantly forward to the Apostle's control column and switched on the power. The crowd mumbled to itself in suspense, with a sound like old women asleep. At another prod, Gumboi's clumsy fingers began to lumber round the typewriter keyboard as he translated and typed Dumayami's demand.

Soames, through his slot, had listened uncomprehendingly to all this, and watched a narrow section of it, with increasing curiosity. His fear that someone present would notice that the Apostle was not functioning and investigate the cause of the trouble soon passed; the only man qualified to realise the truth was Gumboi, who was in no fit state to realise anything.

When the message was typed, Soames leant forward and, working the band of typing paper manually, drew the note into the machine where he could read it. For the first time, he gained some inkling of what had transpired outside. The slip read:

WAT IS 2 BE DON WITH SOMES

An insane desire to howl with laughter assailed Soames. What on earth did these dimwits think an electronic computer, if it were working, would make of that conundrum? But it was essential that the dimwits should suppose it to be working, in case they started to pry.

Leaning forward to the outgoing message writer, Soames disconnected the automatic impulse arm and tapped out an answer on it.

As he did so, a fishy gleam came into his eye, a gleam compounded of the desire to be funny and the urge to settle Dumayami's hash for good. When he had finished he cranked the paper roll till its tongue protruded at the crowd outside. Black hands snatched eagerly at it.

A moment later, opposing parties were staring, each with peculiarly deep feelings of his own, at the legend SOAMES FOR PRESIDENT.

Chapter Fifteen

'Close bosom-friend …'

It was fortunate that Soames' heart was in good working order, for the following day also brought its quota of strain.

In the morning, a double funeral was held. Close by the spot where Soames and Jimpo had recently stood to see the victims of the air crash buried, Soames now stood alone to see Jimpo and Ted Timpleton buried close together. A hot, dry wind blew in his face, rustling the garments of the multitude assembled for this ceremony. While M'Grassi delivered a farewell homily in Goyese, Soames' thoughts wandered gloomily.

He knew now he had been right about the sunshine and the oleander bushes; light and dark lay cheek by jowl. Consciousness was the experiencing of events neither entirely tragic nor comic. It was not, as Hardy had claimed, that:

Tragedy is true guise,
Comedy lies

but rather that the two were always present, mixed as inseparably as copulating octopi; life was at once funny and frightening: what lied was consciousness itself, for it was merely the sunlight painted over the wall of blackness. It was stretched skin-thin, and through it on occasions one could, as now at the funeral, glimpse the spear-sharp shadows beneath.

Timpleton's death at the hands of Dumayami's strong men had been brutally unnecessary. Soames resented it like a blow on the face.

The ceremony was over at last. The Umbalathorp Guards' Brass Band struck up with a lively rendering of 'Kiss the Boys Goodbye', and the crowd began to disperse or buy magic monkeys' paws from one another.

The royal family gave Soames a lift back to the palace in their lorry. All, Soames thought, looked inappropriately convivial. Queen Louise patted his hand in a proprietorial fashion. Princess Cherry said, 'This at least has done the good thing to break up Dumayami's power. To escape just vengeance he is fleeing to the interior quickly to breed chickens and to be becoming generally a harmless old man. You can be happy and quite free here now, Mr Soames.'

She rolled her eyes at Soames. He could see that, despite her youth, the vague outlines of her mother already set up her face; they did her no good. Though he liked her, he found her intriguingly repulsive.

'Will Dumayami not be pursued and punished for his crimes?' Soames asked of the company in general.

'That would be unwise,' M'Grassi said in French, when he had asked for and received a translation of this question. 'By letting Dumayami go, we make him merely an escaping blackguard; by chopping off his head, we would turn him into an object of reverence. The chicken farm will do for him what we could never do: cause him to be forgotten. And now, when we get back to the palace, we must consider your affairs. You will have to be properly groomed for the Presidency; it is not entirely a light-hearted affair, I warn you.'

Soames nodded without speaking, and when the company got back to the palace, he and M'Grassi continued the discussion in the latter's study. These two had spent the last night well into the early hours discussing this matter. The joke Soames had played with the computer had gone wrong: not unforeseeably, for the whole spectrum of humour is something a cautious man does well to shun. Practical jokes are mere childishness; the buffoonery that comes with high spirits is undignified; to crack jokes is an attempt to relieve unworthy tensions; sarcasm is a token of a failure to be aware of one's proper position in society; punning is simply bad taste; while if one is witty, the Anglo-Saxon world at least will hold one to be shallow and insincere. Soames had asked for trouble and got it: he now had to become President.

'You know, and I know,' M'Grassi said, 'that men enjoy dramatic reversals of fortune, especially when these can be watched rather than participated in. For this reason, you should make a popular President; from jail to senate in three days is the kind of success story the hardest-boiled of my subjects will enjoy, believing as they do that evidence of an ability to attract good fortune is worth more than evidence of any other ability.'

'I hope I may be able to give them evidence of more than that,' Soames said, just slightly offended, for against his will he was already visualising himself as a legislator.

'Indeed, I think you will,' M'Grassi said, clapping him convivially on the back and pouring more port into their glasses, 'but you must realise that as a spectacle the people will find it less impressive: an administrator administering does not draw packed houses. The point, though, is not that you will be a good President, but that you will be a President. It is necessary. Otherwise, all I have striven for here all my life falls to the ground. I have taught the Goyese to believe in progress, because that is the step one has to take before one teaches people to disbelieve in progress. This progress is now exemplified by the Apostle Mk II, and I cannot think of a better symbol for it. The computer failed once, in predicting the survival of Jimpo; I cannot afford to let it fail again, or everyone will lose faith. That is why you have to fulfil its prediction and become President.'

177

At this point, Soames almost admitted the truth: that the message from the computer had been a fake. He refrained only because he could see that the truth, as is so frequently the case, would not alter the situation, and might even do harm. Even if M'Grassi knew that Soames himself had typed the crucial message, the people could not be told – or, if told, could not be made to believe.

That secret was best left buried. The Apostle was now repaired and functioning again. Working with the aid of Timpleton's voluminous manuals, Soames had spent the afternoon after the chase remaking the connections he had broken. Gumboi had been away having his arm treated at the hospital, but Soames had been assisted by a subdued L'Panto. The latter had not returned to the palace until several hours after he fled from Dumayami's hut. On running away, he had, he informed Soames apologetically, burst through the bushes by the side of the path and taken a header into the Uiui, which carried him a mile downstream before he could climb out. It then took him some while to work his way back to the palace again.

'Well now,' Soames said, leaning further back in the cane chair so that the fan on M'Grassi's desk blew more concentratedly upon him, 'when the voting for President takes place, you will presumably ensure my success by putting me up as an unopposed candidate – as you said you were going to do with Jimpo.'

'No,' M'Grassi said. 'In your case, it will be better, I consider, to have an opposition, a local man. Your recent lawyer, Obendsi, will stand against you; he has political ambitions. To stand will cost him an initial levy of a thousand doimores, which he will pay: thus we shall receive back again some of the money Timpleton paid him to defend you, which came from the illegal sale of spare parts to Soares. Interesting to see how money circulates, is it not?'

'And suppose Obendsi gets in and becomes President?' Soames asked.

'He will not. A minor reason is that secretly he was a confrère of Dumayami's; and since it was an open secret, he is therefore

178

out of favour at present. A more cogent reason, is, simply, that you have been predicted for President.'

'Yes, but a prediction is a mere – a mere prediction, words. It does not affect the future in any way.'

'Indeed it does, my dear boy,' M'Grassi said. 'The people know from the Apostle's prediction that you will be President; therefore they will give you their vote; who ever cared to set himself deliberately on the losing side?'

'In actual fact,' Soames said, weakly, 'the prediction was not a prediction. It simply said "Soames for President". That is not the same as "Soames will be President".'

'An oracle's concern is with destiny rather than syntax,' M'Grassi replied.

Soames sighed gustily and with pleasure as he accepted more port. He had begun to believe in the prediction himself. And how excellent it was to have all his conscientious objections remorselessly demolished! There is no luxury like having greatness thrust upon one.

He sipped the port greedily. He was beginning to feel rather stewed.

'Do you mind telling me how you stand in all this?' he asked M'Grassi. 'You've been very good to me, but you aren't going to tell me it is all disinterested. What are you hoping to get out of my Presidency?'

'Disinterest is a symptom of illness,' the other said briskly. 'Your chief value will be as another symbol of our progressiveness. Goya is already looked upon as something of an oddity by the world's press; but with a white President, we shall be something more than an oddity. You'll see! The seekers after straws in the wind will be round us like flies. Sociologists will be two a penny here in no time. Goya is going up in the world – and its President with it!'

'But how can I be President of Goya,' Soames exclaimed next, 'when I know so little of its history, mores or jurisdiction?'

'To be informed is not everything,' replied the King; 'one must know first what is going on in other men's minds. To be well-informed can be as dangerous as being well-intentioned; the vital factor here is that you are welcomed.'

'This all sounds too good to be true!' exclaimed Soames, draining his glass again. 'Yet I really cannot see *why* the people should like me. I know a girl told me once – a wonderful girl called Sheila Thurston; you ought to hear about her, M'Grassi! She really was the sweetest – still, that's not what I was going to say. What I was going to say was that Sheila once told me that I should never be popular for the same reason that Shaw's plays weren't popular, because I contained all the ingredients of a Shaw play.'

'It is possibly time for you to go and lie down, to rest from the heat,' M'Grassi said, eyeing Soames' glass without refilling it again, 'but since I knew you were doubtful on this point of your popularity, I have already tried a small practical test, the results of which speak highly in your favour.'

'Another test?' said Soames. 'What was this one?'

'Yesterday afternoon, when you were engaged with L'Panto in checking over the Apostle, I caused a notice to be erected on the notice board outside the palace gates. The notice read, "As a tribute to the nationality of our honoured candidate for the presidential office, all embargoes and sanctions hitherto imposed upon other English nationals dwelling in Umbalathorp are rescinded forthwith".'

'Nicely phrased,' Soames observed sleepily. 'What's it mean, M'Grassi?'

'It means the Pickets are no longer official objects of scorn. They can come and go as they please – at least till father or daughter misbehave themselves again, when the bans will be reimposed. This move is undoubtedly offensive to the nostrils of all good Umbalathorpians; yet they have not scratched the notice down – always their first manifestation of displeasure. They are, in other words, enduring cheerfully for your sake. They are with you one hundred per cent, Soames.'

'Soames for President,' Soames muttered drowsily.

During the next three days, in which Soames was kept well occupied, the desire to become President grew upon him. Like many a man, until the opportunity occurs, he had thought he had no relish for power; now he knew, without the slightest flaw in his conviction, that to rule in Umbalathorp was better than to plough the Unilateral furrow in Oxford Street; that he desired and deserved nothing more than to establish a White House in the black household.

Accordingly, he cabled his resignation to Unilateral, assuring them that he would fulfil his contract by instructing L'Panto and Gumboi in the mysteries of operating the Apostle Mk II. He cabled to his relations, informing them of his good fortune. He cabled his landlady, asking her to send out his collection of long-playing records, to put the rest of his possessions in store and to cancel his subscriptions to *The Spectator*, *History Today* and *Scientific American*.

M'Grassi also did some cabling. The liking, not untinged with curiosity, which he had for Soames made him rejoice that the latter would stay and take the Presidency; but he had other reasons for rejoicing. He felt an affinity with Soames; but even a bosom friend may be turned to mundane advantage. Not only would this new move save the day for him and his computer: it would also – or M'Grassi would see that it would – provide a great deal of publicity for Goya. He had been disingenuous when Soames had taxed him on this point; Soames might well appear a symbol of progress to the outer world, but it would be as a decoy for foreign goods and aid he would serve his chief purpose. The King had not forgotten how another small republic, Monaco, had flared into the headlines when its Prince married an American film star; and although only a blind or perverted taste would think to equate Soames with Princess Grace, still this odd alliance of black and white ought to be received with interest by the vast newsprint-consuming herds of the Western world. The limelight could then be usefully exploited.

With Mayor Wabe, Queen Louise and King M'Grassi frequently at his side, candidate Soames toured Umbalathorp and many small kraals lying nearby, accepting gifts of live, dead and cooked fowl from headmen, patting babies' heads, shaking hands with M'Grassi, speaking in French and smiling in English. As he travelled about, crude polling booths were erected and the local populace exhorted to vote for the Right and the White. A 'Soames song' was invented for the occasion, roughly translatable as:

Big God Computey
He say 'Do Your Duty:
Speak up for Soames
Who loves your homes.'

As M'Grassi had foretold, Obendsi never stood a chance in the unequal contest. Probably the lawyer knew this; yet he threw himself heartily into the fray, the old monkey-faced Ladies Only following like a faithful shadow behind him. Obendsi, like Soames, toured, patted bare bottoms, accepted sucking pigs, swore to make Goya mightier yet, and lustily joined in his own song, of which a rough translation might run:

Assawa Obendsi, bendsi, bendsi,
Is a man like you:
He like you too
He chop the laws up plain and fansi
Assawa Obendsi, bendsi, bendsi.

His song never caught on like Soames' song. Somehow, his pigs were never quite as tender as Soames' fowls. Somehow, his flashy ties and lounge suits struck a less responsive chord in the simple souls of the villagers than Soames' tailored shirts with the cravats neat in their open necks.

The election was a walkover. By four o'clock in the afternoon of the day it was held, Soames was home almost unanimously. The crowds surged into the palace grounds and listened – with good humour but without particular credence – as Soames, from a flower-bedecked balcony, gratefully promised them such laws and reforms as they had never known.

After a certain amount of cheering, and buying of ice cream and groundnuts, the people dispersed. Soames came in from his balcony, huffy as a prima donna failing to receive an expected encore.

'Aren't they going to celebrate, or let off fireworks or anything?' he asked the royal family, trying to keep the disappointment from his voice. Anger towards what he regarded as the ingratitude of the Goyese swept him, burning him as righteously as if the reforms he had merely promised had been converted into fact.

'The day after tomorrow they will make celebrate properly,' Queen Louise said. 'Then you will receive real spirit of festival.'

'Why not celebrate now? It seems the obvious time.'

'Because one item of ritual remains before you become proper, true President,' the Queen said.

'And what is that?' Soames enquired impatiently, visualising some prosaic business of swearing in.

'Why, it takes place at dawn, day after tomorrow,' Princess Cherry said. 'If it is a success, then all day the people will celebrate until midnight. Umbalathorp will be as gay as Piccadilly Circus!'

'Excellent. And what is this bit of ritual?'

'I should have thought you knew of it already,' the Queen said carelessly. 'Have you been told and forgotten about it? The defloration ceremony of course will take place, in which you prove you are potent to rule. I imagine from the rumours which circulate through the palace you will suffer no trouble at that score.'

In the laughter which followed, Princess Cherry also joined, a little shrilly.

Soames did not laugh. His stomach whimpered.

'Defloration ceremony!' he said faintly. This was the first he had heard of it. 'This is the first I have heard of it. M'Grassi, what is this?'

'Why do you look so surprised?' the ex-President asked, taking one of Soames' arms as the Queen took the other. 'The defloration ceremony is merely a simple and wise part of the business of becoming President, although I understand it is omitted in some other republics – notably in the United States, where Presidents are apt to be older than we care for. Consider it this way, if you like: the idea of governing and being governed is reciprocal. Something is needed to balance with the voting which has just taken place, which is a demonstration of the people carrying out their will; the President also has to demonstrate he is capable of carrying out his will. As the Queen says, I don't think that this particular performance is likely to occasion you –'

'But why didn't you tell me about this before?' Soames burst out, as they propelled him gently into the corridor in the direction of the banqueting hall.

'Mon cher ami,' exclaimed the King, 'I have told you: the ceremony – which after all is brief – is just part of the routine, a symbolic act, like a communion. Afterwards, you and I go to the Town Hall to the Mayor, where I relinquish all my rights as President while retaining my prerogatives as King, and you are then officially sworn into office in the presence of witnesses who –'

'Never mind that,' Soames said. 'Don't try and change the subject! You don't know how I feel about this. This is so terribly *sudden* – I mean –'

'Not for a healthy man, it is not sudden for a healthy young man,' Queen Louise said. 'You will perform perfectly well at dawn the day after tomorrow, if only you stay continent just for these two nights. That is not much to ask.'

'I think Mr Soames means,' Princess Cherry interposed coyly, 'that he is given only short time to think about what virgin in the land he will select for the partner at this ceremonial.'

'You'll have all tomorrow to think about that,' M'Grassi said soothingly. 'The day after the voting is always set aside for that, hence its name, Choosing Day. On that day, all suitable virgins come and present themselves to you, in the hope they may be chosen for the honour. You pick the one you find most suitable or attractive. Is that so unpleasant?'

'My God!' groaned Soames. He staggered over to the sideboard as they entered the hall, and poured himself a stiff drink. 'And I suppose somebody will have to witness this ghastly – er, ceremony.'

'Somebody?!' exclaimed M'Grassi. 'Everybody! It is held on the Defloration Field outside the town, and all Goya will be there to watch you perform. For the simple people, it is a great, significant event. You'll be all right! I know *I* rather enjoyed showing off my powers in public. The important thing is not to get stage fright: then your power fails you, and the mob will throw you into the river for being an impostor, a sheep in wolf's clothing.'

Chapter Sixteen

'Then in a wailful choir …'

A few hours later, with a fanfare of Technicolor, the sun sank like an express lift into the world's basements; and night, with the jocular shrewdness of a confidence trickster, stepped out in its best array. Unalarmed by this florid imagery, Soames paced the roof of the palace, lonely and alone. A night bird, with all the zest of a returning earth satellite, hurtled over his head calling 'Crippen! Crippen!'

Under his arm, Soames carried a bulky volume which detailed the statutes of the realm. Princess Cherry had found it for him in the library. He had brought it straight up here to peruse the regulations pertaining to the defloration ceremony. The relevant passage was fairly brief. Translated from a French liberally scattered with misprints, it read:

1. The President shall present himself at dawn upon the appointed day at the Defloration Field, at what time his ministers and his people shall already be present and orderly. He shall then be divested by his retinue of all he wears, save only his shoes, should he care to retain them. He shall then salute the East,

so that the first rays of the sun, lighting and warming his pudendum, shall reveal that he has no artificial aids, props or engines about him.

2. The Chosen Virgin shall meanwhile have been made ready upon the Defloration Couch, whose height shall be adjusted to the requirements of the President, provided it be not raised higher than the general eye level of the spectators. The Chosen Virgin shall be divested of all her garments; such bangles and adornments as she may wear on her arms and legs shall be removed, provided they be removable; necklaces may be retained, provided they be of insufficient length to hamper the proceedings.

3. The Defloration Call shall now be sounded upon bugle or drum. The President shall come forward and, without climbing upon the Couch, shall be allowed two minutes in which to exchange such endearments or caresses with the Virgin as may suitably stiffen his purpose for the task at hand.

4. The Second Defloration Call shall now be sounded, whereupon the President, without undue hesitation, shall be required to mount the Couch and assume an appropriate position with the Chosen Virgin.

5. The Defloration shall now take place. If the season is wet, a thin attendant shall be allowed to hold an umbrella over the accouched couple in such a manner as not to obscure them from the general view; or, if it be dry, a similarly narrow attendant shall fan the couple with a small fan to protect them from the attentions of flies.

6. Upon the President's withdrawal, the Mayor shall investigate the Chosen Virgin, in order to ascertain that matters have reached their just and necessary conclusion. When he has satisfied himself upon this point, he shall declare in a loud voice: 'The candidate for the Presidency is proven capable of filling the opening offered him.' He shall take the right hand of the President and raise it high, showing him this way and

that to the crowds, to announce him victorious. The President shall then assume his dress again.

7. No animals shall be allowed upon the Field. No ice cream or any other foodstuff capable of causing a distraction shall be consumed while the ceremony is in progress. Such betting as may be carried on over the outcome of the event, shall be conducted outside the field.

8. The term 'Virgin' shall be understood to mean any female over the age of six years old; previous experience in love shall not disqualify her, unless she be plainly more than six months gone with child.

9. A silver collection shall be taken directly after the dismounting; proceeds shall go to the Mayor's 'Help the Children' Fund.

10. When the ceremony is successfully completed, the Chosen Virgin shall be considered the lawful wife of the President and shall receive the title of 'Mrs President', and shall live in the palace until her demise or until the expiration of the term of office, whichever term shall prove shorter.

All this, to Soames, made very uncomfortable reading. The absurd glory of becoming President had been killed for him at the moment of its fruition; as the cup of success reached his lips, he had read its label, 'Not Drinking Water'. This horrible, primitive rite he could not go through with.

'It's always the same,' he muttered, half-aloud, wandering behind the tesselations. 'Whatever I do, there's always sex in it. No matter how remotely connected the two things seem, you bet sex will eventually enter. You cannot escape it! As the most solid-looking matter is basically composed of nothing more than waves of force, so the most innocent-seeming circumstance turns out to consist of this peculiar quality. It gives me as much pleasure as it does the next man; thank heaven, I've never been stuck with the idea that sex was dirty – but, my God, it's certainly ubiquitous.'

He stopped suddenly. A slight figure had emerged from behind the covered stair-top and stood on the roof in Soames' path.

'Who's that?' Soames demanded sharply, peering through the dusk.

'Sir, not to be alarmed, sir, is only to be your humble servant, Turdilal Ghosti,' said an oily voice. 'I am come here for to give you helpful advice, sir.'

'I don't want any advice from you, thank you. You can turn round and go right back to where you came from; in fact, why don't you go back to Firpo's, Turdilal?'

'Is impossible, sir. Here I am living in this bloody old town, sir, since seven years, also having with me my wife and six little chickos, and my brother and his family, and my uncle with his relations, also including my senile old mother, sir, lapsing rapidly to death. Is impossible to leave, sir, forgive me.'

'Well, just get off the roof!' Soames said.

The Hindu spread his arms wide.

'Between us, sir, the past has maybe brought much misunderstanding; each and every bit I am regretting with a bristling heart. This I now make up for by make you very good offer, sir, and seal our friendship with love.'

'What do you want?' Soames asked.

'Now, sir, only I am coming to tell you of very lovely fair lady called by name Tulatu. About her I can confidentially tell you many secret things for your advantage, sir. This young lady is of extraordinary, irresistible attractment and also once seen can hardly be believed. On top also is making lovely nice cooking and doing all household work good. Also about this young lady is many symptoms of culture, such as make dance or singing for you either upstairs or in your lower regions or the garden. I tell you, sir, purely with confidence, that this mentionable young lady is blessed also by Heaven with nature most gentle, mild temper and strong white teeth. Sleeping or awake, always I insist you will like her. She makes most dainty motions. This girl for you to take on Defloration Couch is a most ideal only attained by splendid good fortune or the lucky chance of circumstance, blessed by God. Happily, sir, having once set her eyes upon you, she is consummated with bloody eager desire to be taken by you, otherwise she will not consider this matter in any way at all.'

'I see,' Soames remarked, properly impressed by this oration. 'Is she by any chance some sort of relation of yours, Turdilal?'

'Oh, sir, no, sir. Of her only I am speaking in purely self-disinterest. You are too much suspicious for me! This young lady is Dumayami's daughter, sir.'

The wind went from Soames' sails like a homing pigeon homing. Before he could attack the impudence of this suggestion, Turdilal was speaking again.

'Sir, please to consider this poor old man Dumayami that by your power you are casting from his job, sir, to humble chicken farm; he is now being without friends or doimores. So he is thinking humbly in exile each and every day that if you are accepting this paragon of daughter called by name Tulatu he will regain prestige and good name and live to bless you. Also this young daughter is only just a schoolgirl, sir, exceptionally well reversed in all the arts of love and every pleasure of marriage bed, with good fine flesh and moulded exterior make you lucky man all men are envying.'

'I'll think it over,' Soames said. 'Bring Tulatu to me tomorrow, Choosing Day, and I will interview her.' After all, if the office of President was to carry its burdens, it should also carry its pleasures.

When he had lavished more praise on the attractions of Miss Dumayami, the Hindu departed. Soames, however, was not left alone on the roof. No sooner had Turdilal gone, than a light footstep made Soames turn to confront the slender figure approaching him. Peering through the dimness, Soames discerned Ping Hwa.

His heart lightly changed gear as she touched his sleeve and then withdrew her hand.

'Excuse,' she said, hanging her head and obviously filled with a sudden embarrassment. 'I – ai ya, I say little English, cannot say. Best go leave you.'

'Ping Hwa,' Soames said, reaching out and seizing her fragile wrist, for she looked as if she were about to run away. He sat down on a weathered bench, drawing her nearer until her knees touched his legs. 'Ping Hwa, I am glad to see you.'

'Sir, two times I come to see you your room. You not there. I t'ink you not want see this girl,' she said, looking about her uneasily, as if the idea of running away had not yet deserted her.

'I did want to see you, Ping Hwa,' Soames said. 'I didn't know you had come. It was just – well, I have hardly had a moment of peace since I came to Goya. I never seem to get a chance to do the things I want to do. Do you understand?'

'I say my father, "I not want go again see that man, he not like me." My father say, "Go more again one time".'

'You mustn't let him bully you. I'd like to know you better, Ping Hwa, without any strings or conditions attached. Not a business deal, you know – a – a gentleman's agreement. Do you understand what I mean? For your own sake …'

'My father make me come see you. I not speak many word in English. Not say anything of meaning. You not like see me.'

'I don't feel like that,' Soames said. 'You don't know what I'm like. You'll soon learn the language and, besides, two people can do other things besides talk, eh? Let's just keep our father out of this entirely, shall we? Think of each other; do you understand?'

'I say my father, "Here many girl too many." I no speak. You not want see this girl.'

During this conversation, in which both sides might have been addressing different sides of different brick walls, for all the transference of ideas that took place, the Chinese girl looked, in the half-light, so infinitely defenceless and desirable that Soames groaned in despair. He groaned because he surmised that something more impenetrable than the language bar lay between them, because he had experienced this same inability to communicate with English girls perfectly fluent in the language and he perceived that Ping Hwa was unable to grasp all the unsaid things which – whether we like it or not – comprise the greater part of social intercourse. For all her elegance of manner and figure, Ping Hwa was a little fool.

191

He groaned again, a general groan for the way performance so often belies appearance, and a particular groan because none of this had any power whatsoever to alter his urge to lie with her.

'See, you not like me. You want me go 'way,' she said, interpreting, as he pressed her closer, his groans in her own fashion. 'Better I not come at all.'

'What this infinitely foolish girl is trying to say,' Ping Ah exclaimed – bursting from his hiding place, unable to contain his righteous impatience any longer, and causing Soames to jump like a startled gnu – 'is that she holds love in her bosom for you, and will serve always in honourable measure if you choose her for Chosen Virgin.'

'I suppose this is all your idea?' Soames asked sourly, letting the girl go. She stood motionless between the two men, gazing into the imbecile darkness.

'Is a partnership: I have the notion, she have the body,' Ping Ah explained. 'You could do no better than choosing my girl. With this bond between us, Mr Noyes, you and I could control this town for its own good. I have plenty contact. We throw out Portuguese men entirely on their ear.'

'Get out!' Soames said wearily. 'Please get out and take your daughter with you. Quite frankly, the idea of bargaining with women offends me.'

'Please, is only because you are brought up in funny Western way, Mr Noyes,' Ping Ah said. 'Here is occasion to become well familiar with our way. Women must bow to necessities like all other things.'

'Well, just don't make her bow to me,' Soames said; he vaguely suspected he was being foolish, without being able to work out why. The supper gong sounded from below, a tropical, moon-like noise which nevertheless brought with it a reminder of British seaside boarding-houses, and bloateresque high teas at six.

'Excuse me,' Soames said, slipping past the father and the daughter. Ping Ah called after him, but he hurried downstairs without pausing.

*

192

These two interviews with Turdilal and Ping Ah provided a fore-taste of the pattern which repeated itself with many variations during Choosing Day, that most curious day in Soames' life.

He was roused early and given breakfast by himself. He was then escorted to a well-appointed room made available to him for the occasion. A queue of people had already gathered garrulously outside the door to await interviews with him. All these people, Soames marvelled, as his interpreter let them in by ones and twos, were beseeching him to accept an attractive woman as a favour; a couch in the room inspired many of them to suggest that he try out the goods beforehand. It was every young man's most ideal situation, dreamed of, unattainable – and when attained it was found to contain several disadvantages.

To begin with, Soames enjoyed himself to the full, especially as among the first half-dozen applicants for the post were two young Portuguese girls on whom to look was to be reassured that one could pass the morrow's ceremony with flying colours. Their names were Amelia and Isidora; their nubility was terrific. One of them kissed him, one made him a pretty speech in English, in which, among other things, she guaranteed her ability 'never to snore and always to cook English Yorkshire pudding'. There was also a half-caste girl with a squint, a black widow with a dowry of five head of cattle, a pygmy girl of about ten with breasts like pears, and Mrs President Tunna.

The latter entered, sat on the proffered chair and began to weep with the slow, indifferent air with which one picks up a textbook.

'What does she want here?' Soames asked the interpreter. 'Surely she doesn't think I'd … What does she want?'

Gradually, between sobs, an answer was forthcoming. Now that M'Grassi was no longer President, her position as President's wife automatically lapsed. On the morrow, she would be turned out of the palace according to the law. She was old, she admitted it. She was ugly, she knew it. She could not cook, she confessed it. She could not manage servants. She had no knowledge of what

193

might appeal to a white man. She had borne six children, and felt certain no more goodness remained in her womb. Nevertheless, if Soames, by shutting his eyes and using his imagination, could possibly bring himself to take her on the morrow, she could enjoy a further term in her old rank and would, in exchange, be like a mother to him in everything.

'Thank her for the offer,' Soames said to the interpreter with difficulty. 'Tell her I'll bear her in mind.'

He watched sadly as the big bundle of her left the room, still weeping; but he did not add her name to the names of the two Portuguese girls, which stood alone on his short list headed 'Possibles'.

Throughout the day the interviews went on. Soames, among the plain and ugly, saw many attractive women; he often felt that uncounterfeitable stirring of the blood, yet to every beauty some objection seemed to attach itself. Mostly the girls came accompanied by brothers, fathers, mothers; some Soames guessed to be bazaar whores accompanied by their pimps. These escorts were almost invariably of Ping Ah's ilk, hoping for personal gain by a link with the Presidency; they talked or wheedled, while their offerings sat sullenly by without pretence of interest. By lunch time, Soames had realised what he was seeking in the ideal candidate.

'It's quite simple,' he told M'Grassi, when the Sovereign solicitously enquired how he was progressing, 'I just want a girl who is physically presentable and at the same time has a – well, a spark of genuine affection for me.'

'Then you will very likely be disappointed,' M'Grassi said, wolfing down several corn pancakes. 'The system makes it long odds against such a girl turning up here, for most of them are pushed forward by self-seeking relatives; and if there is one such as you seek, she will probably stay away because she can offer you only affection, and does not think that enough to attract a great man like you.'

'If that is what the system does, then the system is wrong,' Soames said.

'No, no, the system is all right, it is simply that your thinking does not fit it. You should do what I did when I was choosing: pick a comfortable one with good health and few brains. Never mind the family connections at all; the family will soon accustom themselves to the idea that they are unable to pull strings, and are not even welcome at the palace.'

'And you, an intelligent man, can really think like that?!' Soames exclaimed, marvelling. 'I have never thought you cynical, but to connive at fixing yourself a marriage without love or respect for your wife is surely the shallowest kind of smartness.'

For a moment, M'Grassi halted the rapid movement of his jaws and looked at Soames askance.

'Now I see where you are going adrift,' he remarked thoughtfully. 'It must be harder than I had suspected to slew off one mode of feeling and take on another; I believed you had done so merely because you have, at least on the surface, accepted our way of life so unprotestingly. What I hoped you had found by instinct, let me therefore help you to by logic. Matrimony, at least as it is conceived in most Western countries, places – if it is to succeed on its own terms – a terrible burden on the husband and a worse one on the wife. She has to be friend and lover, companion and adviser, mother and audience. She must bear her husband's moods when he sulks, his tears when he fails, his lusts at all times. She must bring forth his children, with their wakeful nights and fickle passions the very image of his! In many cases, she must also wash, cook and even work for him. Is this not true?'

'Well,' Soames hedged, 'it is, but you make it sound awful.'

'It is awful! What is more, it does not endure just for the term when, the fires of sexual attraction being strong between them, the husband and wife see no wrong in each other; no, it endures till death! – which is no freedom! Has there ever been woman born whose nature is so intolerably miscellaneous that she can fulfil all these expectations? If there is such, you may be sure she has had sense enough to avoid the exasperations of marriage.'

195

'You are being wildly unfair,' Soames said. 'You are letting your imagination run away with you!'

'That is any man's privilege,' M'Grassi replied, 'but I assure you I was not indulging myself then. All I am saying is that in Western marriage a thousand barriers are placed between the hope of and the achievement of true intimacy. Here, perhaps because we are sceptical of true intimacy between the opposed sexes, except briefly when the blood dictates, we tax our wives with far less. We give them the status of marriage and ask in return only the more modest comforts. For all the intangibles, the butterflies, you are hunting, we turn to mistresses or concubines; they are welcome to trifle with our hearts, while our wives have the more vital job of looking after our stomachs.'

He accepted a steaming bowl of rice and spiced livers from a serving woman and added, 'There, in essence, you have the credo of the balanced man: a wife for this side of his nature, a mistress for that. The practical for public, the poetical for private.'

'That's all sound enough as far as it goes,' Soames said, 'but it excludes the whole idea of love. I cannot go into this thing cool-bloodedly; I must also have *love*. Can't you understand that?'

'I can entirely. I also know you mean, not just love, but romantic love, complete with dizzy feelings and the big gesture. This is fine, my dear Soames, and honourable – if also a little ludicrous in a man over twenty-one; what is less fine is that you are obviously expecting such a passion to spring up within the next twenty-four hours. Surely if such feelings are to be deep, they must also be slow growing?'

'Not necessarily,' Soames replied defensively. 'I'm not sure you can't clap eyes on a girl and be certain that she is the one you have always been seeking.'

'Just as you chose your male friends, by instinct rather than any *reasoned* system, in which case the time factor is really irrelevant?'

'Yes, I think so,' Soames said. 'Intellect is not a very good guide in personal relationships, is it?'

'It may be a fair guide as far as men are concerned; obviously it is more pleasurable to be surrounded by those who think like us than by those with whom we can only disagree. But the best guides to friendship are those mysterious affinities we can sense only instinctively; whoever does not have this power cannot learn it, and is lost, at least by my reckoning. Friends chosen by this method are the true friends, however surprising they may appear to outsiders – who will note our differences rather than the deeper similarities. I sense that we have that sort of friendship, Soames.'

'Thank you; I am flattered. I believe it is so. But may not our differences, which you must admit are many, finally outweigh our similarities?'

'They may, but I think they may not,' M'Grassi said, beckoning for some more sauce. 'If somebody *feels* like you, the chances are he will also *think* like you – which is why I said the intellect is a fair guide: if you pick on someone who thinks as you do, he may feel as you do. But the feeling is the cause, the thinking the effect, not vice versa. All thought is rationalisation.'

Recollecting his present situation, Soames said, 'This is interesting, but it hardly helps me choose a Chosen Virgin.'

'It is indeed interesting,' M'Grassi replied, obviously reluctant to change the subject. 'It is *the* vital subject, for the richness of our lives consists almost entirely in the amount of reciprocity existing between us, our friends and our women. We must talk of this much more in the days ahead … But at the moment, you want a practical application of the theory. Well, what I have said about friends goes equally for lovers – except that though women feel as we do, their thought processes are always alien, because they rationalise differently. My advice is, to try to detect this affinity of which we have been speaking, and see that it's housed in a passable body.'

'That's more or less what I've been trying to do, I think,' Soames said confusedly. 'But in practice it doesn't seem so easy.'

'Well, you must work it out on your own terms, but they seem so muddled I do seriously fear for your performance tomorrow. Please let me press some more of these excellent spiced livers upon you: they are supposed to have aphrodisiacal powers.'

Chapter Seventeen

'Steady thy laden head!'

'There are more attitudes towards love than there are positions for it,' Soames said to himself, as he finished his meal and steeled himself for the afternoon's session of interviews. 'Each man seems to have a different idea about this vital matter when one gets down to examining it. What a thousand pities that the subject still cannot be honestly and openly discussed at home: then we might get some general agreement on it. Well, I can only go by my own heart. Perhaps that's what M'Grassi means.'

His decision, the name of his Choice, had to be communicated to the Mayor of Umbalathorp by ten o'clock that night. He settled down in his room to interview the next applicants.

One of the first to appear was Alastair Picket. Over his long, tolerant face, extending even to his crinkled linen suit, was a look of shamed embarrassment.

'Shan't keep you long, old man,' he said, giving Soames the briefest, dampest handshake. 'Just dropped in in passing, but I can see you're busy. I wanted to tell you, as the only other Englishman in this god-forsaken hole, how much I feel for you in your dreadful predicament. Of course, we are delighted – absolutely delighted

– to hear about your falling into the Presidency. I may say, too, that this delight isn't entirely unselfish either, because after all, who should benefit out of it if not your own countrymen, eh?'

'Who indeed?' echoed Soames blandly, glancing at his watch.

'But what we feel is so typically Goyese – believe me, Soames, I know them to the core, right to the core! – is the way they're forcing you to go through this Defloration business as if you were a blessed black. It's absolutely degrading. Disgusting!'

'Why degrading?' Soames asked who, having felt that way himself, now suddenly felt otherwise. 'If I accept the honour of being elected President, I must accept everything else that goes with it. I must be whole-hearted or nothing. This ceremony, with small variation, has been carried out on the accession of new rulers for hundreds of years; it's their way of guaranteeing they don't get themselves an impotentate; it's certainly not something which has been invented on the spot just to upset me.'

'But you're a *white* man, old man,' Picket said, explaining the cardinal fact with the exaggerated patience one uses to imbeciles. 'It's terrible to think you should have to do this in front of a crowd of these people.'

'Do you know, Picket, I'd much rather do it here tomorrow than in Wembley Stadium. In Wembley, it would merely be an obscene stunt; here, it *means* something to these people.'

'It means degradation for you,' Picket said sharply. He reached at his throat, as if a ghostly dog collar still lingered there, and then, recollecting why he had come, said much more gently, 'It means degradation, I fear, but in the circumstances it is up to us British to pop our heads together to see if we can't in some way mitigate the disgrace. At least we can foil what I cannot help seeing as a blatant attempt at miscegenation on M'Grassi's part. It is a frame-up there is only one way of avoiding. You must perform this ceremony at dawn with my daughter, Grace, Noyes.'

Soames got up and began to walk about behind the desk.

'Grace agrees, does she?' he asked.

The ex-clergyman shook his head and lowered his eyes. This, obviously, was not the reaction he had been counting on.

'As a matter of fact, to be quite frank,' he said, 'I dared not put it to her in case she refused. I thought if I could get you to agree, *you* could put it to her. You must admit my suggestion is the only one worth listening to. Don't you?'

'No, I don't,' Soames said. 'Your arguments strike me as peculiarly objectionable. You don't like the idea of my going on to that field, yet you're quite willing to send your daughter there – provided I will do the dirty work of talking her into it.'

Picket rose, gathering dignity.

'Very well, Noyes, I'll go,' he said; 'if you can't accept a suggestion in the spirit it was offered, I'm sorry for you, that's all I can say. And considering what went on between you and Grace the other evening, I think you're behaving very badly towards her.'

'You are mistaken, Mr Picket. I had not forgotten Grace. From the sentimental point of view, I feel in some ways very attracted to Grace. From a practical point of view, to have an English wife in such exotic surroundings might be more than wise. But to have you as a father-in-law, in any surroundings, is, I think, something I would much prefer to avoid. Good afternoon.'

He felt better after that, and rattled through several applicants without a qualm. Among these applicants were a penitent Soares and his daughter Maria. Soares made the expected speech about the financial advantages which would accrue to both of them out of a union with Maria. Soames, already feeling the strength of his new position, shooed him out and turned to speak with Maria alone.

She flung herself at once into his arms.

'Please, please, forgive,' she said, looking up with tears in her great brown eyes. 'I think perhaps you look in my heart to see what is said there. Help me to escape from my cruel father!'

'He seems to treat you kindly enough,' Soames remarked.

'Ah, you do not know! How can you know! I am treated only to cruelty. I will even submit to this horrible ceremony tomorrow to become free with him. I will always be loving to you – and I can also dance very nicely – if you take me from him. You are a strong man and my father cannot come to the palace if you say "no", isn't it?'

'It is,' Soames agreed, and put her name on his list of possibles. He also, hesitantly, added Grace's name; Picket, too, could be kept away without any objections from his daughter. Later, he added the name of a faun-eyed Galla girl, Roedi, who smiled at him across the desk, holding herself with an appealing mixture of eagerness and shyness. One of M'Grassi's affinities might be there, and anyhow the breasts were good.

Dumayami's daughter, Tulatu, so extolled by Turdilal the previous evening, also appeared. Either the Indian had grossly exaggerated on every point or else Tulatu had changed a good deal during the night: she looked a raddled fifty, with a face like a goat's udder and warts on her dirty hands. Turdilal had had the sense not to appear with her, and Soames dismissed her without wasting a minute.

By teatime, Soames had added only one other name to his list: Miss Betty Noktrauma, a dusky little thing of entangled ancestry who had been a film star in South Africa. She vamped Soames unremittingly, and twitched round the room looking at everything as she talked.

'Here, I tell you what, Mr President,' she said, in a low, quick voice. 'I am a what you call a real fortune-huntress, you know. Boy, man, we could really wake up this town, hey? Do all sorts of things, have fun – I tell you, you and me. But I'm not one of your hard-hearted hussies, you know, not this girl. Soft as they came, is me! Soft all through, yes sir! And you know what I also like a spot of? Ah, boy, man, I show you …'

She leant across Soames and kissed him on the lips, gradually letting herself subside on to him, without slackening the pressure, working her plump hands under his jacket, round to his shoulder blades. This was novel treatment for Soames, and he emerged from it slightly groggy.

'Yes, yes, I think you've got there something I like a very much,' Betty Noktrauma sighed. 'I would like to stay and teach you to

201

release just a bit more easily, Mr President. I make you give out plenty! If I don't know much stuff about men, I know the slow starters make a hot finish. That's you, Mr President! Take the tip from Betty, tomorrow morning at dawn, you will be standing there with your pants down hollering out for the kind of girl who can bring you round to life quick, hey? Believe me, I do that for you, no fooling, is a pleasure. What you say?'

'Ooooh,' Soames murmured, breaking out of a fresh embrace. 'There's a good deal in what you say, Miss Noktrauma. A very good deal indeed. My decision will be announced tonight at ten o'clock.'

After tea, Mrs Picket was shown in. She moved through the door as if on the point of collapse, sitting down on a chair with closed eyes and ashen face.

'Can I get you anything?' Soames asked. 'May I ring for a glass of water – or a whisky?'

She did not answer. After a minute, in which she sat absolutely still, she opened her eyes and said, 'You must go back to England, Mr Noyes. At once. This evening.'

Soames was astounded.

'Go home, Mrs Picket?' he exclaimed. 'I can't go home. Haven't you heard? Tomorrow morning at dawn I am due to go through –'

'I know all that,' Mrs Picket interposed, speaking without emphasis as if every move of her jaw hurt her, 'that is why I made the effort to come here. You must go home. You think of this place as a principality of Africa; I know it better; I know it as a principality of the devil. Quite literally … a principality of the devil.'

'Really,' Soames said, 'what do you expect me to say to that?'

'Say nothing, only go home. If you had lived here as long as I, you would know what I mean. Can you imagine, Mr Noyes, what my life has been like here? I came here as a devout, Christian woman, full of the desire to serve God and my husband. Almost at once, my husband had his faith stolen from him. I am convinced the devil entered him as soon as he arrived here. He spoke blasphemy …'

She paused, closing her eyes again. Dust seemed to lie like powder on her plump cheeks. In a moment she continued to speak, though without opening her eyes.

'Then my husband was seized by unnatural inclinations, Mr Noyes; he began to seduce black boys. Later, my daughter was visited by the same terrible lusts. What could that have been but the work of the devil? And by a thousand other signs about me of nakedness and promiscuity, I have learnt that this is the country of the Powers of Darkness. Now they are about to gather you in too. Go, I say, before it is too late, before you are doomed for ever.'

She opened her eyes, regarding Soames with the sort of expression one generally reserves for Monday mornings at the office. Soames just sat there; it was not till some days later that he realised he should have said to her, 'Madam, you have obviously reached a certain dangerous stage of life; the menopause has allied itself with the unhappy conditions of your marriage to give you delusions.' The shock might have been good for her.

'What I am saying is not making its proper mark on you,' Mrs Picket continued, in the same flat fashion, closing her eyes again. 'This is one of the things the devil has done to me. I have never fallen to his temptations as the other members of my family have done; but the battle has drained my strength over the years. Sometimes I feel I have grown all but invisible to the world. You must disregard this, Mr Noyes; you must heed what I say and go away. I know that my husband came to you earlier. You must disregard his words. He is corruption. He is now the devil's chief agent in Umbalathorp.'

'You aren't well, Mrs Picket,' Soames said, getting up and going to her. 'Let me use my influence to get you a bed in the hospital; I will pay for it. You need a long rest away from everyone.'

'You are speaking for the devil,' she said. 'I must stay in that cursed house on the hill; it is my bounden duty. The devil has now moved in in person, and I have to stay and confront him as best I can.'

'Really, you are imagining things, Mrs Picket. Your health is low, you are mentally overstrained.'

'Naturally you would say that, Mr Noyes, if you are as lost as I now fear you are. You have seen this creature of the night, Pawli, who has now taken over our house, have you not? That is the disguise of the devil! It is he in person – and the terrible thing is that I should have to live with him and pretend I have not recognised him.'

She stood up, weakly fending his hand from her arm. The lids of her closed eyes were dark yellow in the white face.

'You're terribly mistaken,' Soames said. 'I beg you to take that bed just for a week, and see if you don't see things differently afterwards.'

'Go!' she said, 'go quickly, or you are damned for all eternity. Leave for England before dark falls.'

As she left the room, she was, as she had claimed, all but invisible. Her outlines seemed fuzzy. Soames lit a cigarette and let it burn. He did not countenance one word she said: yet he felt uneasy. The modern equivalents of the devil are every bit as efficient as the Old Master.

None of the other girls who paraded before him pleased him. His mind was no longer on his work. At seven o'clock, when daylight died, he rang a bell and had the rest of the applicants dismissed.

As he came slowly out of the room, the Princess Cherry met him in the corridor.

'Your face says you still do not decide,' she said, staring hard at him. 'I am too proud girl to come as candidate for choosing, but remember me, won't you? I have more desires than reading poetry. I think we could make a good pleasure together.'

'Of course,' he said gently, 'I won't forget, Princess. You've always been terribly kind to me. I – often feel very lost here, but I'm always glad to see you. This is a rather awkward sort of thing to say to you, but – well, I hope you'll be forgiving if I don't pick you for tomorrow.'

'Do not worry,' she said. 'After tomorrow are other days for more choosing. No? Your contracts will not forbid you being versatile.'

Soames ate a pensive supper, retired to his room, smoked, emerged to have a bath, returned to his room, thought, dithered.

At a quarter to ten, a clerk knocked at his door, asked him in broken French if he could yet name the Chosen Virgin, and was sharply dismissed. Soames went down to see M'Grassi.

'In a few minutes,' he said, without many preliminaries, 'I'm supposed to be ringing up Mayor Wabe and communicating my decision to him. The truth is, I haven't yet decided. I'm sorry to be so slow about this, but I want a little more time. Would it be all right if I postponed telling him till later?'

'It would be all right in a legal sense,' M'Grassi replied, 'or at least it could be arranged. But I doubt if it would be right from your personal point of view. You will condemn yourself to a sleepless night, which would not be good. Can you not make a snap decision? You must have *some* idea …'

'No idea,' Soames said firmly.

The king sighed and rose to pour them drinks.

'You know I enjoy talking to you like what you would term a "Dutch uncle",' he said, 'and you constantly tempt me to do it again. Let me, just this time, restrain myself, and point out merely that one woman is very like another. The servant girl, the Hollywood film star: much the same in bed.'

'"It is not in our stars but in ourselves" the difference lies,' Soames said. 'I'm sorry to be silly about this, M'Grassi, but if you could get on to Mayor Wabe, I should much appreciate it.'

'Here's your drink,' M'Grassi said resignedly, and went over to the phone. In a short time, he was connected to the Mayor's Parlour and speaking to the Mayor. They conversed in Goyese. As he replaced the receiver, M'Grassi turned to Soames with a slight smile.

'He says you can have your wish; he will go home to bed,' the king said. 'You need not tell him your choice of Virgin till you actually get on to the field at dawn. All the interested females will be there anyway, so the selected one can immediately be – ah, pressed into service. Nor will the people care a hang about this change in protocol provided the essential part of the entertainment goes forth as planned.'

'That's very good of you,' Soames said relievedly. 'I really will make up my mind soon.'

'Not at all. I only wish I could take your place on the field,' M'Grassi said cordially. He raised his glass. 'To the lucky woman!'

'"To whosoe'er she be, That not impossible she", Soames quoted. With a slight shiver, he drank.

Ten o'clock chimed. Eight hours till dawn.

'If you will excuse me, I think I'll go back up to my room,' Soames said apologetically.

He sat on the edge of his bed, swinging one leg nervously, looking at the six names on a little piece of paper.

Amalia
Isidora (the two Portuguese girls)
Maria Soares
Grace
Roedi, the Galla girl
Betty Noktrauma

Surely he could cross one of them off? No, instead he added a seventh name, 'Ping Hwa'. For all her obtuseness, he might have settled for her straight away, were it not that Soames foresaw her father making a considerable nuisance of himself: Ping Ah could not be kept from the palace, as José Soares could be, because he already lived in the palace.

'God, you've no passion, man!' Soames addressed himself furiously when he had stared at this bit of paper for half an hour. 'Your trouble is not that you fancy them all but that you don't fancy any of them enough.'

But the truth was more than that, he realised. He had to choose someone who would be suitable not only for himself but for the whole ceremony. This was a symbolic act, an investiture; at the same time, it was for Soames a divestment: he was getting rid of his old English character. Here was his great chance to become someone newer, bigger, his opportunity to renounce his childhood.

He grew more and more uneasy as time passed.

'Inside me is all the apparatus for making a decision, yet I cannot decide,' he grumbled. 'How apt that I should bear the name Noyes! One half of me says No, one half says Yes. Pull devil, pull baker, I shall never agree with myself.'

He smote his forehead, and attempted to smoke a cigarette without thinking at all. The attempt failed.

'It's this cursed indecisiveness!' he said aloud. 'It runs through me … I can actually feel it – like wildfire. Or ivy. Or rust. Right down inside. It splits me in two. How can I ever be or make myself a whole man when half of me is Mother and half of me is Father? Even *this* boils down to sex: that you have to have male and female to make another generation – so no wonder if the generation's a mixture, half pulling one way, half the other. Why was I not brought forth by parthenogenesis, a bastard on the divine scale? Hell's blood, the business of existence is too much for one man!'

Jumping up, he kicked over a wicker chair and stood with his back to the wall, drumming his fists against it.

'You think you're one person, and then your situation and surroundings change – and you're not, you're someone else. Then in another place or another time, you're someone else again. This damned uncertain bisexual way of building a character insures its instability, as far as I can see. I mean, who am I now? Which part of me do I owe allegiance to? How can I tell? What can help me to tell? – not the religious training I had as a kid; not the *laisser faire* I learnt at the university; not the cautious humanism I had fallen into recently. They applied once, but they are all about as relevant as Ancient Rome to me – *now* in Umbalathorp …'

He fell to thinking of Sheila Thurston, calming himself some-what. Though he had lost touch with her recently, he knew she had not married; that he would have heard about. He had certainly gained both courage and knowledge since coming to Goya; could he not go away, even at this eleventh hour, go back home, and with his new strength seek Sheila out again?

'Mere escapism!' Soames scoffed. And yet the idea of leaving Goya – was not that sound? He could sneak out here and now, get a boat down river.

'Crippen! Crippen!' a bird jeered at his window. Soames ran on to the balcony and shooed it away.

It would not be cowardice to leave. Obscurely, he was aware of the grip Goya was taking on him, perhaps because he was not a sufficiently strong character to withstand it. If he were to retain his old self – selves –? He could do no better than go now.

What had Mrs Picket said? 'This is the Country of the Powers of Darkness; now they are about to gather you in.' It seemed more feasible at this muddy time of night than it had at tea-time. Soames lay on the bed, trying to straighten it out. He flinched from the sort of terms he imagined Mrs Picket would use, but what it all came to was that he was either throwing his soul away or trying, in a fashion just beyond his comprehension, to save it.

'Which brings us back to women again,' Soames breathed, 'because …'

But everything grew more muddled than ever and took him along on a tide of sleep. Outside, the Crippen bird called unheeded.

Chapter Eighteen

'Or on a half-reap'd furrow ...'

Dawn over Goya was no meagre thing. Instead of sneaking in like a belated reveller, daylight leapt into the sky to do battle with the night – and discovered a vast crowd already gathered upon the Defloration Field. It was a gay-coloured crowd, silent in anticipation.

The ranks of the local inhabitants had been swollen by sight-seers from the far corners of Goya, all eager to see their new white President prove himself. In addition, a newsreel camera team and representatives from several newspapers, including the London *Daily Excess*, had arrived, much to M'Grassi's pleasure.

The entire ceremony was conducted almost without a hitch, which was fortunate, considering there had been no undress rehearsal. The Presidential candidate, looking rather pale, arrived upon the scene only a few minutes late, garbed resplendently in the official defloration robes. When he had taken up his stance before the couch, he was divested of his apparel, though still retaining his brown suede shoes, as the regulations permitted. He was seen to look anxiously about, searching the faces of the crowd, where undoubtedly he could recognise everyone he had ever met in Goya.

Finally, he pointed at one of the women he saw among the throng. She hung back momentarily as officials hurried up, prepared her for her part, and laid her upon the couch in readiness. A murmur of interest rose from all sides at the President's choice.

The first defloration call was sounded on a drum. Without any hesitation, the President walked forward, bent over his choice, and said a few words to her. At the second call, he went smoothly into the next and vital stage of the ceremony. Absolute silence fell round the field except for the whir of the movie cameras.

The defloration successfully accomplished, Mayor Wabe made his inspection, took the President's wrist and held his hand high in the air. A spontaneous round of applause burst from the thronged onlookers. As both President and Virgin dressed, the Umbalathorp Guards' Brass Band burst into a lively rendition of that stirring tune, 'Kiss the Boys Goodbye', which, by possessing the sheet music of nothing else, they had made so peculiarly their own.

A few minutes later, the two chief participants in this dramatic and significant ceremony drove off with the royal party. The remainder of the day, for most of Goya's inhabitants, was spent in rejoicing, the eating of sweet cakes and the drinking of sweet wine.

'It was the nicest choice, this I am sure,' Queen Louise said, kissing Soames resoundingly and crying down his cheeks. 'All of us are mightily touched. We are proud of you both.'

The royal parlour was packed with people, all laughing, crying and drinking. Soames himself hardly knew what he was doing, and when someone said, 'Here is the *Daily Excess* reporter to interview you,' he turned and stared at Sheila Thurston for some time without realising it was she.

'Can't we go somewhere quiet?' she shouted.

'Like England you mean?' Soames asked. 'No, I'm staying right here. This is my wonderful country!'

'Soames, however have you managed to get yourself into a scrape like this? I must have a story!'

'Let me alone! I'm a conqueror, can't you see?' Soames exclaimed, riding along on the crest of reaction. 'There's no story!'

'Of course there is. Darling, you've changed so! Can't we go somewhere quiet, just for a minute?'

'You don't want me to repeat my performance on the playing field with you, do you?'

'Soames, you're drunk, you horror!'

'Ha! Bloody funny. How do you expect me to act? Come here, and make it quick! The President deigns to spare you two precious minutes.'

Bellowing, laughing uproariously, he snatched a bottle from Princess Cherry, seized Sheila's wrist, and dragged her through the milling bodies into the quiet of M'Grassi's study. There he locked the door, turned and kissed her vigorously.

'First time you've ever been kissed by a President,' he said. 'How long have you been working for the *Excess*, as if I cared now?'

'Over two years. Soames, what's the matter? Have you gone crazy? That business out on the field – it was *horrible*! How could you – how could *anyone* bring themselves to do it – I mean, there in full daylight, in front of everyone … You used to be so reserved.'

'Yes!' he said, so loudly she flinched. He poured a tumbler full of port, jerked it back and drank it himself when she refused it. 'Yes, I was reserved. Don't ask me *why*. Until today, even after all these years, I think I was still half in love with you. Don't, again, ask me why. Because all we had on each other was a freezing effect!'

'That's not true,' Sheila said freezingly. 'Besides, you've no right to talk about it; it was all over long ago as far as I'm concerned. You don't mean a thing to me.'

'Good,' Soames said equably. 'I wish I could say the same; but at least I realise now that for all the external rigmarole that people put up – the front they present to the world – they also have a subterranean something. And if your subterranean somethings don't chime, it's no good going on, no matter how infatuated or well-meaning or whatever you may be. M'Grassi told me that in

211

different words, and I can see now that he was right. Have a drink, Sheila! Come on, woman, relax!'

'No, thank you. I'm waiting to hear something I can put in my paper.'

'Then hold on tight, because here it comes. I'm staying right out here in Umbalathorp, because this place has got more of this subterranean feeling than anywhere else I know. You wouldn't understand.'

'And I suppose you were in touch with this – subterranean something during that beastly rite?' Sheila asked. She had a pencil and notebook out now, looking very efficient, holding herself prim and trim.

Soames did a tipsy little dance and ended it by sitting heavily on the desk. He felt the need to pretend he was drunk because he had suddenly gone cold sober.

'That beastly little rite meant something, whether you like it or not,' he said. 'What I did out there on that field was an act of authority, a token of fitness. I know it, and everyone else here knows it.'

Sheila made no comment. Turning her back to him, she asked, 'And I suppose you wouldn't have any shame in telling me about this little black girl, Coitala, you – performed with?'

'No, no shame,' Soames agreed. 'Until I got on to that field, I honestly didn't know who to pick. It might have been one of several girls. And then I felt this radiation bounding off the crowd. I've felt it before here. I felt it one night when there was a spot of trouble and I walked through a big kraal after dark. I felt it another night in jail – oh, there's a big spread of muck here for *Excess* readers, Sheila!'

'I doubt if they would be as interested as you think,' Sheila said, 'but do go on.'

'Perhaps you were always as sharp as this, and I just didn't notice,' Soames said. 'Anyhow, as I was saying. There was this thing – quite indefinable really – which comes up and hits you in the bowels. I felt it several times, but most strongly when I slept with Coitala. Unfortunately, the second time she came to me, I scared her off and she wouldn't come again.'

He stopped, staring out of the window, lost in speculation. Soames had been a closed man: now he was open and receptive.

212

What he had heard had been the throb of a gigantic appetite, but to explain it – above all to explain it to this stranger – was impossible.

'So whatever you feel out here is personified in this girl Coitala, is that it?' Sheila asked concisely.

'Yes, that's it,' Soames admitted, worried to find himself agreeing with her. She made it sound very little …

'No, that isn't quite it,' he corrected himself. He paused, confused, and consequently between anger and deflation, struggling with a realisation that whatever had happened to him since he came to Umbalathorp was something which did not go into a neat definition, as Sheila would have it go. He wanted to explain it to her. Yet at the same time he saw that there is a mystery in every human act beyond explanations; your theologians, your psychologists – now even your biochemists – provide explanations: which only postpone the mystery by one step.

'I think we can put this all into something quite reasonable,' Sheila said, without looking at him, scribbling busily on her pad, 'without hurting any feelings anywhere. Page Four stuff.'

'I must go back next door now,' Soames announced, suddenly anxious to get out of this room. Sheila paused.

'Just one question, in which I know our readers would be interested,' she said. 'How do you reconcile your pagan behaviour with the fact that you are a Christian?'

'I'm not a Christian,' Soames told her. 'It just happened I was born in a Christian country and conformed almost automatically to the traditions. Now I'm out of the country, I suppose the traditions just drop away. I was an agnostic, I'm still an agnostic.'

'I see … Which presumably means you don't regret a thing you've done?'

'Regret? Here, drink some of this, Sheila! Nobody who discovers his way of living fully could ever regret it! Perhaps that's the vital difference between Christian and agnostic: the Christian spends his time regretting what he's done, the agnostic what he hasn't done.'

He watched her write something down, stared at her, sought to break her professional composure.

'And I'd blank Coitala in public again tomorrow,' he said, 'if it were necessary.'

'There have been – er, cases like yours before,' she said hurriedly, her cheeks colouring. 'I'm sure you'll regret what you're doing shortly, Soames. I came with a spare seat in the plane, thinking I might be able to rescue you and take you back home. You are certain you still wouldn't like it?'

'Absolutely certain,' he said doubtfully.

'In that case then –'

'Hang on!' he exclaimed. 'There's a girl here called Grace Picket. Perhaps at bottom you two might have quite a bit in common … You can do me a favour and take her with you.'

He opened the door. The volume of sound hit him; he launched himself into it like a retriever taking to water. All round him were grinning black faces, shouting, laughing, toasting him. 'Bakkuds!' Soames bellowed genially, boring among them all, swimming in success, already feeling drunk again. When he saw Coitala smiling unreservedly at him from a corner, he entirely lost the last of that cool, sane feeling in his stomach and head.

Ten days later, Soames and Coitala started on a sort of honeymoon tour of Goya, in a big Ford bought from de Duidos for the purpose. The crimson, scarlet and black colours of Goya fluttered from the pennant on the bonnet.

'It's a wonderful, wonderful country!' Soames exclaimed expansively, as they drove along the bumpy tracks. The gazelle-eyed Coitala made pleasant company; the amount of English she had picked up already was extraordinary. 'You know that English reporter girl, Sheila?' he said, putting an arm round her. 'I should have told her that I could never leave Africa because, on the very first day I got to Umbalathorp, old Dumayami predicted I would stay here for ever!'

'There is old Dumayami!' said Coitala, pointing ahead through the drapes of bright sunshine.

'It can't be,' Soames said; but it was. He stopped the car and leant out of the window. They had come to a fordable river. A shack stood nearby, its roof overhung by trees, an immense cacophony of chickens coming from behind it. On the one mud steps sat Dumayami. He had seen them; he came slowly down into the road, walking steadily towards them, his wrinkled face expressionless.

'I am frightened. Please not speak!' Coitala said. 'Leave him 'lone.'

'Nonsense, trust the President!' Soames said airily; it amused him to refer to himself in the third person in this way. Disengaging Coitala's hand, he sat watching Dumayami till the old man had come close. Jumping out of the car, he went forward with his hand outstretched, consciously the white man doing the white thing.

'Dumayami!' he cried. 'It really is good to see you. This is a chance to say how much I hope you'll let bygones be bygones. You were quite right about me, you know! Here I am, still here, just as you said I would be!'

The old witch doctor took the proffered hand. Though dressed only in a loin cloth, he seemed for a moment oddly European. He had, Soames thought, the self-consciously triumphant air of a friend who has just discovered something nasty about you.

'You must come in my home, take one drink with me,' he said, 'accept one fowl.'

'Fine,' Soames agreed. He signalled to Coitala that he would not be long. 'I'd be glad to. In a way, indirectly, I owe you a great deal, Dumayami, and I hope we'll be friends in future. A man's life turns in many strange and unexpected ways.'

'All is in the gods' hands,' Dumayami said.

'I sometimes wonder if it isn't a matter of how he reacts from moment to moment – a matter of luck if he is feeling silly or sane at any particular crisis.'

'Much is debatable,' Dumayami said.

They walked side by side towards the shack, Soames with his hands in his pockets. His new self-confidence was amazing; only an enemy would equate it with conceit. Feeling wonderful he wanted everyone to feel the same: had he not personally proved that you had only really to want to live and you could live?

'You know, the first thing I did when I got into office,' he said conversationally, 'was to get to the bottom of that business about the railway engine. You remember? We traced the injured driver through the old bowler hat you gave him. He confessed that you and Turdilal Ghosti had planned the whole thing to get Deal Jimpo out of the way – and if I had gone too, so much the better.'

Dumayami made no reply.

'So,' Soames continued, 'Turdilal is now serving a life sentence. We thought it better to let you go free; you are an old man now, and harmless. It was *my* decision not to have you shut away, so you need not bear me any grudges, need you?'

'Carrion birds at last eat all grudges,' Dumayami said.

'Exile is not so bad, is it?' Soames said. 'The air's good here, anyway! Is your daughter looking after you? I'm sorry I never married her, by the way, but you see what a little pet I got instead.'

The sun heavy on their shoulders, they walked in silence through the dust to the shack. By the single mud step, a snake lay motionless in the shade.

'That's the first snake I've seen since I came to Africa,' Soames confided, inspecting it with cautious interest.

'Black mamba. Very deadly; one bite – death come at once,' the witch doctor said gravely. 'This fellow I kill this morning. Kick him, make you feel better, prove your new power.'

'All right,' Soames said, humouring the old man. 'Take that, you sinister-looking –'

The kick never landed, As Soames' boot moved, the casual coils of snake twisted and launched themselves with deadly accuracy. The fangs sank into the flesh just above Soames' ankle. Dumayami, without delay, turned and went up into his shack, as Soames rolled among the oleander bushes.